W9-BWR-602

"ONE OF THE GREATEST LIVING SUSPENSE WRITERS"
—CBS Radio

"His name on the jacket is a guarantee of pleasure."
—Washington Star-News

"One of the most highly acclaimed suspense novelists of the decade"
—The Bookshelf

"Francis is right up there at the top among the best mystery writers in the world."
—Stanley Ellin

"Dick Francis continues to be the hottest author going to the post. He improves with every offering."
—Colombus Enquirer

Books by Dick Francis

Published by POCKET BOOKS

DICK FRANCIS

ODDS AGAINST

PUBLISHED BY POCKET BOOKS NEW YORK

POCKET BOOKS, a Simon & Schuster division of
GULF & WESTERN CORPORATION
1230 Avenue of the Americas, New York, N.Y. 10020

Copyright © 1965 by Dick Francis

Published by arrangement with Harper & Row, Publishers, Inc.

ISBN: 0-671-83350-2

First Pocket Books printing July, 1975

10   9   8   7   6   5   4   3   2

POCKET and colophon are trademarks of Simon & Schuster.

Printed in the U.S.A.

1

I was never particularly keen on my job before the day I got shot and nearly lost it, along with my life. But the .38 slug of lead which made a pepper shaker out of my intestines left me with fire in my belly in more ways than one. Otherwise I should never have met Zanna Martin, and would still be held fast in the spider threads of departed joys, of no use to anyone, least of all myself.

It was the first step to liberation, that bullet, though I wouldn't have said so at the time. I stopped it because I was careless. Careless because bored.

I woke up gradually in the hospital, in a private room for which I got a whacking great bill a few days later. Even before I opened my eyes I began to regret I had not left the world completely. Someone had lit a bonfire under my navel.

A fierce conversation was being conducted in unhushed voices over my head. With woolly wits, the anesthetic still drifting inside my skull like puffball clouds in a summer sky, I tried unenthusiastically to make sense of what was being said.

"Can't you give him something to wake him more quickly?"

"No."

"We can't do much until we have his story, you must see that. It's nearly seven hours since you finished operating. Surely—"

"And he was all of four hours on the table before that. Do you want to finish off what the shooting started?"

"Doctor—"

"I am sorry, but you'll have to wait."

There's my pal, I thought. They'll have to wait. Who wants to hurry back into the dreary world? Why not go to sleep for a month and take things up again after

5

they've put the bonfire out? I opened my eyes reluctantly.

It was night. A globe of electric light shone in the center of the ceiling. That figured. It had been morning when Jones-boy found me still seeping gently onto the office linoleum and went to telephone, and it appeared that about twelve hours had passed since they stuck the first blessed needle into my arm. Would a twenty-four-hour start, I wondered, be enough for a panic-stricken ineffectual little crook to get himself undetectably out of the country?

There were two policemen on my left, one in uniform, one not. They were both sweating, because the room was hot. The doctor stood on the right, fiddling with a tube which ran from a bottle into my elbow. Various other tubes sprouted disgustingly from my abdomen, partly covered by a light sheet. Drip and drainage, I thought sardonically. How absolutely charming.

Radnor was watching me from the foot of the bed, taking no part in the argument still in progress between medicine and the law. I wouldn't have thought I rated the boss himself attendant at the bedside, but then I suppose it wasn't every day that one of his employees got himself into such a spectacular mess.

He said, "He's conscious again, and his eyes aren't so hazy. We might get some sense out of him this time." He looked at his watch.

The doctor bent over me, felt my pulse, and nodded. "Five minutes, then. Not a second more."

The plainclothes policeman beat Radnor to it by a fraction of a second. "Can you tell us who shot you?"

I still found it surprisingly difficult to speak, but not as impossible as it had been when they asked me the same question that morning. Then, I had been too far gone. Now, I was apparently on the way back. Even so, the policeman had plenty of time to repeat his question, and to wait some more, before I managed to answer.

"Andrews."

It meant nothing to the policeman, but Radnor looked astonished and also disappointed.

"Thomas Andrews?" he asked.

6

"Yes."

Radnor explained to the police. "I told you that Halley here and another of my operatives set some sort of a trap intending to clear up an intimidation case we are investigating. I understand they were hoping for a big fish, but it seems now they caught a tiddler. Andrews is small stuff, a weak sort of youth used for running errands. I would never have thought he would carry a gun, much less that he would use it."

Me neither. He had dragged the revolver clumsily out of his jacket pocket, pointed it shakily in my direction, and used both hands to pull the trigger. If I hadn't seen that it was only Andrews who had come to nibble at the bait I wouldn't have ambled unwarily out of the darkness of the washroom to tax him with breaking into the Cromweel Road premises of Hunt Radnor Associates at one o'clock in the morning. It simply hadn't occurred to me that he would attack me in any way.

By the time I realized that he really meant to use the gun and was not waving it about for effect, it was far too late. I had barely begun to turn to flip off the light switch when the bullet hit, in and out diagonally through my body. The force of it spun me onto my knees and then forward onto the floor.

As I went down he ran for the door, stiff-legged, crying out, with circles of white showing wild round his eyes. He was almost as horrified as I was at what he had done.

"At what time did the shooting take place?" asked the policeman formally.

After another pause I said, "One o'clock, about."

The doctor drew in a breath. He didn't need to say it: I knew I was lucky to be alive. In a progessively feeble state I'd lain on the floor through a chilly September night looking disgustedly at a telephone on which I couldn't summon help. The office telephones all worked through a switchboard. This might have been on the moon as far as I was concerned, instead of along the passage, down the curving stairs and through the door to the reception desk, with the girl who worked the switches fast asleep in bed.

7

The policeman wrote in his notebook. "Now sir, I can get a description of Thomas Andrews from someone else so as not to trouble you too much now, but I'd be glad if you can tell me what he was wearing."

"Black jeans, very tight. Olive-green jersey. Loose black jacket." I paused. "Black fur collar, black and white checked lining. All shabby . . . dirty." I tried again. "He had gun in jacket pocket right side . . . took it with him . . . no gloves . . . can't have a record."

"Shoes?"

"Didn't see. Silent, though."

"Anything else?"

I thought. "He had some badges . . . place names, skull and crossbones, things like that . . . sewn on his jacket, left sleeve."

"I see. Right. We'll get on with it then." He snapped shut his notebook, smiled briefly, turned, and walked to the door, followed by his uniformed ally, and by Radnor, presumably for Andrews' description.

The doctor took my pulse again, and slowly checked all the tubes. His face showed satisfaction.

He said cheerfully, "You must have the constitution of a horse."

"No," said Radnor, coming in again and hearing him. "Horses are really quite delicate creatures. Halley has the constitution of a jockey. A steeplechase jockey. He used to be one. He's got a body like a shock absorber . . . had to have to deal with all the fractures and injuries he got racing."

"Is that what happened to his hand? A fall in a steeple-chase?"

Radnor's glance flicked to my face and away again, uncomfortably. They never mentioned my hand to me in the office if they could help it. None of them, that is, except my fellow trap-setter Chico Barnes, who didn't care what he said to anyone.

"Yes," Radnor said tersely. "That's right." He changed the subject. "Well, Sid, come and see me when you are better. Take your time." He nodded uncertainly to me, and he and the doctor, with a joint backward glance, ushered each other out of the door.

So Radnor was in no hurry to have me back. I would have smiled if I'd had the energy. When he first offered me the job I guessed that somewhere in the background my father-in-law was pulling strings; but I had been in a why-not mood at the time. Nothing mattered very much.

"Why not?" I said to Radnor, and he put me on his payroll as an investigator, racing section, ignoring my complete lack of experience, and explained to the rest of the staff that I was there in an advisory capacity, owing to my intimate knowledge of the game. They had taken it very well, on the whole. Perhaps they realized, as I did, that my employment was an act of pity. Perhaps they thought, I should be too proud to accept that sort of pity. I wasn't, I didn't care one way or the other.

Radnor's agency ran Missing Persons, Guard, and Divorce departments, and also a section called Bona Fides, which was nearly as big as the others put together. Most of the work was routine painstaking inquiry stuff, sometimes leading to civil or divorce action, but oftener merely to a discreet report sent to the client. Criminal cases, though accepted, were rare. The Andrews business was the first for three months.

The Racing section was Radnor's special baby. It hadn't existed, I'd been told, when he bought the agency with an army gratuity after the war and developed it from a dingy three-roomed affair into something like a national institution. Radnor printed "Speed, Results, and Secrecy" across the top of his stationery; promised them, and delivered them. A life-long addiction to racing, allied to six youthful rides in point-to-points, had led him not so much to ply for hire from the Jockey Club and the National Hunt Committee as to indicate that his agency was at their disposal. The Jockey Club and the National Hunt Committee tentatively wet their feet, found the water beneficial, and plunged right in. The Racing section blossomed. Eventually private business outstripped the official, especially when Radnor began supplying prerace guards for fancied horses.

By the time I joined the firm, "Bona Fides: Racing" had proved so successful that it had spread from its own big office into the room next door. For a reasonable fee a trainer could check on the character and background of a prospective owner, a bookmaker on a client, a client on a bookmaker, anybody on anybody. The phrase "O.K.'d by Radnor" had pressed into racing slang. Genuine, it meant. Trustworthy. I had even heard it applied to a horse.

They had never given me a Bona Fide assignment. This work was done by a bunch of inconspicuous middle-aged retired policemen who took minimum time to get results. I'd never been sent to sit all night outside the box of a hot favorite, though I would have done it willingly. I had never been put on a racecourse security patrol. If the stewards asked for operators to keep taps on undesirables at race meetings, I didn't go. If anyone had to watch for the pickpockets in Tatterstalls, it wasn't me. Radnor's two unvarying excuses for giving me nothing to do were first that I was too well known to the whole racing world to be inconspicuous, and second, that even if I didn't seem to care, he was not going to be the one to give an ex-champion jockey tasks which meant a great loss of face.

As a result I spent most of my time kicking around the office reading other people's reports. When anyone asked me for the informed advice I was supposedly there to give, I gave it; if anyone asked what I would do in a certain set of circumstances, I told them. I got to know all the operators and gossiped with them when they came into the office. I always had the time. If I took a day off and went to the races nobody complained. I sometimes wondered whether they even noticed.

At intervals I remarked to Radnor that he didn't have to keep me, as I so obviously did nothing to earn my salary. He replied each time that he was satisfied with the arrangement, if I was. I had the impression that he was waiting for something, but if it wasn't for me to leave, I didn't know what. On the day I walked into Andrews' bullet I had been with the agency in this fashion for exactly two years.

A nurse came in to check the tubes and take my blood pressure. She was starched and efficient. She smiled, but

10

didn't speak. I waited for her to say that my wife was outside asking about me anxiously. She didn't say it. My wife hadn't come. Wouldn't come. If I couldn't hold her when I was properly alive, why should my near-death bring her running? Jenny. My wife. Still my wife in spite of three years separation. Regret, I think, held us both back from the final step of divorce: we had been through passion, delight, dissension, anger and explosion. Only regret was left, and it wouldn't be strong enough to bring her to the hospital. She'd seen me in too many hospitals before. There was no more drama, no more impact, in my form recumbent, even with tubes. She wouldn't come. Wouldn't telephone. Wouldn't write. It was stupid of me to want her.

Time passed slowly and I didn't enjoy it, but eventually all the tubes except the one in my arm were removed and I began to heal. The police didn't find Andrews, Jenny didn't come, Radnor's typist sent me a get-well card, and the hospital sent the bill.

Chico slouched in one evening, his hands in his pockets and the usual derisive grin on his face. He looked me over without haste and the grin, if anything, widened.

"Rather you than me, mate," he said.

"Go to bloody hell."

He laughed. And well he might. I had been doing his job for him because he had a date with a girl, and Andrews' bullet should have been his bellyache, not mine.

"Andrews," he said musingly. "Who'd have thought it? Sodding little weasel. All the same, if you'd done what I said and stayed in the washroom, and taken his photo quiet-like on the old infrared, we'd have picked him up later nice and easy and you'd have been lolling on your arse around the office as usual instead of sweating away in here."

"You needn't rub it in," I said. "What would you have done?"

He grinned. "The same as you, I expect. I'd have reckoned it would only take the old one-two for that little worm to come across with who sent him."

"And now we don't know."

11

"No." He sighed. "And the old man ain't too sweet about the whole thing. He did know I was using the office as a trap, but he didn't think it would work, and now this has happened he doesn't like it. He's leaning over backwards, hushing the whole thing up. They might have sent a bomb, not a sneak thief, he said. And of course Andrews bust a window getting in, which I've probably got to pay for. Trust the little sod not to know how to pick a lock."

"I'll pay for the window," I said.

"Yeah," he grinned. "I reckoned you would if I told you."

He wandered round the room, looking at things. There wasn't much to see.

"What's in that bottle dripping into your arm?"

"Food of some sort, as far as I can gather. They never give me anything to eat."

"Afraid you might bust out again, I expect."

"I guess so," I agreed.

He wandered on. "Haven't you got a telly then? Cheer you up a bit, wouldn't it, to see some other silly buggers getting shot?" He looked at the chart on the bottom of the bed. "Your temperature was one hundred and two this morning, did they tell you? Do you reckon you're going to kick it?

"No."

"Near thing, from what I've heard. Jones-boy said there was enough of your life's blood dirtying up the office floor to make a tidy few black puddings."

I didn't appreciate Jones-boy's sense of humor.

Chico said, "Are you coming back?"

"Perhaps."

He began tying knots in the cord of the window blind. I watched him, a thin figure imbued with so much energy that it was difficult for him to keep still. He had spent two fruitless nights watching in the washroom before I took his place, and I knew that if he hadn't been dedicated to his job he couldn't have borne such inactivity. He was the youngest of Radnor's team. About twenty-four, he believed, though as he had been aban-

12

doned as a child on the steps of a police station in a push-chair, no one knew for certain.

If the police hadn't been so kind to him, Chico sometimes said, he would have taken advantage of his later opportunities and turned delinquent. He never grew tall enough to be a copper. Radnor's was the best he could do. And he did very well by Radnor. He put two and two together quickly and no one on the staff had faster physical reactions. Judo and wrestling were his hobbies, and along with the regular throws and holds he had been taught some strikingly dirty tricks. His smallness bore no relation whatever to his effectiveness in his job.

"How are you getting on with the case?" I asked.

"What case? Oh . . . that. Well, since you got shot the heat's off, it seems. Brinton's had no threatening calls or letters since the other night. Whoever was leaning on him must have got the wind up. Anyway, he's feeling a bit safer all of a sudden and he's carping a lot to the old man about fees. Another day or two, I give it, and there won't be no one holding his hand at night. Anyway, I've been pulled off it. I'm flying from Newmarket to Ireland tomorrow, sharing a stall with a hundred thousand pounds' worth of stallion."

Escort duty was another little job I never did. Chico liked it, and went often. As he had once thrown a fifteen-stone would-be nobbler over a seven-foot wall, he was always much in demand.

"You ought to come back," he said suddenly.

"Why?" I was surprised.

"I don't know. . . ." He grinned. "Silly, really, when you do sweet off all, but everybody seems to have got used to you being around. You're missed, kiddo, you'd be surprised."

"You're joking, of course."

"Yeah. . . ." He undid the knots in the window cord, shrugged, and thrust his hands into his trouser pockets. "God, this place gives you the willies. It reeks of warm disinfectant. Creepy. How much longer are you going to lie here rotting?"

"Days," I said mildly. "Have a good trip."

"See you." He nodded, drifting in relief to the door. Do you want anything? I mean books or anything?"

"Nothing, thanks."

"Nothing . . . that's just your form, Sid, mate. You don't want nothing." He grinned and went.

I wanted nothing. My form. My trouble. I'd had what I'd wanted most in the world and lost it irrevocably. I'd found nothing else to want. I stared at the ceiling, waiting for time to pass. All I wanted was to get back onto my feet and stop feeling as though I had eaten a hundredweight of green apples.

Three weeks after the shooting I had a visit from my father-in-law. He came in the late afternoon, bringing with him a small parcel which he put without comment on the table beside the bed.

"Well, Sid, how are you?" He settled himself into an easy chair, crossed his legs and lit a cigar.

"Cured, more or less. I'll be out of here soon."

"Good. Good. And your plans are . . . ?

"I haven't any."

"You can't go back to the agency without some . . . er, convalescence," he remarked.

"I suppose not."

"You might prefer somewhere in the sun," he said, studying the cigar. "But I would like it if you could spend some time with me at Aynsford."

I didn't answer immediately.

"Will . . . ?" I began and stopped, wavering.

"No," he said. "She won't be there. She's gone out to Athens to stay with Jill and Tony. I saw her off yesterday. She sent you her regards."

"Thanks," I said dryly. As usual I did not know whether to be glad or sorry that I was not going to meet my wife. Nor was I sure that this trip to see her sister Jill was not as diplomatic as Tony's job in the Corps.

"You'll come, then? Mrs. Cross will look after you splendidly."

"Yes, Charles, thank you. I'd like to come for a little while."

He gripped the cigar in his teeth, squinted through the smoke, and took out his diary.

"Let's see, suppose you leave here in, say, another week. . . . No point in hurrying out before you're fit to go. That brings us to the twenty-sixth . . . hm . . . now, suppose you come down a week on Sunday, I'll be at home all that day. Will that suit you?"

"Yes, fine, if the doctors agree."

"Right, then." He wrote in the diary, put it away and took the cigar carefully out of his mouth, smiling at me with the usual inscrutable blankness in his eyes. He sat easily in his dark city suit, Rear Admiral Charles Roland, R.N., retired, a man carrying his sixty-six years lightly. War photographs showed him tall, straight, bony almost, with a high forehead and thick dark hair. Time had grayed the hair, which in receding left his forehead higher than ever, and had added weight where it did no harm. His manner was ordinarily extremely charming and occasionally patronizingly offensive. I had been on the receiving end of both.

He relaxed in the armchair, talking unhurriedly about steeplechasing.

"What do you think of that new race at Sandown? I don't know about you, but I think it's framed rather awkwardly. They're bound to get a tiny field with those conditions, and if Devil's Dyke doesn't run after all the whole thing will be a non-crowd puller par excellence."

His interest in this game only dated back a few years, but recently to his pleasure he had been invited by one or two courses to act as a Steward. Listening to his easy familiarity with racing problems and racing jargon, I was in a quiet inward way amused. It was impossible to forget his reaction long ago to Jenny's engagement to a jockey, his unfriendly rejection of me as a future son-in-law, his absence from our wedding, the months afterward of frigid disapproval, the way he had seldom spoken to or even looked at me.

I believed at this time that it was sheer snobbery, but it wasn't as simple as that. Certainly he didn't think me good enough, but not only, or even mainly, on a class distinction level; and probably we would never have understood each other, or come eventually to like each

15

other, had it not been for a wet afternoon and a game of chess.

Jenny and I went to Aynsford for one of our rare, painful Sunday visits. We ate our roast beef in near silence, Jenny's father staring rudely out of the window and drumming his fingers on the table. I made up my mind that we wouldn't go again. I'd had enough. Jenny could visit him alone.

After lunch she said she wanted to sort out some of her books now that we had a new bookcase, and disappeared upstairs. Charles Roland and I looked at each other in dislike, the afternoon stretching drearily ahead and the downpour outside barring retreat into the garden and park beyond.

"Do you play chess?" he asked in a bored, expecting-the-answer-no voice.

"I know the moves," I said.

He shrugged (it was more like a squirm), but clearly thinking that it would be less trouble than making conversation, he brought a chess set out and gestured to me to sit opposite him. He was normally a good player, but that afternoon he was bored and irritated and inattentive, and I beat him quite early in the game. He couldn't believe it. He sat staring at the board, fingering the bishop with which I'd got him in a classic discovered check.

"Where did you learn?" he said eventually, still looking down.

"Out of a book."

"Have you played a great deal?"

"No, not much. Here and there." But I'd played with some good players.

"Hm." He paused. "Will you play again?"

"Yes, if you like."

We played. It was a long game and ended in a draw, with practically every piece off the board. A fortnight later he rang up and asked us, next time we came, to stay overnight. It was the first twig of the olive branch. We went more often and more willingly to Aynsford after that. Charles and I played chess occasionally and won a roughly equal number of games, and he began rather tentatively to go to the races. Ironically from then on our mutual respect grew strong enough to survive even the crash of Jenny's and my marrage, and Charles's interest in racing expanded and deepened with every passing year.

"I went to Ascot yesterday," he was saying, tapping off his cigar. "It wasn't a bad crowd, considering the weather. I had a drink with that handicap fellow, John Pagan. Nice chap. He was very pleased with himself because he got six abreast over the last in the handicap hurdle. There was an objection after the three-mile chase—flagrant bit of crossing on the run-in. Carter swore blind he was leaning and couldn't help it, but you can never believe a word he says. Anyway, the Stewards took it away from him. The only thing they could do. Wally Gibbons rode a brilliant finish in the handicap hurdle and then made an almighty hash of the novice chase."

"He's heavy-handed with novices," I agreed.

"Wonderful course, that."

"The tops." A wave of weakness flowed outward from my stomach. My legs trembled under the bedclothes. It was always happening. Infuriating.

"Good job it belongs to the Queen and is safe from the land-grabbers." He smiled.

"Yes, I suppose so. . . ."

"You're tired," he said abruptly. "I've stayed too long."

"No," I protested. "Really, I'm fine."

He put out the cigar, however, and stood up. "I know you too well, Sid. Your idea of fine is not the same as anyone else's. If you're not well enough to come to Aynsford a week on Sunday you'll let me know. Otherwise I'll see you then."

"Yes, O.K."

He went away, leaving me to reflect that I did still tire infernally easily. Must be old age, I grinned to myself, old age at thirty-one. Old tired battered Sid Halley, poor old chap. I grimaced at the ceiling.

A nurse came in for the evening jobs.

"You've got a parcel," she said brightly, as if speaking to a retarded child. "Aren't you going to open it?"

I had forgotten about Charles's parcel.

17

"Would you like me to open it for you? I mean, you can't find things like opening parcels very easy with a hand like yours."

She was only being kind. "Yes," I said. "Thank you."

She snipped through the wrappings with scissors from her pocket and looked dubiously at the slim dark book she found inside.

"I suppose it is meant for you? I mean somehow it doesn't seem like things people usually give patients."

She put the book into my right hand and I read the title embossed in gold on the cover. *Outline of Company Law*.

"My father-in-law left it on purpose. He meant it for me."

"Oh well, I suppose it's difficult to think of things for people who can't eat grapes and such." She bustled around, efficient and slightly bullying, and finally left me along again.

Outline of Company Law. I riffled through the pages. It was certainly a book about company law. Solidly legal. Not light entertainment for an invalid. I put the book on the table.

Charles Roland was a man of subtle mind, and subtlety gave him pleasure. It hadn't been my parentage that he had objected to so much as what he took to be Jenny's rejection of his mental standards in choosing a jockey for a husband. He'd never met a jockey before, disliked the idea of racing, and took it for granted that everyone engaged in it was either a rogue or a moron. He'd wanted both his daughters to marry clever men, clever more than handsome or wellborn or rich, so that he could enjoy their company. Jill had obliged him with Tony, Jenny disappointed him with me: that was how he saw it, until he found that at least I could play chess with him now and then.

Knowing his subtle habits, I took it for granted that he had not idly brought such a book and hadn't chosen it or left it by mistake. He meant me to read it for a purpose. Intended it to be useful to me—or to him—later on. Did he think he could maneuver me into business, now that I hadn't distinguished myself at the agency? A nudge, that book was. A nudge in some specific direction.

I thought back over what he had said, looking for a clue. He'd been insistent that I should go to Aynsford. He'd sent Jenny to Athens. He'd talked about racing, about the new racing at Sandown, about Ascot, John Pagan, Carter. Wally Gibbons . . . nothing there that I could see had the remotest connection with company law.

I sighed, shutting my eyes. I didn't feel too well. I didn't have to read the book, or go wherever Charles pointed. And yet . . . why not? There was nothing I urgently wanted to do instead. I decided to do my stodgy homework. Tomorrow.

Perhaps.

2

Four days after my arrival at Aynsford I came downstairs from an afternoon's rest to find Charles delving into a large packing case in the center of the hall. Strewn round on the half-acre of parquet was a vast amount of wood shavings, white and curly, and arranged carefully on a low table beside him were the first trophies out of the lucky dip, appearing to me to be dull chunks of rock.

I picked one of them up. One side had been ground into a smooth face and across the bottom of this was stuck a neat label. "Porphyry" it said, and beneath, "Carver Mineralogy Foundation."

"I didn't know you had an obsessive interest in quartz."

He gave me one of his blank stares which I knew didn't mean he hadn't heard or understood what I'd said, but that he didn't intend to explain.

19

"I'm going fishing," he said, plunging his arms back into the box.

So the quartz was bait. I put down the porphyry and picked up another piece. It was small, the size of a squared-off egg, and beautiful, as clear and translucent as glass. The label said simply, "Rock Crystal."

"If you want something useful to do," said Charles, "you can write out what sort they all are on the plain labels you will find on my desk, and then soak the Foundation's labels off and put the new ones on. Keep the old ones, though. We'll have to replace them when all this stuff goes back."

"All right," I agreed.

The next chunk I picked up was heavy with gold. "Are these valuable?" I asked.

"Some are. There's a booklet somewhere. But I told the Foundation they'd be safe enough. I said I'd have a private detective in the house all the time guarding them."

I laughed and began writing new labels, working from the inventory. The lumps of quartz overflowed from the table onto the floor before the box was empty.

"There's another box outside," Charles observed.

"Oh no!"

"I collect quartz," said Charles with dignity, "and don't you forget it. I've collected it for years. Years. Haven't I?"

"Years," I agreed. "You're an authority. Who wouldn't be an authority on rocks, after a life at sea?"

"I've got exactly one day to learn them in," said Charles, smiling. "They've come later than I asked. I'll have to be word perfect by tomorrow night."

He fetched the second lot, which was much smaller and was fastened with important-looking seals. Inside were uncut gem quartz crystals, mounted on small individual black plinths. Their collective value was staggering. The Carver Foundation must have taken the private detective bit seriously. They'd have held tight to their rocks if they'd seen my state of health.

We worked for some time changing the labels while Charles muttered their names like incantations under his

20

breath. "Chrysoprase, aventurine, agate, onyx, chalcedony, tiger's-eye, carnelian, citrine, rose, plasma, basanite, blood-stone, chert. Why the hell did I start this?"

"Well, why?"

I got the blank stare again. He wasn't telling. "You can test me on them," he said.

We carried them piece by piece into the dining room, where I found the glass-doored bookshelves on each side of the fire had been cleared of their yards of leather-bound classics.

"They can go up there later," said Charles, covering the huge dining-room table with a thick felt. "Put them on the table for now."

When they were all arranged he walked slowly round learning them. There were about fifty altogether. I tested him for a while, at his request, and he muddled up and forgot about half of them. They were difficult, because so many looked alike.

He sighed. "It's time we had a noggin and you went back to bed." He led the way into the little sitting room he occasionally referred to as the wardroom, and poured a couple of stiffish brandies. He raised his glass to me and appreciatively took a mouthful. There was a suppressed excitement in his expression, a glint in the unfathomable eyes. I sipped the brandy, wondering with more interest what he was up to.

"I have a few people coming for the weekend," he said casually, squinting at his glass. "A Mr. and Mrs. Rex van Dysart, a Mr. and Mrs. Howard Kraye, and my cousin Viola, who will act as hostess."

"Old friends?" I murmured, having ever heard only of Viola.

"Not very," he said smoothly. "They'll be here in time for dinner tomorrow night. You'll meet them then."

"But I'll make it an odd number. . . . I'll go up before they come and stay out of your way for most of the weekend."

"No," he said sharply. Much too vehemently. I was surprised. Then it came to me suddenly that all he had been doing with his rocks and his offer of a place for my convalescence was to engineer a meeting between

21

me and the weekend guests. He offered me rest. He offered Mr. van Dysart, or perhaps Mr. Kraye, rocks. Both of us had swallowed the hook. I decided to give the line a tug, to see just how determined was the fisherman.

"I'd be better upstairs. You know I can't eat normal meals." My diet at the time consisted of brandy, beef juice, and some vacuum-packed pots of stuff which had been developed for feeding astronauts. Apparently none of these things affected the worst-shot-up bits of my digestive tract.

"People loosen up over the dinner table . . . they talk more, and you get to know them better." He was always carefully unpersuasive.

"They'll talk to you just as well if I'm not there—better in fact. And I couldn't stand watching you all tuck into steaks."

He said musingly, "You can stand anything, Sid. But I think you'd be interested. Not bored, I promise you. More brandy?"

I shook my head and relented. "All right, I'll be there at dinner, if you want it."

He relaxed only a fraction. A controlled and subtle man. I smiled at him, and he guessed that I'd been playing him along.

"You're a bastard," he said.

From him, it was a compliment.

The transistor beside my bed was busy with the morning news as I slowly ate my breakfast pot of astronaut paste.

"The race meeting scheduled for today and tomorrow at Seabury," the announcer said, "has had to be abandoned. A tanker carrying liquid chemical crashed and overturned at dusk yesterday afternoon on a road crossing the racecourse. There was considerable damage to the turf, and after an examination this morning, the Stewards regretfully decided that it was not fit to be raced on. It is hoped to replace the affected turf in time for the next meeting in a fortnight's time, but an announcement will be made about this at a later date. And here is the weather forecast. . . ."

Poor Seabury, I thought, always in the wars. It was only a year since their stable block had been burned down on the eve of a meeting. They had had to cancel then too, because temporary stables could not be erected overnight and the National Hunt Committee in consultation with Radnor had decided that indiscriminate stabling in the surrounding district was too much of a security risk.

It was a nice track to ride on, a long circuit with no sharp bends, but there had been some trouble with the surface in the spring, a drain of some sort had collapsed during a hurdle race: the forefeet of one unfortunate horse had gone right through into it to a depth of about eighteen inches and he had broken a leg. In the resulting pile-up two more horses had been injured and one jockey badly concussed. Maps of the course didn't even warn that the drain existed, and I'd heard trainers wondering whether there were anymore antique waterways ready to collapse with as little notice. The executive, on their side, naturally swore there weren't.

For some time I lay daydreaming, racing round Seabury again in my mind, and wishing uselessly, hopelessly, achingly, that I could do it again in fact.

Mrs. Cross tapped on the door and came in. She was a quiet, unobtrusive mouse of a woman with soft brown hair and a slight outward cast in her gray-green eyes. Although she seemed to have no spirit whatever and seldom spoke, she ran the place like oiled machinery, helped by a largely invisible squad of "dailies." She had the great virtue to me of being fairly new in the job and impartial on the subject of Jenny and me. I wouldn't have trusted her predecessor, who had been fanatically fond of Jenny, not to have added cascara to my beef juice.

"The Admiral would like to know if you are feeling well today, Mr. Halley," said Mrs. Cross primly, picking up my breakfast tray.

"Yes, I am, thank you." More or less.

23

"He said, then, when you're ready would you join him in the dining room?"

"The rocks?"

She gave me a small smile. "He was up before me this morning, and had his breakfast on a tray in there. Shall I tell him you'll come down?"

"Please."

When she had gone, and while I was slowly dressing, the telephone bell rang. Not long afterward, Charles himself came upstairs.

"That was the police," he said abruptly with a frown. "Apparently they've found a body and they want you to go and identify it."

"Whose body, for heaven's sake?"

"They didn't say. They said they would send a car for you immediately though. I gathered they really rang here to locate you."

"I haven't any relatives. It must be a mistake."

He shrugged. "We'll know soon, anyway. Come down now and test me on the quartz. I think I've got it taped at last."

We went down to the dining room, where I found he was right. He went round the whole lot without a mistake. I changed the order in which they stood, but it didn't throw him. He smiled, very pleased with himself.

"Word-perfect," he said. "Let's put them up on the shelves now. At least, we'll put all the least valuable ones up there, and the gem stones in the bookcase in the drawing room—that one with the curtains inside the glass doors."

"They ought to be in a safe." I had said it yesterday evening as well.

"They were quite all right on the dining-room table last night, in spite of your fears."

"As the consultant private detective in the case I still advise a safe."

He laughed. "You know bloody well I haven't got a safe. But as consultant private detective you can guard the things properly tonight. You can put them under your pillow. How's that?"

24

"O.K." I nodded.

"You're not serious?"

"Well, no . . . they'd be too hard under the pillow."

"Damn it. . . ."

"But upstairs, either with you or me, yes. Some of those stones really are valuable. You must have had to pay a big insurance premium on them."

"Er . . . no," admitted Charles. "I guaranteed to replace anything which was damaged or lost."

I goggled. "I know you're rich, but . . . you're an absolute nut. Get them insured at once. Have you any idea what each specimen is worth?"

"No, as a matter of fact . . . no. I didn't ask."

"Well, if you've got a collector coming to stay, he'll expect you to remember how much you paid for each."

"I thought of that," he interrupted. "I inherited them all from a distant cousin. That covers a lot of ignorance, not only costs and values but about crystallography and distribution and rarity, and everything specialized. I found I couldn't possibly learn enough in one day. Just to be able to show some familiarity with the collection should be enough."

"That's fair enough. But you ring the Carver Foundation at once and find out what the stones are worth just the same, and then get straight onto your broker. The trouble with you, Charles, is that you are too honest. Other people aren't. This is the bad, rough world you're in now, not the navy."

"Very well," he said amicably. "I'll do as you say. Hand me that inventory."

He went to telephone and I began putting the chunks of quartz on the empty bookshelves, but before I had done much the front doorbell rang. Mrs. Cross went to answer it and presently came to tell me that a policeman was asking for me.

I put my useless, deformed left hand into my pocket, as I always did with strangers, and went into the hall. A tall, heavy young man in uniform stood there, giving the impression of trying not to be overawed by his rather grand surroundings. I remembered how it felt.

"Is it about this body?" I asked.

"Yes, sir, I believe you are expecting us."

"Whose body is it?"

"I don't know, sir. I was just asked to take you."

"Well . . . where to?"

"Epping Forest, sir."

"But that's miles away," I protested.

"Yes, sir," he agreed, with a touch of gloom.

"Are you sure it's me that's wanted?"

"Oh, positive, sir."

"Well, all right. Sit down a minute while I get my coat and say where I am going.

The policeman drove on his gears, which I found tiring. It took two hours to go from Aynsford, west of Oxford, to Epping Forest, and it was much too long. Finally, however, we were met at a crossroads by another policeman on a motorcycle, and followed him down a twisting secondary road. The forest stretched away all round, bare-branched and mournful in the gray, damp day.

Round the bend we came on a row of two cars and a van, parked. The motorcyclist stopped and dismounted, and the policeman and I got out.

"ETA 12.15," said the motorcyclist, looking at his watch. "You're late. The brass has been waiting here twenty minutes."

"Traffic like caterpillars on the A.40," said my driver defensively.

"You should have used your bell," the motorcyclist grinned. "Come on. It's over this way."

He led us down a barely perceptible track into the wood. We walked on dead brown leaves, rustling. After about half a mile we came to a group of men standing round a screen made of hessian. They were stamping their feet to keep warm and talking in quiet voices.

"Mr. Halley?" One of them shook hands, a pleasant, capable-looking man in middle age who introduced himself as Chief Inspector Cornish. "We're sorry to bring you here all this way, but we want you to see the er . . . remains . . . before we move them. I'd better warn you, it's a perfectly horrible sight." He gave a very human shudder.

"Who is it?" I asked.

26

"We're hoping you can tell us that, for sure. We think . . . but we'd like you to tell us without us putting it into your head. All right? Now?"

I nodded. He showed me round the screen.

It was Andrews. What was left of him. He had been dead a long time, and the Epping Forest scavengers seemed to have found him tasty. I could see why the police had wanted me to see him *in situ*. He was going to fall to pieces as soon as they moved him.

"Well?"

"Thomas Andrews," I said.

They relaxed. "Are you sure? Positive?"

"Yes."

"It's not just the clothes?"

"No. The shape of the hairline. Protruding ears. Exceptionally rounded helix, vestigial lobes. Very short eyebrows, thick near the nose. Spatulate thumbs, white marks across nails. Hair growing on backs of phalanges."

"Good," said Cornish. "That's conclusive, I'd say. We made a preliminary identification fairly early because of the clothes—they were detailed on the wanted-for-questioning list, of course. But our first inquiries were negative. He seems to have no family, and no one could remember that he had any distinguishing marks—no tattoos, no scars, no operations, and as far as we could find out he hadn't been to a dentist all his life."

"It was intelligent of you to check all that before you gave him to the pathologist," I remarked.

"It was the pathologist's idea, actually." He smiled.

"Who found him?" I asked.

"Some boys. It's usually boys who find bodies."

"When?"

"Three days ago. But obviously he's been here weeks, probably from very soon after he took a pot at you."

"Yes. Is the gun still in his pocket?"

Cornish shook his head. "No sign of it."

"You don't know yet how he died?" I asked.

"No, not yet. But now you've identified him we can get on with it."

27

We went out from behind the screen and some of the other men went in with a stretcher. I didn't envy them.

Cornish turned to walk back to the road with me, the driver following at a short distance. We went fairly slowly, talking about Andrews, but it seemed more like eight miles than eight hundred yards. I wasn't quite ready for jolly country rambles.

As we reached the cars he asked me to lunch with him. I shook my head, explained about the diet, and suggested a drink instead.

"Fine," he said. "We could both do with one after that." He jerked his head in the direction of Andrews. "There's a good pub down the road this way. Your driver can follow us."

He climbed into his car and we drove after him.

In the bar, equipped with a large brandy and water for me and a whisky and sandwiches for him, we sat at a black oak table, on chintzy chairs, surrounded by horse brasses, hunting horns, warming pans and pewter pots.

"It's funny, meeting you like this," said Cornish, in between bites. "I've watched you so often racing. You've won a tidy bit for me in your time. I hardly missed a meeting on the old Dunstable course, before they sold it for building. I don't get so much racing now, it's so far to a course. Nowhere now to slip along to for a couple of hours in an afternoon." He grinned cheerfully and went on, "You gave us some rare treats at Dunstable. Remember the day you rode that dingdong finish on Brushwood?"

"I remember," I said.

"You literally picked that horse up and carried him home." He took another bite. "I never heard such cheering. There's no mistake about it, you were something special. Pity you had to give it up."

"Yes. . . ."

"Still, I suppose that's a risk you run steeplechasing. There is always one crash too many."

"That's right."

"Where was it you finally bought it?"

"At Stratford-on-Avon, two years ago last May."

He shook his head sympathetically. "Rotten bad luck."

I smiled. "I'd had a pretty good run, though, before that."

"I'll say you did." He smacked his palm on the table. "I took the Missus down to Kempton on Boxing Day, three or four years ago. . . ." He went on talking with enjoyment about races he had watched, revealing himself as a true enthusiast, one of the people without whose interest all racing would collapse. Finally, regretfully, he finished his whisky and looked at his watch. "I'll have to get back. I've enjoyed meeting you. It's odd how things turn out, isn't it? I don't suppose you ever thought when you were riding that you would be good at this sort of work."

"What do you mean, good?" I asked, surprised.

"Hm? Oh, Andrews of course. That description of his clothes you gave after he had shot you. And identifying him today. Most professional. Very efficient." He grinned.

"Getting shot wasn't very efficient," I pointed out.

He shrugged. "That could happen to anyone, believe me. I shouldn't worry about that."

I smiled, as the driver drove me back to Aynsford, at the thought that anyone could believe me good at detective work. There was a simple explanation of my being able to describe and identify—I had read so many of the Missing Persons and Divorce files. The band of ex-policemen who compiled them knew what to base identification on, the unchanging things like ears and hands, not hair color or the wearing of spectacles or a mustache. One of them had told me without pride that wigs, beards, face-padding, and the wearing of or omission of cosmetics made no impression on him, because they were not what he looked at. "Ears and fingers," he said, "they can't disguise those. They never think of trying. Stick to ears and fingers, and you don't go far wrong."

Ears and fingers were just about all there was left of Andrews to identify. The unappetizing gristly bits.

The driver decanted me at Charles's back door and

I walked along the passage to the hall. When I had one foot on the bottom tread of the staircase Charles himself appeared at the drawing-room door.

"Oh, hullo, I thought it might be you. Come in here and look at these."

Reluctantly leaving the support of the bannisters I followed him into the drawing room.

"There," he said, pointing. He had fixed up a strip of light inside his bookcase and it shone down onto the quartz gems, bringing them to sparkling life. The open doors with their red silk curtains made a softly glowing frame. It was an eye-catching and effective arrangement, and I told him so.

"Good. The light goes on automatically when the doors are open. Nifty, don't you think?" He laughed. "And you can set your mind at rest. They are now insured."

"That's good."

He shut the doors of the bookcase and the light inside went out. The red curtains discreetly hid their treasure. Turning to me, more seriously he said, "Whose body?"

"Andrews'."

"The man who shot you? How extraordinary. Suicide?"

"No, I don't think so. The gun wasn't there, anyway."

He made a quick gesture toward the chair. "My dear Sid, sit down, sit down. You look like d . . . er . . . a bit worn out. You shouldn't have gone all that way. Put your feet up, I'll get you a drink." He fussed over me like a mother hen, fetching me first water, then brandy, and finally a cup of warm beef juice from Mrs. Cross, and sat opposite me watching while I dispatched it.

"Do you like that stuff?" he asked.

"Yes, luckily." I grinned.

"We used to have it when we were children. A ritual once a week. My father used to drain it out of the Sunday joint, propping the dish on the carving fork. We all loved it, but I haven't had any for years."

"Try some?" I offered him the cup.

He took it and tasted it. "Yes, it's good. Takes me back sixty years. . . ." He smiled companionably, relaxing in his chair, and I told him about Andrews and the long-dead state he was in.

"It sounds," he said slowly, "as if he might have been murdered."

"I wouldn't be surprised. He was young and healthy. He wouldn't just lie down and die of exposure in Hertfordshire."

Charles laughed.

"What time are your guests expected?" I asked, glancing at the clock. It was just after five.

"About six."

"I think I'll go up and lie on my bed for a while, then."

"You are all right, Sid, aren't you? I mean, really all right?"

"Oh yes. Just tired."

"Will you come down to dinner?" There was the faintest undercurrent of disappointment in his casual voice. I thought of all his hard work with the rocks and the amount of maneuvering he had done. Besides, I was getting definitely curious myself about his intentions.

"Yes," I nodded, getting up. "Lay me a teaspoon."

I made it upstairs and lay on my bed, sweating. And cursing. Although the bullet had missed everything vital in tearing holes through my gut, it had singed and upset a couple of nerves. They had warned me in the hospital that it would be some time before I felt well. It didn't please me that so far they were right.

I heard the visitors arrive, heard their loud cheerful voices as they were shown up to their rooms, the doors shutting, the bath waters running, the various bumps and murmurs from the adjoining rooms; and eventually the diminishing chatter as they finished changing and went downstairs past my door. I heaved myself off the bed, took off the loose-waisted slacks and jersey shirt I felt most comfortable in, and put on a white cotton shirt and dark gray suit.

My face looked back at me, pale, gaunt and dark-eyed, as I brushed my hair. A bit of a death's-head at the feast. I grinned nastily at my reflection. It was only a slight improvement.

31

3

By the time I got to the foot of the stairs, Charles and his guests were coming across the hall from the drawing room to the dining room. The men all wore dinner jackets and the women, long dresses. Charles deliberately hadn't warned me, I reflected. He knew my convalescent kit didn't include a black tie.

He didn't stop and introduce me to his guests, but nodded slightly and went straight on into the dining room, talking with charm to the rounded, fluffy little woman who walked beside him. Behind came Viola and a tall dark girl of striking good looks. Viola, Charles's elderly widowed cousin, gave me a passing half-smile, embarrassed and worried. I wondered what was the matter: normally she greeted me with affection, and it was only a short time since she had written warm wishes for my recovery. The girl beside her barely glanced in my direction, and the two men bringing up the rear didn't look at me at all.

Shrugging, I followed them into the dining room. There was no mistaking the place laid for me: it consisted, in actual fact, of a spoon, a mat, a glass, and a fork, and it was situated in the centèr of one of the sides. Opposite me was an empty gap. Charles seated his guests, himself in his usual place at the end of the table with fluffy Mrs. van Dysart on his right, and the striking Mrs. Kraye on his left. I sat between Mrs. Kraye and Rex van Dysart. It was only gradually that I sorted everyone out. Charles made no introductions whatever.

The groups at each end of the table fell into animated chat and paid me as much attention as a speed limit. I began to think I would go back to bed.

The manservant whom Charles engaged on these occasions served small individual tureens of turtle soup. My

32

tureen, I found, contained more beef juice. Bread was passed, spoons clinked, salt and pepper were shaken and the meal began. Still no one spoke to me, though the visitors were growing slightly curious. Mrs. van Dysart flicked her sharp china-blue eyes from Charles to me and back again, inviting an introduction. None came. He went on talking to the two women with almost overpowering charm, apparently oblivious.

Rex van Dysart on my left offered me bread, with lifted eyebrows and a faint noncommittal smile. He was a large man with a flat white face, heavy black rimmed spectacles and a domineering manner. When I refused the bread he put the basket down on the table, gave me the briefest of nods, and turned back to Viola.

Even before he brought quartz into his conversation I guessed it was for Howard Kraye that the show was being put on; and I disliked him on sight with a hackle-raising antipathy that disconcerted me. If Charles was planning that I should ever work for, or with, or near Mr. Kraye, I thought, he could think again.

He was a substantial man of about forty-eight to fifty, with shoulders, waist and hips all knocking forty-four. The dinner jacket sat on him with the ease of a second skin, and when he shot his cuffs occasionally he did so without affectation, showing off noticeably well-manicured hands.

He had tidy gray-brown hair, straight eyebrows, narrow nose, small firm mouth, rounded freshly shaven chin, and very high unwrinkled lower eyelids, which gave him a secret, shuttered look.

A neat enclosed face like a mask, with perhaps something rotten underneath. You could almost smell it across the dinner table. I guessed, rather fancifully, that he knew too much about too many vices. But on top he was smooth. Much too smooth. In my book, a nasty type of phony. I listened to him talking to Viola.

". . . So when Doria and I got to New York I looked up those fellows in that fancy crystal palace on First Avenue and got them moving. You have to give the clotheshorse diplomats a lead, you know, they've absolutely no initiative of their own. Look, I told them,

33

unilateral action is not only inadvisable, but impracticable. But they are so steeped in their own brand of pragmatism that informed opinion has as much chance of osmosing as mercury through rhyolite. . . ."

Viola was nodding wisely while not understanding a word. The pretentious rigmarole floated comfortably over her sensible head and left her unmoved. But its flashiness seemed to me part of a gigantic confidence trick: one was meant to be enormously impressed. I couldn't believe that Charles had fallen under his spell; it was impossible. Not my subtle, clever, coolheaded father-in-law. Mr. van Dysart, however, hung on every word.

By the end of the soup his wife at the other end of the table could contain her curiosity no longer. She put down her spoon and with her eyes on me, said to Charles in a low but clearly audible voice, "Who is that?"

All heads turned toward him, as if they had been waiting for the question. Charles lifted his chin and spoke distinctly, so that they should all hear the answer.

"That," he said, "is my son-in-law." His tone was light, amused, and infinitely contemptuous; and it jabbed raw on a nerve I had thought long-dead. I looked at him sharply, and his eyes met mine, blank and expressionless.

My gaze slid up over and passed his head to the wall behind him. There, for some years, and certainly that morning, had hung an oil painting of me on a horse going over a fence at Cheltenham. In its place there was now an old-fashioned seascape, brown with Victorian varnish.

Charles was watching me. I looked back at him briefly and said nothing. I suppose he knew I wouldn't. My only defense against his insults long ago had been silence, and he was counting on my instant reaction being the same again.

Mrs. van Dysart leaned forward a little, and with waking malice murmured, "Do go on, Admiral."

Without hesitation Charles obeyed her, in the same flaying voice. "He was fathered, as far as he knows, by a window cleaner on a nineteen-year-old unmarried girl

34

from the Liverpool slums. She later worked, I believe, as a packer in a biscuit factory."

"Admiral, no!" exclaimed Mrs. van Dysart breathlessly.

"Indeed yes," nodded Charles. "As you might guess, I did my best to stop my daughter making such an unsuitable match. He is small, as you see, and he has a crippled hand. Working class and undersized . . . but my daughter was determined. You know what girls are." He sighed.

"Perhaps she was sorry for him," suggested Mrs. van Dysart.

"Maybe." said Charles. He hadn't finished, and wasn't to be deflected. "If she had met him as a student of some sort, one might have understood it . . . but he isn't even educated. He finished school at fifteen to be apprenticed to a trade. He has been unemployed now for some time. My daughter, I might say, has left him."

I sat like a stone, looking down at the congealed puddle at the bottom of my soup dish, trying to loosen the clamped muscles in my jaw, and to think straight. Not four hours ago he'd shown concern for me and had drunk from my cup. As far as I could ever be certain of anything, his affection for me was genuine and unchanged. So he must have a good reason for what he was doing to me now. At least I hoped so.

I glanced at Viola. She hadn't protested. She was looking unhappily down at her place. I remembered her embarrassment out in the hall, and I guessed that Charles had warned her what to expect. He might have warned me too, I thought grimly.

Not unexpectedly, they were all looking at me. The dark and beautiful Doria Kraye raised her lovely eyebrows and in a flat, slightly nasal voice, remarked, "You don't take offense, then." It was halfway to a sneer. Clearly she thought I ought to take offense, if I had any guts.

"He is not offended," said Charles easily. "Why should the truth offend?"

"Is it true then," asked Doria down her flawless nose, "that you are illegitimate and all the rest?"

35

I took a deep breath and eased my muscles.

"Yes."

There was an uncomfortable short silence. Doria said, "Oh," blankly, and began to crumble her bread.

On cue, and no doubt summoned by Charles's foot on the bell, the manservant came in to remove the plates, and conversation trickled back to the party like cigarette smoke after a cancer scare.

I sat thinking of the details Charles had left out: the fact that my twenty-year-old father, working overtime for extra cash, had fallen from a high ladder and been killed three days before his wedding day, and that I had been born eight months later. The fact that my young mother, finding that she was dying from some obscure kidney ailment, had taken me from grammer school at fifteen, and because I was small for my age had apprenticed me to a racehorse trainer in Newmarket, so that I should have a home and someone to turn to when she had gone. They had been good enough people, both of them, and Charles knew that I thought so.

The next course was some sort of fish smothered in mushroom-colored sauce. My astronauts' delight, coming at the same time, didn't look noticably different, as it was not in its pot, but out on a plate. Dear Mrs. Cross, I thought fervently, I could kiss you. I could eat it this way with a fork, singlehanded. The pots needed to be held—in my case inelegantly hugged between forearm and chest—and at that moment I would have starved rather than taken my left hand out of my pocket.

Fluffy Mrs. van Dysart was having a ball. Clearly she relished the idea of me sitting there practically isolated, dressed in the wrong clothes, and an object of open derision to her host. With her fair frizzy hair, her baby-blue eyes and her rose-pink silk dress embroidered with silver, she looked as sweet as sugar icing. What she said showed that she thoroughly understood the pleasures of keeping a whipping boy.

"Poor relations are such a problem, aren't they?" she said to Charles sympathetically, and intentionally loud enough for me to hear."You can't neglect them in our position, in case the Sunday papers get hold of them and pay them to make a smear. And it's especially difficult if one has to keep them in one's own house. One can't, I suppose, put them to eat in the kitchen, but there are so many occasions when one could do without them. Perhaps a tray upstairs is the best thing."

"Ah, yes," nodded Charles smoothly, "but they won't always agree to that."

I half choked on a mouthful, remembering the pressure he had exerted to get me downstairs. And immediately I felt not only reassured but deeply interested. This, then, was what he had been so industriously planning, the destruction of me as a man in the eyes of his guests. He would no doubt explain why in his own good time. Meanwhile I felt slightly less inclined to go back to bed.

I glanced at Kraye, and found his greenish-amber eyes steady on my face. It wasn't as overt as in Mrs. van Dysart's case, but it was there: pleasure. My toes curled inside my shoes. Interested or not, it was hard to sit tight before that loathsome, taunting half-smile. I looked down, away, blotting him out.

He gave a sound halfway between a cough and a laugh, turned his head, and began talking down the table to Charles about the collection of quartz.

"So sensible of you, my dear chap, to keep them all behind glass, though most tantalizing to me from here. Is that a geode, on the middle shelf? The reflection, you know . . . I can't quite see."

"Er . . ." said Charles, not knowing any more than I did what a geode was. "I'm looking forward to showing them to you. After dinner, perhaps? Or tomorrow?"

"Oh, tonight, I'd hate to postpone such a treat. Did you say that you had any felspar in your collection?"

"No," said Charles uncertainly.

"No, well, I can see it is a small specialized collection. Perhaps you are wise in sticking to silicon dioxide."

Charles glibly launched into the cousinly-bequest alibi for ignorance, which Kraye accepted with courtesy and disappointment.

"A fascinating subject, though, my dear Roland. It repays study. The earth beneath our feet, the fundamental

37

sediment from the Triassic and Jurassic epochs, is our priceless inheritance, the source of all our life and power. . . . There is nothing which interests me so much as land."

Doria on my right gave me the tiniest of snorts, which her husband didn't hear. He was busy constructing another long, polysyllabic and largely unintelligible chat on the nature of the universe.

I sat unoccupied through the steaks, the meringue pudding, the cheese and the fruit. Conversations went on on either side of me and occasionally past me, but a deaf-mute could have taken as much part as I did. Mrs. van Dysart commented on the difficulties of feeding poor relations with delicate stomachs and choosy appetites. Charles neglected to tell her that I had been shot and wasn't poor, but agreed that a weak digestion in dependents was a moral fault. Mrs. van Dysart loved it. Doria occasionally looked at me as if I were an interesting specimen of low life. Rex van Dysart again offered me the bread; and that was that. Finally Viola shepherded Doria and Mrs. van Dysart out to have coffee in the drawing room and Charles offered his guests port and brandy. He passed me the brandy bottle with an air of irritation and compressed his lips in disapproval when I took some. It wasn't lost on his guests.

After a while he rose, opened the glass bookcase doors, and showed the quartzes to Kraye. Piece by piece the two discussed their way along the rows, with van Dysart standing beside them exhibiting polite interest and hiding his yawns of boredom. I stayed sitting down. I also helped myself to some more brandy.

Charles kept his end up very well and went through the whole lot without a mistake. He then transferred to the drawing room, where his gem cabinet proved a great success. I tagged along, sat in an unobtrusive chair and listened to them all talking, but I came to no conclusions except that if I didn't soon go upstairs I wouldn't get there under my own steam. It was eleven o'clock and I had had a long day. Charles didn't look round when I left the room.

Half an hour later, when his guests had come

murmuring up to their rooms, he came quietly through my door and over to the bed. I was still lying on top of it in my shirt and trousers, trying to summon some energy to finish undressing.

He looked down at me, smiling.

"Well?" he said.

"It is you," I said, "who is the dyed-in-the-wool, twenty-four-carat, unmitigated bastard."

He laughed. "I thought you were going to spoil the whole thing when you saw your picture had gone." He began taking off my shoes and socks. "You looked as bleak as the Bering Strait in December. Pajamas?"

"Under the pillow."

He helped me undress in his quick neat naval fashion.

"Why did you do it?" I said.

He waited until I was lying down between the sheets, then he perched on the edge of the bed.

"Did you mind?"

"Hell, Charles . . . of course. At first anyway."

"I'm afraid it came out beastlier than I expected, but I'll tell you why I did it. Do you remember that first game of chess we had? When you beat me out of sight? You know why you won so easily?"

"You weren't paying enough attention."

"Exactly. I wasn't paying enough attention, because I didn't think you were an opponent worth bothering about. A bad tactical error." He grinned. "An admiral should know better. If you underrate a strong opponent you are at a disadvantage. If you grossly underrate him, if you are convinced he is of absolutely no account, you prepare no defense and are certain to be defeated." He paused for a moment, and went on. "It is therefore good strategy to delude the enemy into believing you are too weak to be considered. And that is what I was doing tonight on your behalf."

He looked at me gravely. After some seconds I said, "At what game, exactly, do you expect me to play Howard Kraye?"

He sighed contentedly, and smiled. "Do you remember what he said interested him most?"

I thought back. "Land."

Charles nodded. "Land. That's right. He collects it. Chunks of it, yards of it, acres of it. . . ." He hesitated.

"Well?"

"You can play him," he said slowly, "for Seabury Racecourse."

The enormity of it took my breath away.

"What?" I said incredulously. "Don't be silly. I'm only—"

"Shut up," he interrupted. "I don't want to hear what you think you are only. You're intelligent, aren't you? You work for a detective agency? You wouldn't want Seabury to close down? Why shouldn't you do something about it?"

"But I imagine he's after some sort of take-over bid, from what you say. You want some powerful city chap or other to oppose him, not . . . me."

"He is very much on his guard against powerful chaps in the city, but wide open to you."

I stopped arguing because the implications were pushing into the background my inadequacy for such a task.

"Are you sure he is after Seabury?" I asked.

"Someone is," said Charles. "There has been a lot of buying and selling of the shares lately, and the price per share is up although they haven't paid a dividend this year. The clerk of the course told me about it. He said that the directors are very worried. On paper, there is no great concentration of shares in any one name, but there wasn't at Dunstable either. There, when it came to a vote on selling out to a land developer, they found that about twenty various nominees were in fact all agents for Kraye. He carried enough of the other shareholders with him, and the racecourse was lost to housing."

"It was all legal, though?"

"A wangle; but legal, yes. And it looks like it's happening again."

"But what's to stop him, if it's legal?"

"You might try."

I stared at him in silence. He stood up and straightened the bedcover neatly. "It would be a pity if Seabury went the way of Dunstable." He went toward the door.

"Where does van Dysart fit in?" I asked.

"Oh," he said, turning, "nowhere. It was Mrs. van Dysart I wanted. She has a tongue like a rattlesnake. I knew she would help me tear you to pieces." He grinned. "She'll give you a terrible weekend, I'm glad to say."

"Thanks very much," I said sarcastically. "Why didn't you tell me all this before? When you so carefully left me that book on company law for instance? Or at least this evening when I came back from seeing Andrews, so that I could have been prepared, at dinner?"

He opened the door and smiled across the room, his eyes blank again.

"Sleep well," he said. "Good night, Sid."

Charles took the two men out shooting the following morning and Viola drove their wives into Oxford to do some shopping and visit an exhibition of Venetian glass. I took the opportunity of having a good look round the Krayes' bedroom.

It wasn't until I'd been there for more than ten minutes that it struck me that two years earlier I wouldn't have dreamed of doing such a thing. Now I had done it as a matter of course, without thinking twice. I grinned sardonically. Evidently even in just sitting around in a detective agency one caught an attitude of mind. I realized, moreover, that I had instinctively gone about my search methodically and with a careful touch. In an odd way it was extremely disconcerting.

I wasn't of course looking for anything special: just digging a little into the Krayes' characters. I wouldn't even concede in my own mind that I was interested in the challenge Charles had so elaborately thrown down. But all the same I searched, and thoroughly.

Howard Kraye slept in crimson pajamas with his initials embroidered in white on the pocket. His dressing gown was of crimson brocade with a black quilted collar and black tassels on the belt. His washing things, neatly arranged in a large fitted toilet case in the adjoining bathroom, were numerous and ornate. He used pine-scented aftershave lotion, cologne friction rub, lemon

41

hand cream, and an oily hair dressing, all from gold-topped cut-glass bottles. There were also medicated soap tablets, special formula toothpaste, talcum powder in a gilt container, deodorant, and a supersonic-looking electric razor. He wore false teeth and had a spare set. He had brought a half-full tin of laxatives, some fruit salts, a bottle of mouthwash, some antiseptic foot powder, penicillin throat lozenges, a spot-sealing stick, digestive tablets and an eye bath. The body beautiful, in and out.

All his clothes, down to his vests and pants, had been made to measure, and he had brought enough to cover every possibility of a country weekend. I went through the pockets of his dinner jacket and the three suits hanging beside it, but he was a tidy man and they were all empty, except for a nail file in each breast pocket. His six various pairs of shoes were handmade and nearly new. I looked into each shoe separately, but except for trees they were all empty.

In a drawer I found neatly arranged his stock of ties, handkerchiefs, and socks: all expensive. A heavy chased silver box contained cuff links, studs, and tiepins; mostly of gold. He had avoided jewels, but one attractive pair of cuff links was made from pieces of what I now knew enough to identify as tiger's-eye. The backs of his hair-brushes were beautiful slabs of the gem stone, smoky quartz. A few brown and gray hairs were lodged in between the bristles.

There remained only his luggage, four lavish suitcases standing in a neat row beside the wardrobe. I opened each one. They were all empty except for the smallest, which contained a brown calf attaché case. I looked at it carefully before I touched it, but as Kraye didn't seem to have left any telltales like hairs or pieces of cotton attached, I lifted it out and put it on one of the beds. It was locked, but I had learned how to deal with such drawbacks. A lugubrious ex-police sergeant on Radnor's payroll gave me progessively harder lessons in lock-picking every time he came into the office between jobs, moaning all the while about the damage London soot did to his chrysanthemums. My one-handedness he had seen only as a challenge, and had invented a couple of new techniques and instruments entirely for my benefit. Recently he had presented me with a collection of fine delicate keys which he had once removed from a burglar, and had bullied me until I carried them with me everywhere. They were in my room. I went and fetched them and without much trouble opened the case.

It was as meticulously tidy as everything else, and I was particularly careful not to alter the position or order of any of the papers. There were several letters from a stockbroker, a bunch of share transfer certificates, various oddments, and a series of typed sheets, headed with the previous day's date, which were apparently an up-to-the-minute analysis of his investments. He seemed to be a rich man and to do a good deal of buying and selling. He had money in oils, mines, property and industrial stocks. There was also a sheet headed simply S.R., on which every transaction was a purchase. Against each entry was a name and the address of a bank. Some names occurred three or four times, some only once.

Underneath the papers lay a large thick brown envelope inside which were two packets of new ten-pound notes. I didn't count, but there couldn't have been fewer than a hundred of them. The envelope was at the bottom of the case except for a writing board with slightly used white blotting paper held by crocodile and gold corners. I pulled up the board and found underneath it two more sheets of paper, both covered with dates, initials, and sums of money.

I let the whole lot fall back into place, made sure that everything looked exactly as I had found it, relocked the case, and put it back into its covering suitcase.

The divine Doria, I found, was far from being as tidy as her husband. All her things were in a glorious jumble, which made leaving them undistrubed a difficult job, but also meant that she would be less likely than her husband to notice if anything were slightly out of place.

Her clothes, though they looked and felt expensive, were bought ready-made and casually treated. Her washing things consisted of a plastic zippered case, a flannel, a toothbrush, bath essence, and a puffing bottle of talc. Almost stark beside Howard's collection. No medicine. She appeared to wear nothing in bed, but a pretty white quilted dressing gown hung half off a hanger behind the bathroom door.

She had not completely unpacked. Suitcases propped on chairs and stools still held stirred-up underclothes and various ultra-feminine equipment which I hadn't seen since Jenny left.

The top of the dressing table, though the daily seemed to have done her best to dust it, was an expensive chaos. Pots of cosmetics, bottles of scent and hair spray stood on one side, a box of tissues, a scarf, and the cluttered tray out of the top of a dressing case filled the other. The dressing case itself, of crocodile with gold clips, stood on the floor. I picked it up and put it on the bed. It was locked, I unlocked it, and looked inside.

Doria was quite a girl. She possessed two sets of false eyelashes, spare fingernails, and a hairpiece on a tortoise-shell headband. Her big jewel case, the one tidy thing in her whole luggage, contained on the top layer the sapphire and diamond earrings she had worn the previous evening, along with a diamond sunburst brooch and a sapphire ring; and on the lower layer a second necklace, bracelet, earrings, brooch and ring all of gold, platinum and citrine. The yellow jewels were uncommon, barbaric in design and had no doubt been made especially for her.

Under the jewel case were four paperback novels so pornographic in content as to raise doubts about Kraye's ability as a lover. Jenny had held that a truly satisfied woman didn't need to read dirty sex. Doria clearly did.

Alongside the books was a thick leather-covered diary to which the beautiful Mrs. Kraye had confided the oddest thoughts. Her life seemed to be as untidy as her clothes, a mixture of ordinary social behavior, dream fantasy and a perverted marriage relationship. If the diary were to be believed, she and Howard obtained deeper pleasure, both of them, from his beating her than from the normal act of love. Well, I reflected, at least they were well matched. Some of the divorces which Hunt Radnor Associates dealt with arose because one partner alone was pain-fixated, the other being revolted.

At the bottom of the case were two other objects of interest. First, coiled in a brown velvet bag, the sort of leather strap used by schoolmasters, at whose purpose, in view of the diary, it was easy to guess; and second, in a chocolate box, a gun.

4

Telephoning for the local taxi to come and fetch me, I went to Oxford and bought a camera. Although the shop was starting a busy Saturday afternoon, the boy who served me tackled the problem of a one-handed photographer with enthusiasm and as if he had all the time in the world. Between us we sorted out a miniature German 16 mm. camera, three inches long by one and a half wide, which I could hold, set, snap and wind with one hand with the greatest ease.

He gave me a thorough lesson in how to work it, added an inch to its length in the shape of a screwed-on photoelectric light meter, loaded it with film, and slid it into a black case so small that it made no bulge in my trouser pocker. He also offered to change the film later if I couldn't manage it. We parted on the best of terms.

When I got back everyone was sitting round a cozy fire in the sitting room, eating crumpets. Very tantalizing. I loved crumpets.

No one took much notice when I went in and sat down on the fringe of the circle except Mrs. van Dysart, who began sharpening her claws. She got in a couple of quick digs about spongers marrying girls for their money, and Charles didn't say that I hadn't. Viola looked at me searchingly, worry opening her mouth. I winked, and she shut it again in relief.

I gathered that the morning's bag had been the usual mixture (two brace of pheasant, five wild duck and a hare), because Charles preferred a rough shoot over his own land to organized affairs with beaters. The women had collected a poor opinion of Oxford shop assistants and a booklet on the manufacture of fifteenth-century Italian glass. All very normal for a country weekend. It was my snooping that seemed unreal. That, and the false position Charles had steered me into.

Kraye's gaze, and finally his hands, strayed back to the gem bookshelves. Again the door was opened, Charles's trick lighting working effectively, and one by one the gems were brought out, passed round and closely admired. Mrs. van Dysart seemed much attached to a spectacular piece of rose quartz, playing with it to make light strike sparks from it, and smoothing her fingers over the glossy surface.

"Rex, you must collect some of this for me!" she ordered, her will showing like iron inside the fluff; and masterful-looking Rex nodded his meek agreement.

Kraye was saying, "You know, Roland, these are really remarkably fine specimens. Among the best I've ever seen. Your cousin must have been extremely fortunate and influential to acquire so many fine crystals."

"Oh, indeed he was," agreed Charles equably.

"I should be interested if you ever think of realizing on them . . . a first option, perhaps?"

"You can have a first option by all means," smiled Charles. "But I shan't be selling them, I assure you."

"Ah well, so you say now. But I don't give up easily. . . . I shall try you later. But don't forget, my first option?"

"Certainly," said Charles. "My word on it."

Kraye smiled at the stone he held in his hands, a magnificent raw amethyst like a cluster of petrified violets.

"Don't let this fall into the fire," he said. "It would turn yellow." He then treated everyone to a lecture on amethysts which would have been interesting had he made any attempt at simplicity: but blinding by words was with him either a habit or a policy. I wasn't certain which.

". . . Manganese, of course occurring in geodes or agate nodules in South America or Russia, but with such a world-wide distribution it was only to be expected that elementary societies should ascribe to it supra rational inherencies and attributes. . . ."

I suddenly found him looking straight at me, and I knew my expression had not been one of impressed admiration. More like quizzical sarcasm. He didn't like it. There was a quick flash in his eyes.

"It is symptomatic of the slum mentality," he remarked, "to scoff at what it can't comprehend."

"Sid," said Charles sharply. "I'm sure you must have something else to do. We can let you go until dinner."

I stood up. The natural anger rose quickly, but only as far as my teeth. I swallowed. "Very well," I muttered.

"Before you go, Sid," said Mrs. van Dysart from the depths of a sofa, ". . . Sid, what a deliciously plebeian name, so suitable. . . . Put these down on the table for me."

She held out both hands, one stone in each and another balanced between them. I couldn't manage them all and dropped them.

"Oh dear," said Mrs. van Dysart, acidly sweet, as I knelt and picked them up, putting them one by one on the table, "I forgot you were disabled, so silly of me." She hadn't forgotten. "Are you sure you can't get treatment for whatever is wrong with you? You ought to try some exercises, they'd do you the world of good. All you need is a little perserverance. You owe it to the Admiral, don't you think, to *try*?"

I didn't answer, and Charles at least had the grace to keep quiet.

"I know a very good man," went on Mrs. van Dysart. "He used to work for the army . . . excellent at getting malingerers back into service. Now he's the sort of man who'd do you good. What do you think, Admiral, shall I fix it up for your son-in-law to see him?"

"Er . . . ," said Charles, "I don't think it would work."

"Nonsense." She was brisk and full of smiles. "You can't let him lounge about doing nothing for the rest of his life. A good bracing course of treatment, that's what

47

he needs. Now," she said turning to me, "so that I know exactly what I'm talking about when I make an appointment, let's see this precious crippled hand of yours."

There was a tiny pause. I could feel their probing eyes, their unfriendly curiosity.

"No," I said calmly. "Excuse me, but no."

As I walked across the room and out of the door her voice floated after me. "There you are, Admiral, he doesn't *want* to get better. They're all the same. . . ."

I lay on my bed for a couple of hours rereading the book on company law, especially, now, the section on take-overs. It was no easier going than it had been in the hospital, and now that I knew why I was reading it, it seemed more involved, not less. If the directors of Seabury were worried, they would surely have called in their own investigator. Someone who knew his way round the stock markets like I knew my way round the track. An expert. I wasn't at all the right person to stop Kraye, even if indeed anyone could stop him. And yet . . . I stared at the ceiling, taking my lower lip between my teeth. And yet . . . I did have a wild idea. . . .

Viola came in, knocking as she opened the door.

"Sid, dear, are you all right? Can I do anything for you?" She shut the door, gentle, generous, and worried.

I sat up and swung my legs over the side of the bed. "No, thanks, I'm fine."

She perched on the arm of an easy chair, looked at me with her kind, slightly mournful brown eyes, and said a little breathlessly, "Sid, why are you letting Charles say such terrible things about you? It isn't only when you are there in the room; they've been, oh, almost sniggering about you behind your back. Charles and that frightful Mrs. van Dysart. . . . What has happened between you and him? When you nearly died he couldn't have been more worried if you'd been his own son . . . but now he is so cruel, and terribly unfair."

"Dear Viola, don't worry. It's only some game that Charles is playing, and I go along with him."

"Yes," she said, nodding. "He warned me. He said that you were both going to lay a smoke screen and that I was on no account to say a single word in your defense

48

the whole weekend. But it wasn't true, was it? When I saw your face, when Charles said that about your poor mother, I knew you didn't know what he was going to do."

"Was it so obvious?" I said ruefully. "Well, I promise you I haven't quarreled with him. Will you just be a dear and do exactly as he asked? Don't say a single word to any of them about . . . um . . . the more successful bits of my life history, or about my job at the agency, or about the shooting. You didn't today, did you, on the trip to Oxford?" I finished with some anxiety.

She shook her head. "I thought I'd talk to you first."

"Good." I grinned.

"Oh dear," she cried, partly in relief, partly in puzzlement. "Well, in that case, Charles asked me to pop in and make sure you would come down to dinner."

"Oh he did, did he? Afraid I'd throw a boot at him, I should think, after sending me out of the room like that. Well, you just pop back to Charles and say that I'll come down to dinner on condition that he organizes some chemmy afterwards, and includes me out."

Dinner was a bit of a trial: with their smoked salmon and pheasant the guests enjoyed another round of Sidbaiting. Both the Krayes, egged on by Charles and the fluffy harpy beside him, had developed a pricking skill for this novel weekend parlor game, and I heartily wished Charles had never thought of it. However, he kept his side of the bargain by digging out the chemin-de-fer shoe, and after the coffee, the brandy, and another inspection of the dining-room quartzes, he settled his guests firmly round the table in the drawing-room.

Upstairs, once the shoe was clicking regularly and the players were well involved, I went and collected Kraye's attache case and took it along to my room.

Because I was never going to get another chance and did not want to miss something I might regret later, I photographed every single paper in the case. All the stockbroker's letters and all the investment reports. All the share certificates, and also the two separate sheets under the writing board.

Although I had an ultra-bright light bulb and the exposure meter to help me get the right setting, I took several pictures at different light values of the papers I considered the most important in order to be sure of getting the sharpest possible result. The little camera handled beautifully, and I found I could change the films in their tiny casettes without much difficulty. By the time I had finished I had used three whole films of twenty exposures on each. It took me a long time, as I had put the camera down between each shot to move the next paper into my pool of light, and also had to be very careful not to alter the order in which the papers had lain in the case.

The envelope of ten-pound notes kept me hoping like crazy that Howard Kraye would not lose heavily and come upstairs for replacements. It seemed to me at the time a ridiculous thing to do, but I took two flat blocks of tenners out of the envelope, and photographed them as well. Putting them back I flipped through them: the notes were new, consecutive, fifty to a packet. One thousand pounds to a penny.

When everything was back in the case I sat looking at the contents for a minute, checking their position against my visual memory of how they looked when I first saw them. At last satisfied, I shut the case, locked it, rubbed it over to remove any finger marks I might have left, and put it back where I had found it.

After that I went downstairs to the dining room for the brandy I had refused at dinner. I needed it. Carrying the glass, I listened briefly outside the drawing-room door to the murmurs and clicks from within and went upstairs again, to bed.

Lying in the dark I reviewed the situation. Howard Kraye, drawn by the bait of a quartz collection, had accepted an invitation to a quiet weekend in the country with a retired admiral. With him he had brought a selection of private papers. As he had no possible reason to imagine that anyone in such innocent surroundings would spy on him, the papers might be very private indeed. So private that he felt safest when they were with

50

him? Too private to leave at home? It would be nice to think so.

At that point, imperceptibly, I fell sleep.

The nerves in my abdomen wouldn't give up. About after five hours of fighting them unsuccessfully I decided that staying in bed all morning thinking about it was doing no good, and got up and dressed.

Drawn partly against my will, I walked along the passage to Jenny's room, and went in. It was the small sunny room she had had as a child. She had gone back to it when she left me and it was all hers alone. I had never slept there. The single bed, the relics of childhood, girlish muslin frills on curtains and dressing table, everything shut me out. The photographs round the room were of her father, her dead mother, her sister, brother-in-law, dogs and horses, but not of me. As far as she could, she blotted out her marriage.

I walked slowly round touching her things, remembering how much I had loved her. Knowing, too, that there was no going back, and that if she walked through the door at that instant we would not fall into each other's arms in tearful reconciliation.

Removing a one-eyed teddy bear I sat down for a while on her pink armchair. It's difficult to say just where a marriage goes wrong, because the accepted reason often isn't the real one. The rows Jenny and I had had were all ostensibly caused by the same thing: my ambition. Grown finally too heavy for flat racing, I had switched entirely to steeplechasing the season before we were married, and I wanted to be champion jumping jockey. To this end I was prepared to eat little, drink less, go to bed early, and not make love if I were racing the next day. It was unfortunate that she liked late-night parties and dancing more than anything else. At first she gave them up willingly, then less willingly, and finally in fury. After that, she started going on her own.

In the end she told me to choose between her and racing. But by then I was indeed champion jockey, and had been for some time, and I couldn't give it up. So Jenny left. It was just life's little irony that six months later I lost the racing as well. Gradually since then I had come to realize that a marriage didn't break up just because one half liked parties and the other didn't. I thought now that Jenny's insistence on a gay time was the result of my having failed her in some basic, deeply necessary way. Which did nothing whatsoever for my self-respect or my self-confidence.

I sighed, stood up, replaced the teddy bear, and went downstairs to the drawing room. Eleven o'clock on a windy autumn morning.

Doria was alone in the big comfortable room, sitting on the window seat and reading the Sunday papers, which lay around her on the floor in a haphazard mess.

"Hello," she said, looking up. "What hole did you crawl out of?"

I walked over to the fire and didn't answer.

"Poor little man, are his feelings hurt then?"

"I do have feelings, the same as anyone else."

"So you actually can talk?" she said mockingly. "I'd begun to wonder."

"Yes, I can talk."

"Well, now, tell me your troubles, little man."

"Life is just a bowl of cherries."

She uncurled herself from the window seat and came across to the fire, looking remarkably out of place in skin-tight leopard-printed pants and a black silk shirt.

She was the same height as Jenny, the same height as me, just touching five foot six. As my smallness had always been an asset for racing, I never looked on it as a handicap for life in general, either physical or social. Neither had I ever really understood why so many people thought that height for its own sake was important. But it would have been naïve not to take note of the widespread extraordinary assumption that the mind and heart could be measured by tallness. The little man with the big emotion was a stock comic figure. It was utterly irrational. What difference did three or four inches of leg bone make to a man's essential nature? Perhaps I had been fortunate in coming to terms early with the effect of poor nutrition in a difficult childhood; but it did not stop me understanding why other short men struck back

52

in defensive aggression. They were the pinpricks, for instance, of girls like Doria calling one "little" and intending it as an insult.

"You've dug yourself into a cushy berth here, haven't you?" she said, taking a cigarette from the silver box on the mantelpiece.

"I suppose so."

"If I were the Admiral I'd kick you out."

"Thank you," I said, neglecting to offer her a light. With a mean look she found a box of matches and struck one for herself.

"Are you ill, or something?"

"No. Why?"

"You eat those faddy health foods, and you look such a sickly little creature. . . . I just wondered." She blew the smoke down her nose. "The Admiral's daughter must have been pretty desperate for a wedding ring."

"Give her her due," I said mildly. "At least she didn't pick a rich father figure twice her age."

I thought for a moment she meant to go into the corny routine of smacking my face, but as it happened she was holding the cigarette in the hand she needed.

"You little shit," she said instead. A charming girl, altogether.

"I get along."

"Not with me, you don't." Her face was tight. I had struck very deep, it seemed.

"Where is everyone else?" I asked, gesturing around the empty room.

"Out with the Admiral somewhere. And you can take yourself off again too. You're not wanted in here."

"I'm not going. I live here, remember?"

"You went quick enough last night," she sneered. "When the Admiral says jump, you jump. But fast, little man. And that I like to see."

"The Admiral," I pointed out, "is the hand that feeds. I don't bite it."

"Bootlicking little creep."

I grinned at her nastily and sat down in an armchair. I still didn't feel too good. Pea green and clammy, to

53

be exact. Nothing to be done though, but wait for it to clear off.

Doria tapped ash off her cigarette and looked at me down her nose, thinking up her next attack. Before she could launch it, however, the door opened and her husband came in.

"Doria," he said happily, not immediately seeing me in the armchair, "where have you hidden my cigarette case? I shall punish you for it."

She made a quick movement toward me with her hand and Howard saw me and stopped dead.

"What are you doing here?" he said brusquely, the fun-and-games dying abruptly out of his face and voice.

"Passing the time."

"Clear out, then. I want to talk to my wife."

I shook my head and stayed put.

"Short of picking him up and throwing him out bodily," said Doria, "you won't get rid of him. I've tried."

Krayé shrugged. "Roland puts up with him. I suppose we can too." He picked up one of the newspapers and sat down in an armchair facing me. Doria wandered back to the window seat, pouting. Kraye straightened up the paper and began to read the front page. Across the back page, the racing page, facing me across the fireplace, the black, bold headlines jumped out.

"ANOTHER HALLEY?"

Underneath, side by side, were two photographs: one of me, and the other of a boy who had won a big race the day before.

It was by then essential that Kraye should not discover how Charles had misrepresented me; it had gone much too far to be explained away as a joke. The photograph was clearly printed for once. I knew it well. It was an old one which the papers had used several times before, chiefly because it was a good likeness. Even if none of the guests read the racing column, as Doria obviously hadn't, it might catch their eye in passing, through being in such a conspicuous place.

Kraye finished reading the front page and began to turn the paper over.

"Mr. Kraye," I said. "Do you have a very big quartz collection yourself?"

He lowered the paper a little and gave me an unenthusiastic glance.

"Yes, I have," he said briefly.

"Then could you please tell me what would be a good thing to give the Admiral to add to his collection? And where would I get it, and how much would it cost?"

The paper folded over, hiding my picture. He cleared his throat and with strained politeness started to tell me about some obscure form of crystal which the Admiral didn't have. Press the right button, I thought . . . Doria spoiled it. She walked jerkily over to Kraye and said crossly, "Howard, for God's sake. The little creep is buttering you up. I bet he wants something. You're a sucker for anyone who will talk about rocks."

"People don't make a fool of me," said Kraye flatly, his eyes narrowing in irritation.

"No. I only want to please the Admiral," I explained.

"He's a sly little beast," said Doria. "I don't like him."

Kraye shrugged, looked down at the newspaper and began to unfold it again.

"It's mutual," I said casually. "You daddy's doll."

Kraye stood up slowly and the paper slid to the floor, front page up.

"What did you say?"

"I said I didn't think much of your wife."

He was outraged, as well he might be. He took a single step across the rug, and there was suddenly something more in the room than three guests sparring round a Sunday-morning fire.

Even though I was as far as he knew an insignificant fly to swat, a clear quality of menace flowed out of him like a radio signal. The calm social mask had disappeared along with the wordy, phony, surface personality. The vague suspicion I had gained from reading his papers, together with the antipathy I had felt for him all along, clarified into belated recognition: this was not just a

55

smooth speculator operating near the legal border line, but a full-blown, powerful, dangerous big-time crook.

Trust me, I thought, to prod an anthill and find a hornets' nest. Twist the tail of a grass snake and find a boa constrictor. What on earth would he be like, I wondered, if one did more to cross him than disparage his choice of wife?

"He's sweating," said Doria, pleased. "He's afraid of you."

"Get up," he said.

As I was sure that if I stood up he would simply knock me down again, I stayed where I was.

"I'll apologize," I said.

"Oh, no," said Doria, "that's much too easy."

"Something subtle," suggested Kraye, staring down.

"I know!" Doria was delighted with her idea. "Let's get that hand out of his pocket."

They both saw from my face that I would hate that more than anything. They both smiled. I thought of bolting, but it meant leaving the paper behind.

"That will do very nicely," said Kraye. He leaned down, twined one hand into the front of my jersey shirt and the other into my hair, and pulled me to my feet. The top of my head reached about to his chin. I wasn't in much physical shape for resisting, but I took a half-hearted swipe at him as I came up. Doria caught my swinging arm and twisted it up behind my back, using both or hers and an uncomfortable amount of pressure. She was a strong, healthy girl with no inhibitions about hurting people.

"That'll teach you to be rude to me," she said with satisfaction.

I thought of kicking her shins, but it would only have brought more retaliation. I also wished Charles would come back at once from wherever he was.

He didn't.

Kraye transferred his grip from my hair to my left forearm and began to pull. That arm was no longer much good, but I did my best. I tucked my elbow tight against my side, and my hand stayed in my pocket.

"Hold him harder," he said to Doria. "He's stronger

56

than he looks." She levered my arm up another inch and I started to roll round to get out of it. But Kraye still had his grasp on the front of my jersey, with his forearm leaning across under my throat, and between the two of them I was properly stuck. All the same, I found, I couldn't just stand still and let them do what I so much didn't want them to.

"He squirms, doesn't he?" said Doria cheerfully.

I squirmed and struggled a good deal more—until they began getting savage with frustration, and I was panting. It was my wretched stomach which finished it. I began to feel too ill to go on. With a terrific jerk Kraye dragged my hand out.

"Now," he said triumphantly.

He gripped my elbow fiercely and pulled the jersey sleeve up from my wrist. Doria let go of my right arm and came to look at their prize. I was shaking with rage, pain, humiliation . . . heaven knows what.

"Oh," said Doria blankly. "Oh."

She was no longer smiling, nor was her husband. They looked steadily at the wasted, flabby, twisted hand, and at the scars on my forearm, wrist and palm, not only the terrible jagged marks of the original injury but the several tidier ones of the operations I had had since. It was a mess, a right and proper mess.

"So that's why the Admiral lets him stay, the nasty little beast," said Doria, screwing up her face in distaste.

"It doesn't excuse his behavior," said Kraye. "I'll make sure he keeps that tongue of his still, in future."

He stiffened his free hand and chopped the edge of it down across the worst part, the inside of my wrist. I jerked in his grasp.

"Ah . . . ," I said. "Don't."

"He'll tell tales to the Admiral," said Doria warningly, "if you hurt him too much. It's a pity, but I should think that's about enough."

"I don't agree, but—"

There was a scrunch on the gravel outside, and Charles's car swept past the window, coming back.

Kraye let go of my elbow with a shake. I went weakly

57

down on my knees on the rug, and it wasn't all pretense.

"If you tell the Admiral about this, I'll deny it," said Kraye, "and we know who he'll believe."

I did know who he'd believe, but I didn't say so. The newspaper which had caused the rumpus lay close beside me on the rug. The car doors slammed distantly. The Krayes turned away from me toward the window, listening. I picked up the paper, got to my feet, and set off for the door. They didn't try to stop me in any way. They didn't mention the newspaper either. I opened the door, went through, shut it, and steered a slightly crooked course across the hall to the wardroom. Upstairs was too far. I shut the wardroom door behind me, hid the newspaper, slid into Charles's favorite armchair, and waited for my various miseries, mental and physical, to subside.

Some time later Charles came in to fetch some fresh packages of cigarettes.

"Hullo," he said over his shoulder, opening the cupboard. "I thought you were still in bed. Mrs. Cross said you weren't very well this morning. It isn't at all warm in here. Why don't you come into the drawing room?"

"The Krayes . . ." I stopped.

"They won't bite you." He turned round, cigarette in hand. He looked at my face. "What's so funny?" and then more sharply, looking closer. "What's the matter?"

"Oh, nothing. Have you seen today's Sunday *Hemisphere?*"

"No, not yet. Do you want it? I thought it was in the drawing room with the other papers."

"No, it's in the top drawer of your desk. Take a look."

Puzzled, he opened the drawer, took out the paper, and unfolded it. He went to the racing section unerringly.

"My God!" he said, aghast. "Today of all days." His eyes skimmed down the page and he smiled. "You've read this, of course?"

I shook my head. "I just took it to hide it."

He handed me the paper. "Read it then. It'll be good for your ego. They won't let you die! 'Young Finch,' " he quoted, "'showed much of the judgment and miraculous precision of the great Sid.' How about that? And that's just the start."

"Yeah, how about it?" I grinned. "Count me out for lunch, if you don't mind, Charles. You don't need me there any more."

"All right, if you don't feel like it. They'll be gone by six at the latest, you'll be glad to hear." He smiled and went back to his guests.

I read the newspaper before putting it away again. As Charles had said, it was good for the ego. I thought the columnist, whom I'd known for years, had somewhat exaggerated my erstwhile powers. A case of the myth growing bigger than the reality. But still, it was nice. Particularly in view of the galling, ignominious end to the roughhouse in which the great Sid had so recently landed himself.

On the following morning Charles and I changed back the labels on the chunks of quartz and packed them up ready to return to the Carver Foundation. When we had finished we had one label left over.

"Are you sure we haven't put one stone in the box without changing the label?" said Charles.

"Positive."

"I suppose we'd better check. I'm afraid that's what we've done."

We took all the chunks out of the big box again. The gem collection, which Charles under protest had taken to bed with him each night, was complete; but we looked through them again too to make sure the missing rock had not got among them by mistake. It was nowhere to be found.

"St. Lukes stone," I read from the label. "I remember where that was, up on the top shelf on the right-hand side."

"Yes," agreed Charles, "a dull-looking lump about the size of a fist. I do hope we haven't lost it."

"We have lost it," I remarked. "Kraye's pinched it."

"Oh no," Charles exclaimed. You can't be right."

59

"Go and ring up the Foundation, and ask them what the stone is worth."

He shook his head doubtfully, but went to the telephone and came back frowning.

"They say it hasn't any intrinsic value, but it's an extremely rare form of meteorite. It never turns up in mines or quarrying of course. You have to wait for it to fall from the heavens, and then find it. Very tricky."

"A quartz which friend Kraye didn't have."

"But he surely must know I'd suspect him?" Charles protested.

"You'd never have missed it, if it had really been part of your cousin's passed-on collection. There wasn't any gap on the shelf just now. He'd moved the others along. He couldn't know you would check carefully almost as soon as he had gone."

Charles sighed. "There isn't a chance of getting it back."

"No," I agreed.

"Well, it's a good thing you insisted on the insurance," he said. "Carver's valued that boring-looking lump more than all the rest put together. Only one other meteorite like it has ever been found: the St. Mark's stone." He smiled suddenly. "We seem to have mislaid the equivalent of the penny black."

5

Two days later I went back through the porticoed, columned doorway of Hunt Radnor Associates a lot more alive than when I last came out.

I got a big hullo from the girl on the switchboard, went up the curving staircase very nearly whistling, and was greeted by a barrage of ribald remarks from the Racing Section. What most surprised me was the feeling I had of coming home: I had never thought of myself as really belonging to the agency before, even though down at Aynsford I had realized that I very much didn't want to leave it. A bit late, that discovery. The skids were probably under me already.

Chico grinned widely. "So you made it."

"Well . . . yes."

"I mean, back here to the grindstone."

"Yeah."

"But," he cast a rolling eye at the clock, "late as usual."

"Go stuff yourself," I said.

Chico threw out an arm to the smiling department. "Our Sid is back, his normal charming bloody self. Work in the agency can now begin."

"I see I still haven't got a desk," I observed, looking round. No desk. No roots. No real job. As ever.

"Sit on Dolly's, she's kept it dusted for you."

Dolly looked at Chico, smiling, the mother-hunger showing too vividly in her great blue eyes. She might be the second-best head of department the agency possessed, with a cross-referencing filing-index mind like a computer, she might be a powerful, large, self-assured woman of forty-odd with a couple of marriages behind her and an ever hopeful old bachelor at her heels, but she still counted her life a wasteland because her body couldn't produce children. Dolly was a terrific worker, overflowing with intensely female vitality, excellent drinking company, and very, very sad.

Chico didn't want to be mothered. He was prickly about mothers. All of them in general, not just those who abandoned their tots in push-chairs at police stations near Barnes Bridge. He jollied Dolly along and deftly avoided her tentative maternal invitations.

I hitched a hip onto a long-accustomed spot on the edge of Dolly's desk, and swung my leg.

"Well, Dolly, my love, how's the sleuthing trade?" I said.

"What we need," she said with mock tartness, "is a bit more work from you and a lot less lip."

"Give me a job, then."

"Ah, now." She pondered. "You could . . . ," she

61

began, then stopped. "Well, no . . . perhaps not. And it had better be Chico who goes to Lambourn; some trainer there wants a doubtful lad checked on. . . ."

"So there's nothing for me?"

"Er . . . well . . . ," said Dolly. "No." She had said no a hundred times before. She had never once said yes.

I made a face at her, picked up her telephone, pressed the right button, and got through to Radnor's secretary.

"Joanie? This is Sid Halley. Yes . . . back from Beyond, that's right. Is the old man busy? I'd like a word with him."

"Big deal," said Chico.

Joanie's prim voice said, "He's got a client with him just now. When she's gone I'll ask him, and ring you back."

"O.K." I put down the receiver.

Dolly raised her eyebrows. As head of the department she was my immediate boss, and in asking direct for a session with Radnor I was blowing agency protocol a raspberry. But I was certain that her constant refusal to give me anything useful to do was a direct order from Radnor. If I wanted the drain unblocked I would have to go and pull out the plug. Or go on my knees to stay at all.

"Dolly, love, I'm tired of kicking my heels. Even against your well-worn desk, though the view from here is ravishing." She was wearing, as she often did, a crossover cream silk shirt: it crossed over at a point which on a young girl would have caused a riot. On Dolly it still looked pretty potent, owing to the generosity of nature and the disposal of her arrangements.

"Are you chucking it in?" said Chico, coming to the point.

"It depends on the old man," I said. "He may be chucking me out."

There was a brief, thoughtful silence in the department. They all knew very well how little I did. How little I had been content to do. Dolly looked blank, which wasn't helpful.

Jones-boy clattered in with a tray of impeccable un-

62

chipped tea mugs. He was sixteen; noisy, rude, anarchistic, callous, and probably the most efficient office boy in London. His hair grew robustly heavy down to his shoulders, wavy and fanatically clean, dipping slightly in an expensive styling at the back. From behind he looked like a girl, which never disconcerted him. From in front his bony, acned face proclaimed him unprepossessing male. He spent half his pay packet and his Sundays in Carnaby Street and the other half on week nights chasing girls. According to him, he caught them. No girls had so far appeared in the office to corroborate his story.

Under the pink shirt beat a stony heart; inside the sprouting head hung a big "So what?" Yet it was because this amusing, ambitious, unsocial creature invariably arrived well before his due hour to get his office arrangements ready for the day that he had found me before I died. There was a moral there, somewhere.

He gave me a look. "The corpse has returned, I see."

"Thanks to you," I said idly, but he knew I meant it. He didn't care, though.

He said, "Your blood and stuff ran through a crack in the linoleum and soaked the wood underneath. The old man was wondering if it would start dry rot or something."

"Jones-boy," protested Dolly, looking sick. "Get the hell out of here, and shut up."

The telephone rang on her desk. She picked it up and listened, said "All right," and disconnected.

"The old man wants to see you. Right away."

"Thanks." I stood up.

"The flipping boot?" asked Jones-boy interestedly.

"Keep your snotty nose out," said Chico.

"And balls to you. . . ."

I went out smiling, hearing Dolly start to deal once again with the running dogfight Chico and Jones-boy never tired of. Downstairs, across the hall, into Joanie's little office and through into Radnor's.

He was standing by the window, watching the traffic doing its nut in Cromwell Road. This room, where the clients poured out their troubles, was restfully painted a quiet gray, carpeted and curtained in crimson and furnished with comfortable armchairs, handy little tables with ash trays, pictures on the walls, ornaments, and vases of flowers. Apart from Radnor's small desk in the corner, it looked like an ordinary sitting room, and indeed everyone believed that he had bought the room intact with the lease, so much was it what one would expect to find in a graceful, six-storied, late Victorian town house. Radnor had a theory that people exaggerated and distorted facts less in such peaceful surroundings than in the formality of a more orthodox office.

"Come in, Sid," he said. He didn't move from the window, so I joined him there. He shook hands.

"Are you sure you're fit enough to be here? You haven't been as long as I expected. Even knowing you . . ." He smiled slightly, with watching eyes.

I said I was all right. He remarked on the weather, the rush hour and the political situation, and finally worked round to the point we both knew was at issue.

"So, Sid, I suppose you'll be looking around a bit now?"

Laid on the line, I thought.

"If I wanted to stay here . . ."

"If? Hm, I don't know." He shook his head very slightly.

"Not on the same terms, I agree."

"I'm sorry it hasn't worked out." He sounded genuinely regretful, but he wasn't making it easy.

I said with careful calm, "You've paid me for nothing for two years. Well, give me a chance now to earn what I've had. I don't really want to leave."

He lifted his head slightly like a pointer to a scent, but he said nothing. I ploughed on.

"I'll work for you for nothing, to make up for it. But only if it's real, decent work. No more sitting around. It would drive me mad."

He gave me a hard stare and let out a long breath like a sigh.

"Good God. At last," he said. "And it took a bullet to do it."

"What do you mean?"

"Sid, have you ever seen a zombie wake up?"

"No," I said ruefully, understanding him. "It hasn't been as bad as that?"

He shrugged one shoulder. "I saw you racing, don't forget. You notice when a fire goes out. We've had the pleasant, flippant ashes drifting round this office, that's all." He smiled deprecatingly at his flight of fancy: he enjoyed making pictures of words. It wasted a lot of office time, on the whole.

"Consider me alight again, then." I grinned. "And I've brought a puzzle back with me. I want very much to sort it out."

"A long story?"

"Fairly, yes."

"We'd better sit down, then."

He waved me to an armchair, sank into one himself, and prepared to listen with the stillness and concentration which sent him time and time again to the core of a problem.

I told him about Kraye's dealing in racecourses. Both what I knew and what I guessed. When at length I finished he said calmly, "Where did you get hold of this?"

"My father-in-law, Charles Roland, tossed it at me while I was staying with him last weekend. He had Kraye as a house guest." The subtle old fox, I thought, throwing me in at the deep end: making me wake up and swim.

"And Roland got it from where?"

"The clerk of the course at Seabury told him that the directors were worried about too much share movement, that it was Kraye who got control of Dunstable, and they were afraid he was at it again."

"But the rest, what you've just told me, is your own supposition?"

"Yes."

"Based on your appraisal of Kraye over one week-end?"

"Partly on what he showed me of his character, yes. Partly on what I read of his papers. . . ." With some hesitation I told him about my snooping and the photography. ". . . The rest, I suppose, a hunch."

65

"Hmm. It needs checking. . . . Have you brought the films with you?"

I nodded, took them out of my pocket, and put them on the little table beside me.

"I'll get them developed." He drummed his fingers lightly on the arm of the chair, thinking. Then, as if having made a decision, said more briskly, "Well, the first thing we need is a client."

"A client?" I echoed absent-mindedly.

"Of course. What else? We are not the police. We work strictly for profit. Ratepayers don't pay the overheads and salaries in this agency. The clients do."

"Oh . . . , yes, of course."

"The most likely client in this case is either Seabury Racecourse executive, or perhaps the National Hunt Committee. I think I should sound out the Senior Steward first, in either case. No harm in starting at the top."

"He might prefer to try the police," I said, "free."

"My dear Sid, one thing people want when they employ private investigators is privacy. They pay for privacy. When the police investigate something, everyone knows about it. When we do, they don't. That's why we sometimes get criminal cases when it would undoubtedly be cheaper to go to the police."

"I see. So you'll try the Senior Steward—"

"No," he interrupted. "You will."

"I?"

"Naturally. It's your case."

"But it's your agency—he is used to negotiating with you."

"You know him too," he pointed out.

"I used to ride for him, and that puts me on a bad footing for this sort of thing. I'm a jockey to him, an ex-jockey. He won't take me seriously."

Radnor shrugged a shoulder. "If you want to take on Kraye, you need a client. Go and get one."

I knew very well that he never sent even senior operatives, let alone inexperienced ones, to arrange or angle for an assignment, so that for several moments I couldn't really believe that he intended me to go. But

66

he said nothing else, and eventually I stood up and went toward the door.

"Sandown races are on today," I said tentatively. "He's sure to be there."

"A good opportunity." He looked straight ahead, not at me.

"I'll try it, then."

"Right."

He wasn't letting me off. But then he hadn't kicked me out either. I went through the door and shut it behind me, and while I was still hesitating in disbelief I heard him inside the room give a sudden guffaw, a short, sharp, loud, triumphant snort of laughter.

I walked back to my flat, collected the car, and drove down to Sandown. It was a pleasant day, dry, sunny, and warm for November, just right for drawing a good crowd for steeplechasing.

I turned in through the racecourse gates, spirits lifting, parked the car (a Mercedes 230 SL with automatic gears, power-assisted steering, and a strip on the back saying NO HAND SIGNALS), and walked round to join the crowd outside the weighing-room door. I could no longer go through it. It had been one of the hardest things to get used to, the fact that all the changing rooms and weighing rooms which had been my second homes for fourteen years were completely barred to me from the day I rode my last race. You didn't lose just a job when you handed in your jockey's license, you lost a way of life.

There were a lot of people to talk to at Sandown, and as I hadn't been racing for six weeks I had a good deal of gossip to catch up on. No one seemed to know about the shooting, which was fine by me, and I didn't tell them. I immersed myself very happily in the racecourse atmosphere and for an hour Kraye retreated slightly into the background.

Not that I didn't keep an eye on my purpose, but until the third race the Senior Steward, Viscount Hagbourne, was never out of a conversation long enough for me to catch him.

Although I had ridden for him for years and had found him undemanding and fair, he was in most respects still a stranger. An aloof, distant man, he seemed to find it difficult to make ordinary human contacts, and unfortunately he had not proved a great success as Senior Steward. He gave the impression, not of power in himself, but of looking over his shoulder at power behind: I'd have said he was afraid of incurring the disapproval of the little knot of rigidly determined men who in fact ruled racing themselves, regardless of who might be in office at the time. Lord Hagbourne postponed making decisions until it was almost too late to make them, and there was still a danger after that that he would change his mind. But all the same he was the front man until his year of office ended, and with him I had to deal.

At length I fielded him neatly as he turned away from the clerk of the course and forestalled a trainer who was advancing upon him with a grievance. Lord Hagbourne, with one of his rare moments of humor, deliberately turned his back on the grievance and consequently greeted me with more warmth than usual.

"Sid, nice to see you. Where have you been lately?"

"Holidays," I explained succinctly. "Look sir, can I have a talk with you after the races? There's something I want to discuss urgently."

"No time like the present," he said, one eye on the grievance. "Fire away."

"No, sir. It needs time and all your attention."

"Hm?"

The grievance was turning away. "Not today, Sid, I have to get home. What is it? Tell me now."

I want to talk to you about the take-over bid for Seabury racecourse."

He looked at me, startled. "You want . . . ?"

"That's right. It can't be said out here where you will be needed at any moment by someone else. If you could just manage twenty minutes at the end of the afternoon . . . ?"

"Er . . . what is your connection with Seabury?"

"None in particular, sir. I don't know if you remember, but I've been connected" (a precise way of putting it)

68

"with Hunt Radnor Associates for the last two years. Various . . . er . . . facts about Seabury have come our way and Mr. Radnor thought you might be interested. I am here as his representative."

"Oh, I see. Very well, Sid, come up to the Stewards' tearoom after the last. If I'm not there, wait for me. Right?"

"Yes. Thank you."

I walked down the slope and then up the iron staircase to the jockeys' box in the stand, smiling at myself. Representative. A nice big important word. It covered anything from an ambassador down. Commercial travelers had rechristened themselves with its rolling syllables years ago; they had done it because of jokes, of course. It didn't sound the same, somehow, starting off with "Did you hear the one about the representative who stopped at a lonely farmhouse? . . ." Rodent officers, garbage disposal and sanitary staff: pretty new names for rat catchers, dustmen, and road sweepers. So why not for me?

"Only idiots laugh at nothing," said a voice in my ear. "What the hell are you looking so pleased about all of a sudden? And where the blazes have you been this last month?"

"Don't tell me you've missed me?" I grinned, not needing to look round. We went together through the door of the high-up jockeys' box, two of a kind, and stood looking out over the splendid racecourse.

"Best view in Europe." He sighed. Mark Witney, thirty-eight years old, racehorse trainer. He had a face battered like a boxer's from too many racing falls, and in the two years since he hung up his boots and stopped wasting he had put on all of forty pounds. A fat, ugly man. We had a host of memories in common, a host of hard-ridden races. I liked him a lot.

"How's things?" I said.

"Oh, fair, fair. They'll be a damn sight better if that animal of mine wins the fifth."

"He must have a good chance."

"He's a damn certainty, boy. A certainty. If he doesn't fall over his goddamned legs. Clumsiest sod this side of Hades." He lifted his race glasses and looked at the number board. "I see poor old Charlie can't do the weight again on that thing of Bob's. . . . That boy of Plumtree's is getting a lot of riding just now. What do you think of him?"

"He takes too many risks," I said. "He'll break his neck."

"Look who's talking. No, seriously, I'm considering taking him on. What do you think?" He lowered his glasses. "I need someone available regularly from now on and all the ones I'd choose are already tied up."

"Well, you could do better, you could do worse, I suppose. He's a bit flashy for me, but he can ride, obviously. Will he do as he's told?"

He made a face. "You've hit the bull's-eye. That's the snag. He always knows best."

"Pity."

"Can you think of anyone else?"

"Um . . . what about that boy Cotton? He's too young really. But he's got the makings. . . ." We drifted out in amiable chat, discussing his problem, while the box filled up around us and the horses went down to the start.

It was a three-mile chase, and one of my ex-mounts was favorite. I watched the man who had my old job ride a very pretty race, and with half my mind thought about housing estates. Sandown itself had survived, some years ago, a bid to cover its green tempting acres with little boxes. Sandown had powerful friends. But Hurst Park, Manchester and Birmingham racecourses had all gone under the rolling tide of bricks and mortar, lost to the double-barreled persuasive arguments that shareholders liked capital gains and people needed houses. To defend itself from such a fate Cheltenham Racecourse had transformed itself from a private, dividend-paying company into a non-profit-making holdings trust, and other racecourses had followed their lead.

But not Seabury. And Seabury was deep in a nasty situation. Not Dunstable, and Dunstable Racecourse was now a tidy dormitory for the Vauxhall workers of Luton.

Most British racecourses were, or had been, private companies, in which it was virtually impossible for an outsider to acquire shares against the will of the members. But four—Dunstable, Seabury, Sandown and Chepstow—were public companies, and their shares could be bought in open market, through the stock exchange.

Sandown had been played for in a straightforward and perfectly honorable way, and plans to turn it into suburban housing had been turned down by the local and county councils. Sandown flourished, made a good profit, paid a 10 per cent dividend, and was probably now impregnable. Chepstow was surrounded by so much other open land that it was in little danger from developers. But little Dunstable had been an oasis inside a growing industrial area.

Seabury was on the flat part of the south coast, flanked on every side by miles of warm little bungalows representing the dreams and savings of people in retirement. At twelve bungalows to the acre—elderly people liked tiny gardens—there must be room on the spacious racecourse for over three thousand more. Add six or seven hundred pounds to the building price of each bungalow for the plot it stood on, and you scooped something in the region of two million.

The favorite won and was duly cheered, I clattered down the iron staircase with Mark, and we went and had a drink together.

"Are you sending anything to Seabury next week?" I asked. Seabury was one of his nearest meetings.

"Perhaps. I don't know. It depends if they can hold it at all, of course. But I've got mine entered at Lingfield as well, and I think I'll send them there instead. It's a much more prosperous-looking place, and the owners like it better. Good lunch and all that. Seabury's so dingy these days. I had a hard job getting old Carmicheal to agree to me running his horse there at the last meeting—and look what happened. The meeting was off and we'd missed the other engagement at Worcester too. It wasn't my fault, but I'd persuaded him that he stood more chance at Seabury, and he blamed me because in the end the horse stayed at home eating his head off for

71

nothing. He says there's a jinx on Seabury, and I've a couple more owners who don't like me entering their horses there. I've told them that it's a super track from the horses' point of view, but it doesn't make much difference, they don't know it like we do."

We finished our drinks and walked back toward the weighing room. His horse scrambled home in the fifth by a whisker and I saw him afterward in the unsaddling enclosure beaming like a Halloween pumpkin.

After the last race I went to the Stewards' tearoom. There were several Stewards with their wives and friends having tea, but no Lord Hagbourne. The Stewards pulled out a chair, gave me a welcome, and talked, as ever, about the racing. Most of them had ridden as amateurs in their day, one against me in the not too distant past, and I knew them all well.

"Sid, what do you think of the new-type hurdles?"

"Oh, much better. Far easier for a young horse to see."

"Do you know of a good young chaser I could buy?"

"Didn't you think Hayward rode a splendid race?"

"I watched the third down at the Pond, and believe me that chestnut took off outside the wings. . . ."

". . . do you think we ought to have had him in, George?"

". . . heard that Green bust his ribs again yesterday . . ."

"Don't like that breed, never did, not genuine. . . "

"Miffy can't seem to go wrong, he'd win with a cart horse. . . ."

"Can you come and give a talk to our local pony club, Sid? I'll write you the details. What date would suit you?"

Gradually they finished their tea, said good-bye, and left for home. I waited. Eventually he came, hurrying, apologizing, explaining what had kept him.

"Now," he said, biting into a sandwich. "What's it all about, eh?"

"Seabury."

"Ah yes, Seabury. Very worrying. Very worrying indeed."

"A Mr. Howard Kraye has acquired a large number of shares—"

"Now hold on a minute, Sid. That's only a guess, because of Dunstable. We've been trying to trace the buyer of Seabury shares through the stock exchange, and we can find no definite lead to Kraye."

"Hunt Radnor Associates do have that lead."

He stared. "Proof?"

"Yes."

"What sort?"

"Photographs of share transfer certificates." And heaven help me, I thought, if I've messed them up.

"Oh," he said somberly. "While we weren't sure, there was some hope we were wrong. Where did you get these photographs?"

"I'm not at liberty to say, sir. But Hunt Radnor Associates would be prepared to make an attempt to forestall the takeover of Seabury."

"For a fat fee, I suppose," he said dubiously.

"I'm afraid so, sir, yes."

"I don't connect you with this sort of thing, Sid." He moved restlessly and looked at his watch.

"If you would forget about me being a jockey, and think of me as having come from Mr. Radnor, it would make things a lot easier. How much is Seabury worth to National Hunt racing?"

He looked at me in surprise, but he answered the question, though not in the way I meant.

"Er . . . well, you know it's an excellent course, good for horses and so on."

"It didn't show a profit this year, though."

"There was a great deal of bad luck."

"Yes. Too much to be true, don't you think?"

"What do you mean?"

"Has it ever occurred to the National Hunt Committee that bad luck can be . . . well, arranged?"

"You aren't seriously suggesting that Kraye . . . I mean that anyone would damage Seabury on purpose? In order to make it show a loss?"

73

"I am suggesting that it is a possibility. Yes."

"Good God." He sat down rather abruptly.

"Malicious damage," I said. "Sabotage, if you like. There's a great deal of industrial precedent. Hunt Radnor Associates investigated a case of it only last year in a small provincial brewery where the fermentation process kept going wrong. A prosecution resulted, and the brewery was able to remain in business."

He shook his head. "It is quite ridiculous to think that Kraye would be implicated in anything like that. He belongs to one of my clubs. He's a wealthy, respected man."

"I know, I've met him," I said.

"Well then, you must be aware of what sort of person he is."

"Yes." Only too well.

"You can't seriously suggest—" he began.

"There would be no harm in finding out," I interrupted. "You'll have studied the figures. Seabury's quite a prize."

"How do you see the figures, then?" It seemed he genuinely wanted to know, so I told him.

"Seabury Racecourse has an issued share capital of eighty thousand pounds in fully paid-up one-pound shares. The land was bought when that part of the coast was more or less uninhabited, so that this sum bears absolutely no relation to the present value of the place. Any company in that position is just asking for a take-over.

"A buyer would in theory need fifty-one per cent of the shares to be certain of gaining control, but in practice, as was found at Dunstable, forty would be plenty. It could probably be swung on a good deal less, but from the point of view of the buyer, the more he got his hands on before declaring his intentions, the bigger would be his profit.

"The main difficulty in taking over a racecourse company—its only natural safeguard, in fact—is that the shares seldom come on the market. I understand that it isn't always by any means possible to buy even a few on the stock exchange, as people who own them tend to be fond

74

of them, and as long as the shares pay any dividend, however small, they won't sell. But it's obvious that not everyone can afford to have bits of capital lying around unproductively, and once the racecourse starts showing a loss, the temptation grows to transfer to something else.

"Today's price of Seabury shares is thirty shillings, which is about four shillings higher than it was two years ago. If Kraye can manage to get hold of a forty per cent holding at an average price of thirty shillings, it will cost him only about forty-eight thousand pounds.

"With a holding that size, aided by other shareholders tempted by a very large capital gain, he can outvote any opposition, and sell the whole company to a land developer. Planning permission would almost certainly be granted, as the land is not beautiful, and is surrounded already by houses. I estimate that a developer would pay roughly a million for it, as he could double that by selling off all those acres in tiny plots. There's the capital gains tax, of course, but Seabury shareholders stand to make eight hundred per cent on their original investment, if the scheme goes through. Four hundred thousand gross for Mr. Kraye, perhaps. Did you ever find out how much he cleared at Dunstable?"

He didn't answer.

I went on, "Seabury used to be a busy, lively, successful place, and now it isn't. It's a suspicious coincidence that as soon as a big buyer comes along the place goes downhill fast. They paid a dividend of only sixpence per share last year, a gross yield of under one and three-quarters per cent at today's price, and this year they showed a loss of three thousand, seven hundred and fourteen pounds. Unless something is done soon, there won't be a next year."

He didn't reply at once. He stared at the floor for a long time with the half-eaten sandwich immobile in his hand.

Finally he said, "Who did the arithmetic? Radnor?"

"No . . . I did. It's very simple. I went to Company House in the city yesterday and looked up the Seabury balance sheets for the last few years, and I rang for a

75

quotation of today's share price from a stockbroker this morning. You can easily check it."

"Oh, I don't doubt you. I remember now, there was a rumor that you made a fortune on the stock exchange by the time you were twenty."

"People exaggerate so." I smiled. "My old governor, where I was apprenticed, started me off investing, and I was a bit lucky."

"Hm."

There was another pause while he hesitated over his decision. I didn't interrupt him, but I was much relieved when finally he said, "You have Radnor's authority for seeing me, and he knows what you have told me?"

"Yes."

"Very well." He got up stiffly and put down the unfinished sandwich. "You can tell Radnor that I agree to an investigation being made, and I think I can vouch for my colleagues agreeing. You'll want to start at once, I suppose."

I nodded.

"The usual terms?"

"I don't know," I said. "Perhaps you would get onto Mr. Radnor about that."

As I didn't know what the usual terms were, I didn't want to discuss them.

"Yes, all right. And Sid . . . it's understood that there is to be no leak about this? We can't afford to have Kraye slapping a libel or slander action on us."

"The agency is always discreet," I said, with an outward and an inward smile. Radnor was right. People paid for privacy. And why not?

6

The racing section was quiet when I went in next morning, mostly because Chico was out on an escort job. All the other heads, including Dolly's, were bent studiously over their desks.

She looked up and said with a sigh, "You're late again." It was ten to ten. "The old man wants to see you."

I made a face at her and retraced my way down the staircase. Joanie looked pointedly at her watch.

"He's been asking for you for half an hour."

I knocked and went in. Radnor was sitting behind his desk, reading some papers, pencil in hand. He looked at me and frowned.

"Why are you so late?"

"I had a pain in me tum," I said flippantly.

"Don't be funny," he said sharply, and then, more reasonably, "Oh . . . I suppose you're not being funny."

"No. But I'm sorry about being late." I wasn't a bit sorry, however, that it had been noticed; before, no one would have said a thing if I hadn't turned up all day.

"How did you get on with Lord Hagbourne?" Radnor asked. "Was he interested?"

"Yes. He agreed to an investigation. I said he should discuss terms with you."

"I see." He flicked a switch on the small box on his desk. "Joanie, see if you can get hold of Lord Hagbourne. Try the London flat number first."

"Yes, sir," her voice came tinnily out of the speaker.

"Here," said Radnor, picking up a shallow brown cardboard box. "Look at these."

The box contained a thick wad of large glossy photographs. I looked at them one by one and heaved a sigh of relief. They had all come out sharp and clear, except some of the ones I had duplicated at varying exposures.

The telephone on Radnor's desk rang once, quietly. He lifted the receiver.

"Oh, good morning, Lord Hagbourne. Radnor here. Yes, that's right. . . ." He gestured to me to sit down, and I stayed there listening while he negotiated terms in a smooth, civilized, deceptively casual voice.

"And of course in a case like this, Lord Hagbourne, there's one other thing: we make a small surcharge if our operatives have to take out-of-the-ordinary risks. . . . Yes, as in the Canlas case, exactly. Right then, you shall have a preliminary report from us in a few days. Yes . . . good-bye."

He put down the receiver, bit his thumbnail thoughtfully for a few seconds, and said finally, "Right, then, Sid. Get on with it."

"But—" I began.

"But nothing," he said. "It's your case. Get on with it."

I stood up, holding the packet of photographs. "Can I . . . can I use Bona Fides and so on?"

He waved his hand permissively. "Sid, use every resource in the agency you need. Keep an eye on expenses though, we don't want to price ourselves out of business. And if you want legwork done, arrange it through Dolly or the other department heads. Right?"

"Won't they think it odd? I mean . . . I don't amount to much round here."

"And whose fault is that? If they won't do what you ask, refer them to me." He looked at me expressionlessly.

"All right." I walked to the door. "Er . . . who . . ." I said, turning the knob, "gets the danger money? The operative or the agency?"

"You said you would work for nothing," he observed dryly.

I laughed. "Just so. Do I get expenses?"

"That car of yours drinks petrol."

"It does twenty," I protested.

"The agency rate is based on thirty. You can have that. And other expenses, yes. Put in a chit to accounts."

"Thanks."

He smiled suddenly, the rare sweet smile so incongruous to his military bearing, and launched into another elaborate metaphor.

"The tapes are up," he said. "What you do with the race depends on your skill and .timing, just as it always used to. I've backed you with the agency's reputation for getting results, and I can't afford to lose my stake. Remember that."

"Yes," I said soberly. "I will."

I thought, as I took my stupidly aching stomach up two stories to Bona Fides, that it was time Radnor had a lift installed; and was glad I wasn't bound for Missing Persons away in the rarefied air of the fifth floor. There was a lot more character, I supposed, in the splendidly proportioned, solidly built town house that Radnor had chosen on a corner site on Cromwell Road, but a flat half acre of modern office block would have been easier on his staff. And about ten times as expensive, no doubt.

The basement, to start at the bottom, was—except for the kitchen—given over entirely to files and records. On the ground floor, besides Radnor himself and Joanie, there were two interview-cum-waiting rooms, and also the Divorce Section. On the first floor, the Racing Section, Accounts, another interview room and the general secretarial department. Up one was Bona Fides, and above that, on the two smaller top floors, Guard and Missing Persons. Missing Persons alone had room to spare. Bona Fides, splitting at the seams, was encroaching on Guard. Guard was sticking in its toes.

Jones-boy, who acted as general messenger, must have had legs like iron from pounding up and down the stairs, though thanks to a tiny service lift used long ago to take nursery food to top-floor children, he could haul his ten trays up from landing to landing instead of carrying them.

In Bona Fides there was the usual chatter of six people talking on the telephone all at once. The department head, receiver glued to one ear and finger stuck in the other, was a large bald-headed man with half-moon spectacles sitting halfway down a prominent nose. As always, he was in his shirt sleeves, teamed with a frayed pullover and baggy gray flannels. No tie. He seemed to have an inexhaustible supply of old clothes but never any new ones, and Jones-boy had a theory that his wife dressed him from jumble sales.

I waited until he had finished a long conversation with a managing director about the character of the proposed production manager of a glass factory. The invaluable thing about Jack Copeland was his quick and comprehensive grasp of what dozens of jobs entailed. He was speaking to the glass manufacturer as if he had grown up in the industry; and in five minutes, I knew, he might be advising just as knowledgeably on the suitability of a town clerk. His summing up of a man went far beyond the basic list of honesty, conscientiousness, normality and prudence, which was all that many employers wanted. He liked to discover his subject's reaction under stress, to find out what he disliked doing, and what he often forgot. The resulting footnotes to his reports were usually the most valuable part of them, and the faith large numbers of industrial firms had in him bore witness to his accuracy.

He wielded enormous power but did not seem conscious of it, which made him much liked. After Radnor, he was the most important person in the agency.

"Jack," I said, as he put down the receiver. "Can you check a man for me, please?"

"What's wrong with the Racing Section, pal?" he said, jerking his thumb toward the floor.

"He isn't a racing person."

"Oh? Who is it?"

"A Howard Kraye. I don't know if he has a profession. He speculates on the stock market. He is a rabid collector of quartz." I added Kraye's London address.

He scribbled it all down fast.

"O.K., Sid. I'll put one of the boys on to it and let you have a prelim. Is it urgent?"

"Fairly."

"Right." He tore the sheet off the pad. "George? You still doing that knitting-wool client's report? When you've finished, here's your next one."

"George," I said. "Be careful."

They both looked at me, suddenly still.

"An unexploded bomb," I observed. "Don't set him off."

George said cheerfully, "Makes a nice change from knitting wool. Don't worry, Sid. I'll walk on eggs."

Jack Copeland peered at me closely through the half specs.

"You've cleared it with the old man, I suppose?"

"Yes." I nodded. "It's a query fraud. He said to check with him if you wanted to."

He smiled briefly. "No need, I guess. Is that all then?"

"For the moment, yes, thanks."

"Just for the record, is this your own show, or Dolly's, or whose?"

"I suppose . . . mine."

"Uh-huh," he said accenting the second syllable. "The winds of change, if I read it right?"

I laughed. "You never know."

Down in the Racing Section I found Dolly supervising the reshuffling of the furniture. I asked what was going on, and she gave me a flashing smile.

"It seems you're in, not out. The old man just rang to say you needed somewhere to work, and I've sent Jones-boy upstairs to pinch a table from Missing Persons. That'll do for now, won't it? There isn't a spare desk in the place."

A series of bangs from outside heralded the return of Jones-boy, complete with a spindly plywood affair in a sickly lemon color. "How that lot ever find a missing person I'll never know. I bet they don't even find their missing junk."

He disappeared and came back shortly with a chair. "The things I do for you!" he said, setting it down

81

in front of me. "A dim little bird in the typing pool is now squatting on a stool. I chatted her up a bit."

"What this place needs is some more equipment," I murmured.

"Don't be funny," said Dolly. "Every time the old man buys one desk he takes on two assistants. When I first came here fifteen years ago we had a whole room each, believe it or not."

The rearranged office settled down again, with my table wedged into a corner next to Dolly's desk. I sat behind it and spread out the photographs to sort them. The people who developed and printed all the agency's work had come up with their usual excellent job, and it amazed me that they had been able to enlarge the tiny negatives up to nine-by-seven-inch prints and get a clearly readable result.

I picked out all the fuzzy ones, the duplicates at the wrong exposures, tore them up, and put the pieces in Dolly's wastepaper basket. That left me with fifty-one pictures of the contents of Kraye's attaché case. Innocent enough to the casual eye, but they turned out to be dynamite.

The two largest piles, when I had sorted them out, were Seabury share transfer certificates, and letters from Kraye's stockbroker. The paper headed S.R. revealed itself to be a summary in simple form of the share certificates, so I added it to that pile. I was left with the photographs of the bank notes, of share dealings which had nothing to do with Seabury, and the two sheets of figures I had found under the writing board at the bottom of the case.

I read through all the letters from the stockbroker, a man called Ellis Bolt, who belonged to a firm known as Charing, Street and King. Bolt and Kraye were on friendly terms; the letters referred sometimes to social occasions on which they had met; but for the most part the typewritten sheets dealt with the availability and prospects of various shares (including Seabury), purchases made or proposed, and references to tax, stamp duty, and commission.

Two letters had been written in Bolt's own hand. The first, dated ten days ago, said briefly:

Dear H.
Shall wait with interest for the news on Friday.

E.

The second, which Kraye must have received on the morning he went to Aynsford, read:

Dear H.
I have put the final draft in the hands of the printers, and the leaflets should be out by the end of next week, or the Tuesday following at the latest. Two or three days before the next meeting, anyway. That should do it, I think. There would be a lot of unrest should there be another hitch, but surely you will see to that.

E.

"Dolly," I said. "May I borrow your phone?"
"Help yourself."
I rang upstairs to Bona Fides. "Jack? Can I have a rundown on another man as well? Ellis Bolt, stockbroker, works for a firm called Charing, Street and King." I gave him the address. "He's a friend of Kraye's. Same care needed, I'm afraid."
"Right. I'll let you know."
I sat staring down at the two harmless-looking letters.
"Shall wait with interest for the news on Friday." It could mean any news, anything at all. It also could mean the News; and on the radio on Friday I had heard that Seabury Races were off because a lorry carrying chemicals had overturned and burned the turf.
The second letter was just as tricky. It could easily refer to a shareholder's meeting at which a hitch should be avoided at all costs. Or it could refer to a race meeting—at Seabury—where another hitch could affect the sale of shares yet again.
It was like looking at a conjuring trick: from one side you saw a normal object, but from the other, a sham.

If it were a sham, Mr. Ellis Bolt was in a criminal career up to his eyebrows. If it was just my suspicious mind jumping to hasty conclusions I was doing an old-established respectable stockbroker a shocking injustice.

I picked up Dolly's telephone again and got an outside line.

"Charing, Street and King, good morning," said a quiet female voice.

"Oh, good morning. I would like to make an appointment to see Mr. Bolt and discuss some investments. Would that be possible?"

"Certainly, yes. This is Mr. Bolt's secretary speaking. Could I have your name?"

"Halley. John Halley."

"You would be a new client, Mr. Halley?"

"That's right."

"I see. Well, now, Mr. Bolt will be in the office tomorrow afternoon, and I could fit you in at three thirty. Would that suit you?"

"Thank you. That's fine. I'll be there."

I put down the receiver and looked tentatively at Dolly.

"Would it be all right with you if I go out for the rest of the day?"

She smiled. "Sid, dear, you're very sweet, but you don't have to ask my permission. The old man made it very clear that you're on your own now. You're not accountable to me or anyone else in the agency, except the old man himself. I'll grant you I've never known him give anyone quite such a free hand before, but there you are, my love, you can do what you like. I'm your boss no longer."

"You don't mind?" I asked.

"No," she said thoughtfully. "Come to think of it, I don't. I've a notion that what the old man has always wanted of you in this agency is a partner."

"Dolly!" I was astounded. "Don't be ridiculous."

"He's not getting any younger," she pointed out.

I laughed. "So he picked on a broken-down jockey to help him out."

"He picks on someone with enough capital to buy

84

a partnership, someone who's been to the top of one profession and has the time in years to get to the top of another."

"You're raving, Dolly, dear. He nearly chucked me out yesterday morning."

"But you're still here, aren't you? More here than ever before. And Joanie said he was in a fantastically good mood all day yesterday, after you'd been in to see him."

I shook my head, laughing. "You're too romantic. Jockeys don't turn into investigators any more than they turn into . . ."

"Well, what?" she prompted.

"Into auctioneers, then . . . or accountants."

She shook her head. "You've already turned into an investigator, whether you know it or not. I've been watching you these two years, remember? You look as if you're doing nothing, but you've soaked up everything the bloodhounds have taught you like a hungry sponge. I'd say, Sid love, if you don't watch out, you'll be part of the fixtures and fittings for the rest of your life."

But I didn't believe her, and I paid no attention to what she had said.

I grinned. "I'm going down to take a look at Seabury Racecourse this afternoon. Like to come?"

"Are you kidding?" she sighed. Her in-tray was six inches deep. "I could have just done with a ride in that rocket car of yours, and a breath of sea air."

I stacked the photographs together and returned them to the box, along with the negatives. There was a drawer in the table, and I pulled it open to put the photographs away. It wasn't empty. Inside lay a packet of sandwiches, some cigarettes, and a flat half bottle of whisky.

I began to laugh. "Someone," I said, "will shortly come rampaging down from Missing Persons looking for his missing lunch."

Seabury Racecourse lay about half a mile inland, just off a trunk road to the sea. Looking backward from the top of the stands one could see the wide silver sweep of the English Channel. Between and on both sides the

85

crowded rows of little houses seemed to be rushing toward the coast like Gadarene swine. In each little unit a retired schoolmaster or civil servant or clergyman—or their widows—thought about the roots they had pulled up from wherever it had been too cold or too dingy for their old age, and sniffed the warm south salt-laden air.

They had made it. Done what they'd always wanted. Retired to a bungalow by the sea.

I drove straight in through the open racecourse gate and stopped outside the weighing room. Climbing out, I stretched, and walked over to knock on the door of the racecourse manager's office.

There was no reply. I tried the handle. It was locked. So was the weighing-room door, and everything else.

Hands in pockets, I strolled round the end of the stands to look at the course. Seabury was officially classified in Group Three: that is to say, lower than Doncaster and higher than Windsor when it came to receiving aid from the Betting Levy Board.

It had less than Grade Three stands: wooden steps with corrugated tin roofs for the most part, and drafts from all parts of the compass. But the track itself was a joy to ride on, and it had always seemed a pity to me that the rest of the amenities didn't match it.

There was no one about near the stands. Down at one end of the course, however, I could see some men and a tractor, and I set off toward them, walking down inside the rails, on the grass. The going was just about perfect for November racing, soft but springy underfoot, exactly right for tempting trainers to send their horses to the course in droves. In ordinary circumstances, that was. But as things stood at present, more trainers than Mark Witney were sending their horses elsewhere. A course which didn't attract runners didn't attract crowds to watch them. Seabury's gate receipts had been falling off for some time, but its expenses had risen; and therein lay its loss.

Thinking about the sad tale I had read in the balance sheets, I reached the men working on the course. They were digging up a great section of it and loading it onto

86

a trailer behind the tractor. There was a pervasive un-pleasant smell in the air.

An irregular patch about thirty yards deep, stretching nearly the whole width of the course, had been burned brown and killed. Less than half of the affected turf had already been removed, showing the grayish chalky mud underneath, and there was still an enormous amount to be shifted. I didn't think there were enough men working on it for there to be a hope of its being returfed and ready to race on in only eight days' time.

"Good afternoon," I said to the men in general. "What a horrible mess."

One of them thrust his spade into the earth and came over, rubbing his hands on the sides of his trousers.

"Anything you want?" he said, with fair politeness.

"The racecourse manager. Captain Oxon."

His manner shifted perceptibly toward the civil. "He's not here today, sir. Hey! Aren't you Sid Halley?"

"That's right."

He grinned, doing another quick change, this time toward brotherhood. "I'm the foreman. Ted Wilkins." I shook his outstretched hand. "Captain Oxon's gone up to London. He said he wouldn't be back until tomorrow."

"Never mind," I said. "I was just down in this part of the world and I thought I'd drop in and have a look at the poor old course."

He turned with me to look at the devastation. "Shame, isn't it?"

"What happened, exactly?"

"The tanker overturned on the road over there." He pointed, and we began to walk toward the spot, edging round the dug-up area. The road, a narrow secondary one, ran across near the end of the racecourse, with a wide semi-circle of track on the far side of it. During the races the hard road surface was covered thickly with tan or peat, or with thick green matting, which the horses galloped over without any trouble. Although not ideal, it was an arrangement to be found on many courses throughout the country, most famously with the

Melling Road at Aintree, and reaching a maximum with five road crossings at Ludlow.

"Just here," said Ted Wilkins, pointing. "Worst place it could possibly have happened, right in the middle of the track. The stuff just poured out of the tanker. It turned right over, see, and the hatch thing was torn open in the crash."

"How did it happen?" I asked. "The crash, I mean?"

"No one knows, really."

"But the driver? He wasn't killed, was he?"

"No, he wasn't even hurt much. Just shook up a bit. But he couldn't remember what happened. Some people in a car came driving along after dark and nearly ran into the tanker. They found the driver sitting at the side of the road, holding his head and moaning. Concussion, it was, they say. They reckon he hit his head somehow when lorry went over. Staggers me how he got out of it so lightly, the cab was fair crushed, and there was glass everywhere."

"Do tankers often drive across here?" Lucky it's never happened before, if they do."

"They used not to," he said, scratching his head. "But they've been over here quite regularly now for a year or two. The traffic on the London road's getting chronic, see?"

"Oh . . . did it come from a local firm, then?"

"Down the coast a bit. Intersouth Chemicals, that's the firm it belonged to."

"How soon do you think we'll be racing here again?" I asked, turning back to look at the track. "Will you make it by next week?"

He frowned. "Strictly between you and me, I don't think there's a bleeding hope. What we needed, as I said to the Captain, was a couple of bulldozers, not six men with spades."

"I would have thought so too."

He sighed. "He just told me we couldn't afford them and to shut up and get on with it. And that's what we've done. We'll just about have cut out all the dead turf by next Wednesday, at this rate of going on."

"That doesn't leave any time for new turf to settle," I remarked.

"It'll be a miracle if it's laid, let alone settled," he agreed gloomily.

I bent down and ran my hand over a patch of brown grass. It was decomposing and felt slimy. I made a face, and the foreman laughed.

"Horrible, isn't it? It stinks, too."

I put my fingers to my nose and wished I hadn't. "Was it slippery like this right from the beginning?"

"Yes, that's right. Hopeless."

"Well, I won't take up any more of your time," I said, smiling.

"I'll tell Captain Oxon you came. Pity you missed him."

"Don't bother him. He must have a lot to worry about just now."

"One bloody crisis after another." He nodded. "So long, then." He went back to his spade and his heart-breaking task, and I retraced the quarter mile up the straight to the deserted stands.

I hesitated for a while outside the weighing room, wondering whether to pick the lock and go in, and knowing it was mainly nostalgia that urged me to do it, not any conviction that it would be a useful piece of investigation. There would always be the temptation, I supposed, to use dubious professional skills for one's own pleasure. Like doctors sniffing ether. I contented myself with looking through the windows.

The deserted weighing room looked the same as ever: a large bare expanse of wooden board floor, with a table and some upright chairs in one corner, and the weighing machine itself on the left. Racecourse weighing machines were not all of one universal design. There weren't any left of the old type where the jockeys stood on a platform while weights were added to the balancing arm. That whole process was much too slow. Now there were either seats slung from above, in which one felt much like a bag of sugar, or chairs bolted to a base plate on springs: in both these cases the weight was quickly indicated by a pointer which swung round a gigantic clock face. In essence, modern kitchen scales vastly magnified.

The scales at Seabury were the chair-on-base-plate type, which I'd always found simplest to use. I recalled a few of the before-and-after occasions when I had sat on that particular spot. Some good, some bad, as always with racing.

Shrugging, I turned away. I wouldn't, I thought, ever be sitting there again. And no one walked over my grave.

Climbing into the car, I drove to the nearest town, looked up the whereabouts of Intersouth Chemicals, and an hour later was speaking to the personnel manager. I explained that on behalf of the National Hunt Committee I had just called in passing to find out if the driver of the tanker had fully recovered, or had remembered anything else about the accident.

The manager, fat and fiftyish, was affable but unhelpful. "Smith's left," he said briefly. "We gave him a few days off to get over the accident, and then he came back yesterday and said his wife didn't fancy him driving chemicals any more, and he was packing it in." His voice held a grievance.

"Had he been with you long?" I asked sympathetically.

"About a year."

"A good driver, I suppose?"

"Yes, about average for the job. They have to be good drivers, or we don't use them, you see. Smith was all right, but nothing special."

"And you still don't really know what happened?"

"No," he sighed. "It takes a lot to tip one of our tankers over. There was nothing to learn from the road. It was covered with oil and petrol and chemical. If there had ever been any marks, skid marks I mean, they weren't there after the breakdown cranes had lifted the tanker up again, and the road was cleared."

"Do your tankers use that road often?"

"They have done recently, but not any more after this. As a matter of fact, I seem to remember it was Smith himself who found that way round. Going over the

90

racecourse missed out some bottleneck at a junction, I believe. I know some of the drivers thought it a good idea."

"They go through Seabury regularly, then?"

"Sure, often. Straight line to Southampton and round to the oil refinery at Fawley."

"Oh? What exactly was Smith's tanker carrying?"

"Sulfuric acid. It's used in refining petrol, among other things."

Sulfuric acid. Dense, oily, corrosive to the point of charring. Nothing more instantly lethal could have poured out over Seabury's turf. They could have raced had it been a milder chemical, put sand or tan on the dying grass and raced over the top. But no one would risk a horse on ground soaked with sulfuric acid.

I said, "Could you give me Smith's address? I'll call round and see if his memory has come back."

"Sure." He searched in a file and found it for me. "Tell him he can have his job back if he's interested. Another of the men gave notice this morning."

I said I would, thanked him, and went to Smith's address, which proved to be two rooms upstairs in a suburban house. But Smith and his wife no longer lived there. Packed up and gone yesterday, I was told by a young woman in curlers. No, she didn't leave a forwarding address, and if I was her I wouldn't worry about his health as he'd been laughing and drinking and playing records till all hours the day after the crash, his concussion having cured itself pretty quick. Reaction, he'd said when she complained of the noise, against not being killed.

It was dark by then, and I drove slowly back to London against the stream of headlights pouring out. Back to my flat in a modern block a short walk from the office, down the ramp into the basement garage, and up in the lift to the fifth floor, home.

There were two rooms facing south, bedroom and sitting room, and two behind them, bathroom and kitchen, with windows into an inner well. A pleasant sunny place, furnished in blond wood and cool colors, centrally heated, cleaning included in the rent. A regular order of groceries arrived week by week directly into the kitchen through a hatch, and rubbish disappeared down a chute. Instant living. No fuss, no mess, no strings. And damnably lonely, after Jenny.

Not that she had ever been in the place; she hadn't. The house in the Berkshire village where we mostly lived had been too much of a battleground, and when she walked out I sold it, with relief. I'd moved into the new flat shortly after going to the agency, because it was close. It was also expensive, but I had no fares to pay.

I mixed myself a brandy with ice and water, sat down in an armchair, put my feet up, and thought about Seabury. Seabury, Captain Oxon, Ted Wilkins, Intersouth Chemicals, and a driver called Smith.

After that I thought about Kraye. Nothing pleasant about him, nothing at all. A smooth, phony crust of sophistication hiding ruthless greed; a seething passion for crystals, ditto for land; an obsession with the cleanliness of his body to compensate for the murk in his mind; unconventional sexual pleasures; and the abnormal quality of being able to look carefully at a crippled hand and *then hit it*.

No, I didn't care for Howard Kraye one little bit.

7

"Chico." I said. "How would you overturn a lorry on a predetermined spot?"

"Huh? That's easy. All you'd need would be some heavy lifting gear. A big hydraulic jack. A crane. Anything like that."

"How long would it take?"

"You mean, supposing the lorry and the crane were both in position?"

"Yes."

"Only a minute or two. What sort of lorry?"

"A tanker."

"A petrol job?"

"A bit smaller than the petrol tankers. More the size of milk ones."

"Easy as kiss your hand. They've got a low center of gravity, mind. It'd need a good strong lift. But dead easy, all the same."

I turned to Dolly. "Is Chico busy today, or could you spare him?"

Dolly leaned forward, chewing the end of a pencil and looking at her day's chart. The crossover blouse did its stuff.

"I could send someone else to Kempton. . . ." She caught the direction of my eyes and laughed, and retreated a whole half inch. "Yes, you can have him." She gave him a fond glance.

"Chico," I said. "Go down to Seabury and see if you can find any trace of heavy lifting gear having been seen near the racecourse last Friday . . . those little bungalows are full of people with nothing to do but watch the world go by. You might check whether anything was hired locally, but I suppose that's a bit much to hope for. The road would have to have been closed for a few minutes before the tanker went over, I should think. See if you can find anyone who noticed anything like that . . . detour signs, for instance. And after that, go to the council offices and see what you can dig up among their old maps on the matter of drains." I told him the rough position on the subsiding trench which had made a slaughterhouse of the hurdle race, so that he should know what to look for on the maps. "And be discreet."

"Teach your grandmother to suck eggs." He grinned.

"Our quarry is rough."

"And you don't want him to hear us creep up behind him?"

"Quite right."

"Little Chico," he said truthfully, "can take care of himself."

After he had gone I telephoned Lord Hagbourne and described to him in no uncertain terms the state of Seabury's turf.

"What they need is some proper earth-moving equipment, fast, and apparently there's nothing in the kitty to pay for it. Couldn't the Levy Board . . . ?"

"The Levy Board is no fairy godmother," he interrupted. "But I'll see what can be done. Less than half cleared, you say? Hmm. However, I understand that Captain Oxon assured Weatherbys that the course would be ready for the next meeting. Has he changed his mind?"

"I didn't see him, sir. He was away for the day."

"Oh," Lord Hagbourne's voice grew a shade cooler. "Then he didn't ask you to enlist my help?"

"No."

"I don't see that I can interfere then. As racecourse manager it is his responsibility to decide what can be done and what can't, and I think it must be left like that. Mm, yes. And of course he will consult the clerk of the course if he needs advice."

"The clerk of the course is Mr. Fotherton, who lives in Bristol. He is clerk of the course there, too, and he's busy with the meetings there tomorrow and Monday."

"Er, yes, so he is."

"You could ring Captain Oxon up in an informal way and just ask how the work is getting on," I suggested.

"I don't know—"

"Well, sir, you can take my word for it that if things dawdle on at the same rate down there, there won't be any racing at Seabury next weekend. I don't think Captain Oxon can realize just how slowly those men are digging."

"He must," he protested. "He assured Weatherbys—"

"Another last minute cancellation will kill Seabury off," I said with some force.

There was a moment's pause. Then he said reluctantly. "Yes, I suppose it might. All right then. I'll ask Captain Oxon and Mr. Fotherton if they are both satisfied with the way things are going."

And I couldn't pin him down to any more direct action than that, which was certainly not going to be enough. Protocol would be the death of Seabury, I thought.

Monopolizing Dolly's telephone, I next rang up the Epping police and spoke to Chief Inspector Cornish.

"Any more news about Andrews?" I asked.

"I suppose you have a reasonable personal interest." His chuckle came down the wire. "We found he did have a sister after all. We called her at the inquest yesterday for identification purposes as she is a relative, but if you ask me she didn't really know. She took one look at the bits in the mortuary and was sick on the floor."

"Poor girl, you couldn't blame her."

"No. She didn't look long enough to identify anyone. But we had your identification for sure, so we hadn't the heart to make her go in again."

"How did he die? Did you find out?"

"Indeed we did. He was shot in the back. The bullet ricocheted off a rib and lodged in the sternum. We got the experts to compare it with the one they dug out of the wall of your office. Your bullet was a bit squashed by the hard plaster, but there's no doubt that they are the same. He was killed with the gun he used on you."

"And was it there, underneath him?"

"Not a sign of it. They brought in 'murder by persons unknown.' And between you and me, that's how it's likely to stay. We haven't a lead to speak of."

"What lead do you have?" I asked.

His voice had a smile in it. "Only something his sister told us. She has a bed-sitter in Islington, and he spent the evening there before breaking into your place. He showed her the gun. She says he was proud of having it; apparently he was a bit simple. All he told her was that a big chap had lent it to him to go out and fetch something, and he was to shoot anyone who got in his way. She didn't believe him. She said he was always making things up, always had, all his life. So she didn't ask him anything about the big chap, or about where he was going, or anything at all."

"A bit casual," I said. "With a loaded gun under her nose."

"According to the neighbors she was more interested in a stream of men friends than in anything her brother did."

"Sweet people, neighbors."

"You bet. Anyway we checked with anyone we could find who had seen Andrews that week he shot you, and he hadn't said a word to any of them about a gun or a 'big chap,' or an errand in Cromwell Road."

"He didn't go back to his sister afterwards?"

"No, she'd told him she had a guest coming."

"At one in the morning? The neighbors must be right. You tried racecourses, of course? Andrews is quite well known there, as a sort of spivvy odd-job messenger boy."

"Yes, we mainly tried the racecourses. No results. Everyone seemed surprised that such a harmless person should have been murdered."

"Harmless!"

He laughed. "If you hadn't thought him harmless you'd have kept out of his way."

"You're so right," I said with feeling. "But now I see a villain in every respectable citizen. It's very disturbing."

"Most of them are villains, in one way or another," he said cheerfully. "Keeps us busy. By the way, what do you think of Sparkle's chances this year in the Henessy? . . ."

When eventually I put the telephone down Dolly grabbed it with a sarcastic "Do you mind?" and asked the switchboard girl to get her three numbers in a row, "without interruptions from Halley." I grinned, got the packet of photographs out of the plywood table drawer, and looked through them again. They didn't tell me any more than before. Ellis Bolt's letters to Kraye. Now you see it, now you don't. A villain in every respectable citizen. Play it secretly, I thought, close to the chest, in case the eyes looking over you shoulder give you away. I wondered why I was so oppressed by a vague feeling of apprehension, and decided in irritation that a bullet in the stomach had made me nervous.

When Dolly finished her calls I took the receiver out of her hand and got through to my bank manager.

"Mr. Harper? This is Sid Halley . . . yes, fine thanks,

96

and you? Good. Now, would you tell me just how much I have in both my accounts, deposit and current?"

"They're quite healthy, actually," he said in his gravelly base voice. "You've had several dividends in lately. Hang on a minute, and I'll send for the exact figures." He spoke to someone in the background and then came back. "It's time you reinvested some of it."

"I do have some investments in mind," I agreed. "That's what I want to discuss with you. I'm planning to buy some shares this time from another stockbroker, not through the bank. Er . . . please don't think that I'm dissatisfied; how could I be, when you've done so well for me. It's something to do with my work at the agency."

"Say no more. What exactly do you want?"

"Well, to give you as a reference," I said. "He's sure to want one, but I would be very grateful if you would make it as impersonal and as strictly financial as possible. Don't mention either my past occupation or my present one. That's very important."

"I won't, then. Anything else?"

"Nothing . . . oh, yes. I've introduced myself to him as John Halley. Would you refer to me like that if he gets in touch with you?"

"Right. I'll look forward to hearing from you one day what it's all about. Why don't you come in and see me? I've some very good cigars." The deep voice was amused. "Ah, here are the figures. . . ." He told me the total, which for once was bigger than I expected. That happy state of affairs wouldn't last very long, I reflected, if I had to live for two years without any salary from Radnor. And no one's fault but my own.

Giving Dolly back her telephone with an ironic bow, I went upstairs to Bona Fides. Jack Copeland's mud-colored jersey had a dark blue darn on the chest and a fraying stretch of ribbing on the hip. He was picking at a loose thread and making it worse.

"Anything on Kraye yet?" I asked. "Or is it too early?"

"George has got something on the prelim, I think,"

he answered. "Anybody got any scissors?" A large area of jersey disintegrated into ladders. "Blast."

Laughing, I went over to George's desk. The prelim was a sheet of handwritten notes in George's concertinaed style. "Leg mat, 2 yrs. 2 prev, 1 div, 1 sui dec.," it began, followed by a list of names and dates.

"Oh, yeah?" I said.

"Yeah." He grinned. Kraye was legally married to Doria Dawn, nee Easterman, two years ago. Before that he had two other wives. One killed herself; the other divorced him for cruelty." He pointed to the names and dates.

"So clear," I agreed. "When you know how."

"If you weren't so impatient you'd have had a legible typed report. But as you're here . . ." He went on down the page pointing. "Geologists think him a bit eccentric . . . quartz has no intrinsic value, most of it's much too common, except for the gem stones, but Kraye goes round trying to buy chunks of it if they take his fancy. They know him quite well along the road at the Geology Museum. But not a breath of any dirty work. Clubs: he belongs to these three, not over-liked, but most members think he's a brilliant fellow, talks very well. He gambles at Crockfords, ends up about all square over the months. He travels, always first class, usually by boat, not air. No job or profession, can't trace him on any professional or university lists. Thought to live on investments, playing the stock market, etc. Not much liked, but considered by most a clever, cultured man, by one or two a hypocritical gasbag."

"No talk of him being crooked in any way?"

"Not a word. You want him dug deeper?"

"If you can do it without him finding out."

George nodded. "Do you want him tailed?"

"No, I don't think so. Not at present." A twenty-four-hour tail was heavy on man-power, and expensive to the client, quite apart from the risk of the quarry noticing and being warned of the hunt. "Anything on his early life?" I asked.

George shook his head. "Nothing. Nobody who knows him now has known him longer than about ten years.

98

He either wasn't born in Britain, or his name at birth wasn't Kraye. No known relatives."

"You've done marvels, George. All this in one day."

"Contacts, chum, contacts. A lot of phoning, a bit of pubbing, a touch of gossip with the local tradesmen —nothing to it."

Jack, moodily poking his fingers through the cobweb remains of his jersey, looked at me over the half-moon specs and said that there wasn't a prelim on Bolt yet because ex-sergeant Lamar, who was working on it, hadn't phoned in.

"If he does," I said, "let me know? I've an appointment with Bolt at three thirty. It would be handy to know the setup before I go."

"O.K."

After that I went down and looked out of the windows of the Racing Section for half an hour, idly watching life go by in Cromwell Road and wondering just what sort of mess I was making of the Kraye investigation. A novice chaser in the Grand National, I thought wryly; that was me. Though, come to think of it, I had once ridden a novice in the National, and got round, too. Slightly cheered, I took Dolly out to a drink and a sandwich in the snack bar at the Air Terminal, where we sat and envied the people starting off on their travels. So much expectation in the faces, as if they could fly away and leave their troubles on the ground. An illusion, I thought sourly. Your troubles flew with you; a drag in the mind . . . a deformity in the pocket.

I laughed and joked with Dolly, as usual. What else can you do?

The firm of Charing, Street and King occupied two rooms in a large block of offices belonging to a bigger firm, and consisted entirely of Bolt, his clerk and a secretary.

I was shown the door of the secretary's office, and went into a dull, tidy, fog-colored box of a room with cold fluorescent lighting and a close-up view of the fire escape through the grimy window. A woman sat at a desk by the right-hand wall, facing the window, with her back toward me. A yard behind her chair was a door with ELLIS BOLT painted on a frosted glass panel. It occurred to me that she was most awkwardly placed in the room, but that perhaps she liked sitting in a potential draft and having to turn around every time someone came in.

She didn't turn round, however. She merely moved her head round a fraction toward me and said, "Yes?"

"I have an appointment with Mr. Bolt," I said. "At three thirty."

"Oh, yes, you must be Mr. Halley. Do sit down. I'll see if Mr. Bolt is free now."

She pointed to an easy chair a step ahead of me, and flipped a switch on her desk. While I listened to her telling Mr. Bolt I was there, in the quiet voice I had heard on the telephone, I had time to see she was in her late thirties, slender, upright in her chair, with a smooth wing of straight, dark hair falling down beside her cheek. If anything, it was too young a hair style for her. There were no rings on her fingers, and no nail varnish either. Her clothes were dark and uninteresting. It seemed as though she were making a deliberate attempt to be unattractive, yet her profile, when she half turned and told me Mr. Bolt would see me, was pleasant enough. I had a glimpse of one brown eye quickly cast down, the beginning of a smile on pale lips, and she presented me again squarely with the back of her head.

Puzzled, I opened Ellis Bolt's door and walked in. The inner office wasn't much more inspiring than the outer; it was larger and there was a new green square of carpet on the linoleum, but the grayish walls prevailed, along with the tidy dullness. Through the two windows was a more distant view of the fire escape of the building across the alley. If a drab conventional setting equaled respectability, Bolt was an honest stockbroker; and Lamar, who had phoned in just before I left, had found nothing too suggest otherwise.

Bolt was on his feet behind his desk, hand outstretched. I shook it, he gestured me to a chair with arms, and offered me a cigarette.

"No, thank you, I don't smoke."

"Lucky man," he said benignly, tapping ash off one

he was half through and settling his pin-striped bulk back into his chair.

His face was rounded at every point, large round nose, round cheeks, round heavy chin; no planes, no impression of bone structure underneath. He had exceptionally heavy eyebrows, a full, mobile mouth, and a smug, self-satisfied expression.

"Now, Mr. Halley, I believe in coming straight to the point. What can I do for you?"

He had a mellifluous voice, and he spoke as if he enjoyed the sound of it.

I said, "An aunt has given me some money now rather than leave it to me in her will, and I want to invest it."

"I see. And what made you come to me? Did someone recommend . . . ?" He tailed off, watching me with eyes that told me he was no fool.

"I'm afraid . . ." I hesitated, smiling apologetically to take the offense out of the words, "that I literally picked you with a pin. I don't know any stockbrokers. I didn't know how to get to know one, so I picked up a classified directory and stuck a pin into the list of names, and it was yours."

"Ah," he said paternally, observing the bad fit of Chico's second-best suit, which I had borrowed for the occasion, and listening to me reverting to the accent of my childhood.

"Can you help me?" I asked.

"I expect so, I expect so. How much is this, er, gift?" His voice was minutely patronizing, his manner infinitesimally bored. His time, he suspected, was being wasted.

"Fifteen hundred pounds."

He brightened a very little. "Oh, yes, definitely, we can do something with that. Now, do you want growth stock or a high rate of yield?"

I looked vague. He told me quite fairly the difference between the two and offered no advice.

"Growth, then," I said, tentatively. "Turn it into a fortune in time for my old age."

He smiled without much mirth, and drew a sheet of paper toward him.

"Could I have your full name?"

"John Halley . . . John Sidney Halley," I said truthfully. He wrote it down.

"Address?" I gave it.

"And your bank?" I told him that too.

"And I'll need a reference, I'm afraid."

"Would the bank manager do?" I asked. "I've had an account there for two years. He knows me quite well."

"Excellent." He screwed up his pen. "Now, do you have any idea what companies you'd like shares in, or will you leave it to me?"

"Oh, I'll leave it to you. If you don't mind, that is. I don't know anything about it, you see, not really. Only it seems silly to leave all that money around doing nothing."

"Quite, quite." He was bored with me. I thought with amusement that Charles would appreciate my continuing his strategy of the weak front. "Tell me, Mr. Halley, what do you do for a living?"

"Oh . . . um . . . I work in a shop," I said. "In the men's wear. Very interesting, it is."

"I'm sure it is." There was a yawn stuck in his throat.

"I'm hoping to be made an assistant buyer next year," I said eagerly.

"Splendid. Well done." He'd had enough. He got cumbrously to his feet and ushered me to the door. "All right, Mr. Halley, I'll invest your money safely for you in good long-term growth stock, and send you the papers to sign in due course. You'll hear from me in a week or ten days. All right?"

"Yes, Mr. Bolt, thank you very much indeed," I said. He shut the door gently behind me.

There were now two people in the outer office. The woman with her back still turned, and a spare, middle-aged man with a primly folded mouth, and tough stringy tendons pushing his collar away from his neck. He was quite at home, and with an incurious, unhurried glance at me he went past into Bolt's office. The clerk, I presumed.

The woman was typing addresses on envelopes. The

102

twenty or so that she had done lay in a slithery stack on her left; on her right an open file provided a list of names. I looked over her shoulder casually, and then with quickened interest. She was working down the first page of a list of Seabury shareholders.

"Do you want something, Mr. Halley?" she asked politely, pulling one envelope from the typewriter and inserting another with a minimum of flourish.

"Well, er, yes," I said diffidently. I walked round to the side of her desk and found that one couldn't go on round to the front of it: a large old-fashioned table with bulbous legs filled all the space between the desk and the end of the room. I looked at this arrangement with some sort of understanding and with compassion.

"I wondered," I said, "if you could be very kind and tell me something about investing money, and so on. I didn't like to ask Mr. Bolt too much, he's a busy man. And I'd like to know a bit about it."

"I'm sorry, Mr. Halley." Her head was turned away from me, bent over the Seabury investors. "I've a job to do, as you see. Why don't you read the financial columns in the papers, or get a book on the subject?"

I had a book all right. *Outline of Company Law.* One thing I had learned from it was that only stock-brokers—apart from the company involved—could send circulars to shareholders. It was illegal if private citizens did it. Illegal for Kraye to send letters to Seabury shareholders offering to buy them out: legal for Bolt.

"Books aren't as good as people at explaining things," I said. "If you are busy now, could I come back when you've finished work and take you out for a meal? I'd be so grateful if you would, if you possibly could."

A sort of shudder shook her. "I'm sorry, Mr. Halley, but I'm afraid I can't."

"If you will look at me, so that I can see all of your face," I said, "I will ask you again."

Her head went up with a jerk at that, but finally she turned round and looked at me.

I smiled. "That's better. Now, how about coming out with me this evening?"

"You guessed?"

103

I nodded. "The way you've got your furniture organized. Will you come?"

"You still want to?"

"Well, of course. What time do you finish?"

"About six, tonight."

"I'll come back. I'll meet you at the door, down in the street."

"All right," she said. "If you really mean it, thank you. I'm not doing anything else tonight. . . ."

Years of hopeless loneliness showed raw in the simple words. Not doing anything else, tonight or most nights. Yet her face wasn't horrific; not anything as bad as I had been prepared for. She had lost an eye, and wore a false one. There had been some extensive burns and undoubtedly some severe fracture of the facial bones, but plastic surgery had repaired the damage to a great extent, and it had all been a long time ago. The scars were old. It was the inner wound which hadn't healed. Well . . . I knew a bit about that myself, on a smaller scale.

8

She came out of the door at ten past six wearing a neat well-cut dark overcoat and with a plain silk scarf covering her hair, tied under her chin. It hid only a small part of the disaster to her face, and seeing her like that, defenseless, away from the shelter she had made in her office, I had an uncomfortably vivid vision of the purgatory she suffered day in and day out on the journeys to work.

She hadn't expected me to be there. She didn't look round for me when she came out, but turned directly up the road toward the tube station. I walked after her and touched her arm. Even in low heels she was taller than I.

"Mr. Halley!" she said. "I didn't think—"

"How about a drink first?" I said. "The pubs are open."

"Oh no—"

"Oh yes. Why not?" I took her arm and steered her firmly across the road into the nearest bar. Dark oak, gentle lighting, brass pump handles, and the lingering smell of lunchtime cigars: a warm beckoning stop for city gents on their way home. There were already half a dozen of them, prosperous and dark-suited, adding fizz to their spirits.

"Not here," she protested.

"Here." I held a chair for her to sit on at a small table in a corner, and asked her what she would like to drink.

"Sherry, then . . . dry."

I took the two glasses over one at a time, sherry for her, brandy for me. She was sitting on the edge of the chair, uncomfortably, and it was not the one I had put her in. She had moved round so that she had her back to everyone except me.

"Good luck, Miss . . . ?" I said, lifting my glass.

"Martin. Zanna Martin."

"Good luck, Miss Martin." I smiled.

Tentatively she smiled back. It made her face much worse: half the muscles on the disfigured right side didn't work and could do nothing about lifting the corner of her mouth or crinkling the skin round the socket of her eye. Had life been even ordinarily kind she would have been a pleasant-looking, assured woman in her late thirties with a loving husband and a growing family: years of heartbreak had left her a shy, lonely spinster who dressed and moved as though she would like to be invisible. Yet, looking at the sad travesty of her face, one could neither blame the young men who hadn't married her nor condemn her own efforts at effacement.

"Have you worked for Mr. Bolt long?" I asked peaceably, settling back lazily into my chair and watching her gradually relax into her own.

"Only a few months. . . ." She talked for some time about her job in answer to my interested questions, but

105

unless she was supremely artful, she was not aware of anything shady going on in Charing, Street and King. I mentioned the envelopes she had been addressing, and asked what was going into them.

"I don't know yet," she said. "The leaflets haven't come from the printers."

"But I expect you typed the leaflet anyway," I said idly.

"No, actually I think Mr. Bolt did that one himself. He's quite helpful in that way, you know. If I'm busy he'll often do letters himself."

Will he, I thought. Will he, indeed. Miss Martin, as far as I was concerned, was in the clear. I bought her another drink and extracted her opinion about Bolt as a stockbroker. Sound, she said, but not busy. She had worked for other stockbrokers, it appeared, and knew enough to judge.

"There aren't many stockbrokers working on their own any more," she explained, "and . . . well, I don't like working in a big office, you see . . . and it's getting more difficult to find a job which suits me. So many stockbrokers have joined up into partnerships of three or more; it reduces overheads terrifically, of course, and it means that they can spend more time in the House. . . ."

"Where are Mr. Charing, Mr. Street, and Mr. King?" I asked.

Charing and Street were dead, she understood, and King had retired some years ago. The firm now consisted simply and solely of Ellis Bolt. She didn't really like Mr. Bolt's offices being contained inside of those of another firm. It wasn't private enough, but it was the usual arrangement nowadays. It reduced overhead so much. . . .

When the city gents had mostly departed to the bosoms of their families, Miss Martin and I left the pub and walked through the empty city streets toward the Tower. We found a quiet little restaurant where she agreed to have dinner. As before, she made a straight line for a corner table and sat with her back to the room.

"I'm paying my share," she announced firmly when she had seen the prices on the menu. "I had no idea this

106

place was so expensive or I wouldn't have let you choose it. Mr. Bolt mentioned that you worked in a shop."

"There's Aunty's legacy," I pointed out. "The dinner's on Aunty."

She laughed. It was a happy sound if you didn't look at her, but I found I was already able to talk to her without continually, consciously thinking about her face. One got used to it after a very short while. Sometime, I thought, I would tell her so.

I was still on a restricted diet, which made social eating difficult enough without one-handedness thrown in, but did very well on clear soup and Dover sole, expertly removed from the bone by a waiter. Miss Martin, shedding inhibitions visibly, ordered lobster cocktail, fillet steak, and peaches in kirsch. We drank wine, coffee and brandy, and took our time.

"Oh!" she said ecstatically at one point. "It is so long since I had anything like this. My father used to take me out now and then, but since he died . . . well, I can't go to places like this by myself. I sometimes eat in a café round the corner from my rooms, they know me there . . . it's very good food really, chops, eggs and chips . . . you know . . . things like that." I could picture her there, sitting alone with her ravaged head turned to the wall. Lonely unhappy Miss Martin. I wished I could do something—anything—to help her.

Eventually, when she was stirring her coffee, she said simply, "It was a rocket, this." She touched her face. "A firework. The bottle it was standing in tipped over just as it went off, and it came straight at me. It hit me on the cheek bone and exploded. It wasn't anybody's fault. I was sixteen."

"They made a good job of it," I said.

She shook her head, smiling the crooked tragic smile. "A good job from what it was, I suppose, but . . . they said if the rocket had struck an inch higher it would have gone through my eye into my brain and killed me. I often wish it had."

She meant it. Her voice was calm. She was stating a fact.

"Yes," I said.

107

"It's strange, but I've almost forgotten about it this evening, and that doesn't often happen when I'm with anyone."

"I'm honored."

She drank her coffee, put down her cup, and looked at me thoughtfully.

She said, "Why do you keep your hand in your pocket all the time?"

I owed it to her, after all. I put my hand palm upward on the table, wishing I didn't have to.

She said "Oh!" in surprise, and then, looking back at my face, "So you do know. That's why I feel so . . . so easy with you. You do understand."

I shook my head. "Only a little. I have a pocket; you haven't. I can hide." I rolled my hand over (the back of it was less off-putting) and finally retreated it onto my lap.

"But you can't do the simplest things," she exclaimed. Her voice was full of pity. "You can't tie your shoelaces, for instance. You can't even eat steak in a restaurant without asking someone else to cut it up for you—"

"Shut up," I said abruptly. "Shut up, Miss Martin. Don't you dare to do to me what you can't bear yourself."

"Pity . . . ," she said, biting her lip and staring at me unhappily. "Yes, it's so easy to give—"

"And embarrassing to receive." I grinned at her. "And my shoes don't have shoelaces. They're out of date, for a start."

"You can know as well as I do what it feels like, and yet do it to someone else . . ." She was very upset.

"Stop being miserable. It was kindness. Sympathy."

"Do you think;" she said hesitantly, "that pity and sympathy are the same thing?"

"Very often, yes. But sympathy is discreet and pity is tactless. Oh . . . I'm so sorry." I laughed. "Well, it was sympathetic of you to feel sorry I can't cut up my own food, and tactless to say so. The perfect example."

"It wouldn't be so hard to forgive people for just being tactless," she said thoughtfully.

"No," I agreed, surprised. "I suppose it wouldn't."

"It might not hurt so much . . . just tactlessness?"

"It mightn't."

"And curiosity—that might be easier, too, if I just thought of it as bad manners, don't you think? I mean tactlessness and bad manners wouldn't be so hard to stand. In fact *I* could be sorry for *them,* for not knowing better how to behave. Oh why, why didn't I think of that years ago, when it seems so simple now. So sensible."

"Miss Martin," I said with gratitude. "Have some more brandy. You're a liberator."

"How do you mean?"

"Pity is bad manners and can be taken in one's stride, as you said."

"*You* said it," she protested.

"Indeed I didn't, not like that."

"All right," she said with gaiety, "we'll drink to a new era. A bold front to the world. I will put my desk back to where it was before I joined the office, facing the door. I'll let every caller see me. I'll—" Her brave voice nearly cracked. "I'll just think poorly of their manners if they pity me too openly. That's settled."

We had some more brandy. I wondered inwardly whether she would have the same resolve in the morning, and doubted it. There had been so many years of hiding. She too, it seemed, was thinking along the same lines.

"I don't know that I can do it alone. But if you will promise me something, then I can."

"Very well," I said incautiously. "What?"

"Don't put your hand in your pocket tomorrow. Let everyone see it."

I couldn't. Tomorrow I would be going to the races. I looked at her, appalled, and really understood only then what she had to bear, and what it would cost her to move her desk. She saw the refusal in my face, and some sort of light died in her own. The gaiety collapsed, the defeated, defenseless look came back, the liberation was over.

"Miss Martin . . ." I swallowed.

"It doesn't matter," she said tiredly. "It doesn't matter. And anyway, it's Saturday tomorrow. I only go in for a short while to see to the mail and anything urgent from today's transactions. There wouldn't be any point in changing the desk."

"And on Monday?"

"Perhaps." It meant no.

"If you'll change it tomorrow and do it all next week, I'll do what you ask," I said, quaking at the thought of it.

"You can't," she said sadly. "I can see that you can't."

"If you can, I must."

"But I shouldn't have asked you . . . you work in a shop."

"Oh." That I had forgotten. "It won't matter."

An echo of her former excitement crept back.

"Do you really mean it?"

I nodded. I had wanted to do something—anything—to help her. Anything. My God.

"Promise?" she said doubtfully.

"Yes. And you?"

"All right," she said, with returning resolution. "But I can only do it if I know you are in the same boat. I couldn't let you down then, you see."

I paid the bill, and although she said there was no need, I took her home. We went on the underground to Finchley. She made straight for the least conspicuous seat and sat presenting the good side of her face to the carriage. Then, laughing at herself, she apologized for doing it.

"Never mind," I said, "the new era doesn't start until tomorrow," and hid my hand like a proper coward.

Her room was close to the station (a deliberately short walk, I guessed) in a large, properous-looking suburban house. At the gate she stopped.

"Will . . . er . . . I mean, would you like to come in? It's not very late . . . but perhaps you are tired."

She wasn't eager, but when I accepted she seemed pleased.

"This way, then."

We went through a bare tidy garden to a black-painted front door adorned with horrible stained-glass panels.

Miss Martin fumbled endlessly in her bag for her key and I reflected idly that I could have picked that particular lock as quickly as she opened it legally. Inside there was a warm hall smelling healthily of air freshener, and at the end of a passage off it, a door with a card saying "Martin."

Miss Martin's room was a surprise. Comfortable, large, close carpeted, newly decorated, and alive with color. She switched on a standard lamp and a rosy table lamp, and drew burnt orange curtains over the black expanse of French windows. With satisfaction she showed me the recently built tiny bathroom leading out of her room, and the suitcase-sized kitchen beside it, both of which additions she had paid for herself. The people who owned the house were very understanding, she said. Very kind. She had lived there for eleven years. It was home.

Miss Martin had no mirrors in her home. Not one.

She bustled in her little kitchen, making more coffee: for something to do, I thought. I sat relaxed on her long comfortable modern sofa and watched how, from long habit, she leaned forward most of the time so that the heavy shoulder-length dark hair swung down to hide her face. She brought the tray and set it down, and sat on the sofa carefully on my right. One couldn't blame her.

"Do you ever cry?" she said suddenly.

"No."

"Not . . . from frustration?"

"No." I smiled. "Swear."

She sighed. "I used to cry often. I don't any more, though. Getting older, of course. I'm nearly forty. I've got resigned now to not getting married. I knew I was resigned to it when I had the bathroom and kitchen built. Up to then, you see, I'd always pretended to myself that one day . . . one day, perhaps . . . but I don't expect it any more, not any more."

"Men are fools," I said inadequately.

"I hope you don't mind me talking like this? It's so seldom that I have anyone in here, and practically never anyone I can really talk to. . . ."

I stayed for an hour, listening to her memories, her

111

experiences, her whole shadowed life. What, I chided myself, had ever happened to me that was one tenth as bad? I had had far more ups than downs.

At length she said, "How did it happen with you? Your hand. . . ."

"Oh, an accident. A sharp bit of metal." A razor-sharp racing horseshoe attached to the foot of a horse galloping at thirty miles an hour, to be exact. A hard kicking slash as I rolled on the ground from an easy fall. One of those things.

Horses race in thin light shoes called plates, not the heavy ones they normally wear; blacksmiths change them before and after, every time a horse runs. Some trainers save a few shillings by using the same racing plates over and over again, so that the leading edge gradually wears down to the thickness of a knife. But jagged knives, not smooth. They can cut you open like a hatchet.

I'd really known at once when I saw my stripped wrist, with the blood spurting out in a jet and the broken bones showing white, that I was finished as a jockey. But I wouldn't give up hope, and insisted on the surgeons' sewing it all up, even though they wanted to take my hand off there and then. It would never be any good, they said; and they were right. Too many of the tendons and nerves were severed. I persuaded them to try twice later on to rejoin and graft some of them and both times it had been a useless agony. They had refused to consider it again.

Miss Martin hesitated on the brink of asking for details, and fortunately didn't. Instead she said, "Are you married? Do you know, I've talked so much about myself that I don't know a thing about you."

"My wife's in Athens, visiting her sister."

"How lovely," Miss Martin sighed. "I wish . . ."

"You'll go one day," I said firmly. "Save up, and go in a year or two. On a bus tour or something. With people anyway. Not alone."

I looked at my watch, and stood up. "I've enjoyed this evening a great deal. Thank you so much for coming out with me."

She stood and formally shook hands, not suggesting

another meeting. So much humility, I thought, so little expectation. Poor, poor Miss Martin.

"Tomorrow morning . . ." she said tentatively, at the door.

"Tomorrow," I nodded. "Move that desk. And I . . . I promise I won't forget."

I went home cursing that fate had sent me someone like Miss Martin. I had expected Charing, Street and King's secretary to be young, perhaps pretty, a girl I could take to a café and the pictures and flirt with, with no great involvement on either side. Instead it looked as if I should have to pay more than I'd meant to for my inside information on Ellis Bolt.

9

"Now look," said Lord Hagbourne, amid the bustle of Kempton races, "I've had a word with Captain Oxon and he's satisfied with the way things are going. I really can't interfere any more. Surely you understand that?"

"No, sir, I don't. I don't think Captain Oxon's feelings are more important than Seabury Racecourse. The course should be put right quickly, even if it means overruling him."

"Captain Oxon," he said with a touch of sarcasm, "knows more about his job than you do. I give more weight to his assurance than to your quick look at the track."

"Then couldn't you go and see for yourself? While there is still time."

He didn't like being pushed. His expression said so, plainly. There was no more I could say, either, without risking his ringing up Radnor to cancel the whole investigation.

"I may . . . er . . . I may find time on Monday," he said at last, grudgingly. "I'll see. Have you found

113

anything concrete to support your idea that Seabury's troubles were caused maliciously?"

"Not yet, sir."

"A bit farfetched, if you ask me," he said crossly. "I said so to begin with, as you remember. If you don't turn something up pretty soon . . . it's all expense, you know."

He was intercepted by a passing Steward who took him off to another problem, leaving me grimly to reflect that so far there was a horrid lack of evidence of any sort. What there was was negative.

George had still found no chink in Kraye's respectability, ex-sergeant Lamar had given Bolt clearance, and Chico had come back from Seabury with no results all along the line.

We'd met in the office that morning before I went to Kempton.

"Nothing," said Chico. "I wagged my tongue off, knocking at every front door along that road. Not a soggy flicker. The bit that crosses the racecourse wasn't closed by diversion notices, that's for sure. There isn't much traffic along there, of course. I counted it. Only forty to the hour, average. Still, that's too much for at least some of the neighbors not to notice if there'd been anything out of the ordinary."

"Did anyone see the tanker before it overturned?"

"They're always seeing tankers nowadays. Several complaints about it, I got. No one noticed that one, especially."

"It can't be coincidence. Just at that spot at that time where it would do most harm. And the driver packing up and moving a day or two afterwards with no forwarding address."

"Well . . ." Chico scratched his ear reflectively. "I got no dice with the hiring of lifting gear either. There isn't much to be had, and what there was was accounted for. None of the little bungalows saw anything in that line, except the breakdown cranes coming to lift the tanker up again."

"How about the drains?"

"No drains," he said. "A blank back to doomsday."

"Good."

"Come again?"

"If you'd found them on a map the hurdle race accident would have been a genuine accident. This way, they reek of tiger traps."

"A spot of spadework after dark? Dodgy stuff."

I frowned. "Yes. And it had to be done long enough before the race meeting for the ground to settle, so that the line of the trench didn't show."

"And strong enough for a tractor to roll over it."

"Tractor?"

"There was one on the course yesterday, pulling a trailer of dug-up turf."

"Oh yes, of course. Yes, strong enough to hold a tractor . . . but wheels wouldn't pierce the ground like a horse's legs. The weight is more spread."

"True enough."

"How fast was the turf-digging going?" I asked.

"Fast? You're joking."

It was depressing. So was Lord Hagbourne's shilly-shallying. So, acutely, was the whole day, because I kept my promise to Miss Martin. Pity, curiosity, surprise, embarrassment and revulsion. I encountered the lot. I tried hard to look on some of the things that were said as tactlessness or bad manners, but it didn't really work. Telling myself it was idiotic to be so sensitive didn't help either. If Miss Martin hadn't kept her side of the bargain, I thought miserably, I would throttle her.

Halfway through the afternoon I had a drink in the big upstairs bar with Mark Witney.

"So that's what you've been hiding all this time in pockets and gloves," he said.

"Yes."

"Bit of a mess," he commented.

"I'm afraid so."

"Does it hurt still?"

"No, only if I knock it. And it aches sometimes."

"Mm," he said sympathetically. "My ankle still aches too. Joints are always like that; they mend, but they never forgive you." He grinned. "The other half? There's time; I haven't a runner until the fifth."

115

We had another drink, talking about horses and I reflected that it would be easy if they were all like him.

"Mark," I said as we walked back to the weighing room, "do you remember whether Dunstable ran into any sort of trouble before it packed up?"

"That's going back a bit." He pondered. "Well, it certainly wasn't doing so well during the last year or two, was it? The attendances had fallen off, and they weren't spending any money on paint."

"But no specific disasters?"

"The clerk of the course took an overdose, if you call that a disaster. Yes, I remember now, the collapse of the place's prosperity was put down to the clerk's mental illness. Brinton, I think his name was. He'd been quietly going loco and making hopeless decisions all over the place."

"I'd forgotten," I said glumly. Mark went into the weighing room and I leaned against the rails outside. A suicidal clerk of the course could hardly have been the work of Kraye, I thought. It might have given him the idea of accelerating the demise of Seabury, though. He'd had plenty of time over Dunstable, but owing to a recent political threat of nationalization of building land, he might well be in a hurry to clinch Seabury. I sighed, disregarded as best I could a stare of fascinated horror from the teen-age daughter of a man I used to ride for, and drifted over to look at the horses in the parade ring.

At the end of the too-long afternoon I drove back to my flat, mixed a bigger drink than usual, and spent the evening thinking, without any world-shattering results. Late the next morning, when I was similarly engaged, the doorbell rang, and I found Charles outside.

"Come in," I said with surprise: he rarely visited the flat and was seldom in London at weekends. "Like some lunch? The restaurant downstairs is quite good."

"Perhaps. In a minute." He took off his overcoat and gloves and accepted some whisky. There was something unsettled in his manner, a ruffling of the smooth, urbane exterior, a suggestion of a troubled frown on the high domed forehead.

116

"O.K.," I said. "What's the matter?"

"Er . . . I've just driven up from Aynsford. No traffic at all, for once. Such a lovely morning, I thought the drive would be . . . oh damn it," he finished explosively, putting down his glass with a bang. "To get it over quickly, Jenny telephoned from Athens last night. She's met some man there. She asked me to tell you she wants a divorce."

"Oh," I said. How like her, I thought, to get Charles to wield the ax. Practical Jenny, eager for a new fire, hacking away the deadwood. And if some of the wood was still alive, too bad.

"I must say," said Charles, relaxing, "you make a thorough job of it."

"Of what?"

"Of not caring what happens to you."

"I do care."

"No one would suspect it," he sighed. "When I tell you your wife wants to divorce you, you just say, 'Oh.' When that happened"—he nodded to my arm—"the first thing you said to me afterwards when I arrived full of sorrow and sympathy was, if I remember correctly, and I do, 'Cheer up, Charles. I had a good run for my money.' "

"Well, so I did." Always, from my earliest childhood, I had instinctively shied away from too much sympathy. I didn't want it. I distrusted it. It made you soft inside, and an illegitimate child couldn't afford to be soft. One might weep at school, and one's spirit would never recover from so dire a disgrace. So the poverty and the snickers, and later the lost wife and the smashed career, had to be passed off with a shrug, and what one really felt about it had to be locked up tightly inside, out of view. Silly, really, but there it was.

We lunched companionably together downstairs, discussing in civilized tones the mechanics of divorce. Jenny, it appeared, did not want me to use the justified grounds of desertion. I, she said, should "arrange things" instead. I must know how to do it, working for the agency. Charles was apologetic: Jenny's prospective

117

husband was in the diplomatic service like Tony, and would prefer her not to be the guilty party.

Had I, Charles inquired delicately, already been . . . er . . . unfaithful to Jenny? No, I replied, watching him light his cigar, I was afraid I hadn't. For much of the time, owing to one thing and another, I hadn't felt well enough. That, he agreed with amusement, was a reasonable excuse.

I indicated that I would fix things as Jenny wanted, because it didn't affect my future as it did hers. She would be grateful, Charles said. I thought, knowing her, she would very likely take it for granted.

When there was little else to say on that subject, we switched to Kraye. I asked Charles if he had seen him again during the week.

"Yes, I was going to tell you. I had lunch with him in the Club on Thursday. Quite accidentally. We both just happened to be there alone."

"That's where you met him first, in your club?"

"That's right. Of course he thanked me for the weekend and so on. Talked about the quartz. Very interesting collection, he said. But not a murmur about the St. Luke's stone. I would have liked to have asked him straight out, just to see his reaction." He tapped off the ash, smiling. "I did mention you, though, in passing, and he switched on all the charm and said you had been extremely insulting to him and his wife, but that of course you hadn't spoiled his enjoyment. Very nasty, I thought it. He was causing bad trouble for you. Or at least, he intended to."

"Yes," I said cheerfully. "But I did insult him, and I also spied on him. Anything he says of me is fully merited." I told Charles how I had taken the photographs, and all that I had discovered or guessed during the past week. His cigar went out. He looked stunned.

"Well, you wanted me to, didn't you?" I said. "You started it. What did you expect?"

"It's only that I had almost forgotten . . . this is what you used to be like, always. Determined. Ruthless, even." He smiled. "My game for convalescence has turned out better than I expected."

118

"God help your other patients," I said, "if Kraye is standard medicine."

We walked along the road toward where Charles had left his car. He was going straight home again.

I said, "I hope that in spite of the divorce I shall see something of you? I should be sorry not to. As your ex-son-in-law, I can hardly come to Aynsford any more."

He looked startled. "I'll be annoyed if you don't, Sid. Jenny will be living all round the world, like Jill. Come to Aynsford whenever you want."

"Thank you," I said. I meant it, and it sounded like it.

He stood beside his car, looking down at me from his straight six feet.

"Jenny," he said casually, "is a fool."

I shook my head. Jenny was no fool. Jenny knew what she wanted, and it wasn't me.

When I went into the office (on time) the following morning, the girl on the switchboard caught me and said Radnor wanted me straight away.

"Good morning," he said. "I've just had Lord Hagbourne on the telephone telling me it's time we got results and that he can't go to Seabury today because his car is being serviced. Before you explode, Sid . . . I told him that you would take him down there now, at once, in your own car. So get a move on."

I grinned. "I bet he didn't like that."

"He couldn't think of an excuse fast enough. Get round and collect him before he comes up with one."

"Right."

I made a quick detour up to the Racing Section where Dolly was adjusting her lipstick. No crossover blouse today. A disappointment.

I told her where I was going and asked if I could use Chico.

"Help yourself," she said resignedly. "If you can get a word in edgeways. He's along in Accounts arguing with Jones-boy."

Chico, however, listened attentively and repeated what I had asked him. "I'm to find out exactly what mistakes

119

the clerk of the course at Dunstable made, and make sure that they and nothing else were the cause of the course losing money."

"That's right. And dig out the file on Andrews and the case you were working on when I got shot."

"But that's all dead," he protested, "the file's down in records in the basement."

"Send Jones-boy down for it," I suggested, grinning. "It's probably only a coincidence, but there is something I want to check. I'll do it tomorrow morning. O.K.?"

"If you say so, chum."

Back at my flat, I filled up with Extra and made all speed round to Beauchamp Place. Lord Hagbourne, with a civil but cool good morning, lowered himself into the passenger seat, and we set off for Seabury. It took him about a quarter of an hour to get over having been maneuvered into something he didn't want to do, but at the end of that time he sighed and moved in his seat and offered me a cigarette.

"No, thank you, sir. I don't smoke."

"You don't mind if I do?" He took one out.

"Of course not."

"This is a nice car," he remarked, looking round.

"It's nearly three years old now. I bought it the last season I was riding. It's the best I've ever had, I think."

"I must say," he said inoffensively, "that you manage extremely well. I wouldn't have thought that you could drive a car like this with only one effective hand."

"Its power makes it easier, actually. I took it across Europe last spring . . . good roads, there."

We talked on about cars and holidays, then about theaters and books, and he seemed for once quite human. The subject of Seabury we carefully bypassed. I wanted to get him down there in a good mood—the arguments, if any, could take place on the way back—and it seemed as if he was of the same mind.

The state of Seabury's track reduced him to silent gloom. We walked down to the burnt piece with Captain Oxon, who was bearing himself stiffly and being pointedly polite. I thought he was a fool: he should have fallen on the Senior Steward and begged for instant help.

Captain Oxon, whom I had not met before, though he said he knew me by sight, was a slender, pleasant-looking man of about fifty, with a long pointed chin and a slight tendency to watery eyes. The present offended obstinacy of his expression looked more like childishness than real strength. A colonel *manqué,* I thought uncharitably, and no wonder.

"I know it's not really my business," I said, "but surely a bulldozer would shift what's left of the burnt bit in a couple of hours? There isn't time to settle new turf, but you could cover the whole area with some tons of tan and race over it quite easily, like that. You must be getting tan anyway, to cover the road surface. Surely you could just increase the order?"

Oxon looked at me with irritation. "We can't afford it."

"You can't afford another cancellation at the last minute, I corrected.

"We are insured against cancellations."

"I doubt whether an insurance company would stand this one," I said. "They'd say you could have raced if you'd tried hard enough."

"It's Monday now," remarked Lord Hagbourne thoughtfully. "Racing's due on Friday. Suppose we call in a bulldozer tomorrow; the tan can be unloaded and spread on Wednesday and Thursday. Yes, that seems sound enough."

"But the cost—" began Oxon.

"I think the money must be found," said Lord Hagbourne. "Tell Mr. Fotherton when he comes over that I have authorized the expenditure. The bills will be met, in one way or another. But I do think there is no case for not making an effort."

It was on the tip of my tongue to point out that if Oxon had arranged for the bulldozer on the first day he could have saved the price of casual labor from six hand-diggers for a week, but as the battle was already won, I nobly refrained. I continued to think, however, that Oxon was a fool. Usually the odd custom of giving the managerships of racecourses to ex-army officers worked out well, but conspicuously not in this case.

The three of us walked back up to the stands, Lord Hagbourne pausing and pursing his lips at their dingy appearance. I reflected that it was a pity Seabury had a clerk of the course whose heart and home were far away on the thriving course at Bristol. If I'd been arranging things, I'd have seen to it a year ago, when the profits turned to loss, that Seabury had a new clerk entirely devoted to its own interests, someone moreover whose livelihood depended on its staying open. The bungle, delay, muddle, too much politeness and failure to take action showed by the Seabury executive had been of inestimable value to the quietly burrowing Kraye.

Mr. Fotherton might have been worried, as he said, but he had done little except mention it in passing to Charles in his capacity as Steward at some other meeting. Charles, looking for something to divert my mind from my stomach, and perhaps genuinely anxious about Seabury, had tossed the facts to me. In his own peculiar way, naturally.

The casualness of the whole situation was horrifying. I basely wondered whether Fotherton himself had a large holding in Seabury shares and therefore a vested interest in its demise. Planning a much closer scrutiny of the list of shareholders, I followed Lord Hagbourne and Captain Oxon round the end of the stands, and we walked the three hundred yards or so through the racecourse gates and down the road to where Captain Oxon's flat was situated above the canteen in the stable block.

On Lord Hagbourne's suggestion he rang up a firm of local contractors while we were still there, and arranged for the urgent earth-moving to be done the following morning. His manner was still ruffled, and it didn't improve things when I declined the well-filled ham and chutney sandwiches he offered, though I would have adored to have eaten them, had he but known. I had been out of hospital for a fortnight, but I had another fortnight to go before things like new bread, ham, mustard and chutney were due back on the agenda. Very boring.

After the sandwiches Lord Hagbourne decided on a tour of inspection, so we all three went first round the stable block, into the lads' hostel, through the canteen too the kitchen, and into all the stable administrative offices. Everywhere the story was the same. Except for the rows of wooden boxes which had been thrown up cheaply after the old ones burned down, there was no recent maintenance and no new paint.

Then we retraced our steps up the road, through the main gate, and across to the long line of stands with the weighing room, dining rooms, bars and cloakrooms built into the back. At one end were the secretary's office, the press room and the Stewards' room; at the other, the first-aid room and a store. A wide tunnel like a passage ran centrally through the whole length of the building, giving secondary access on one side to many of the rooms, and on the other to the steps of the stands themselves. We painstakingly covered the lot, even down to the boiler room and the oil bunkers, so I had my nostalgic look inside the weighing room and changing room after all.

The whole huge block was dankly cold, very drafty, and smelled of dust. Nothing looked new, not even the dirt. For inducing depression it was hard to beat, but the dreary buildings along in the cheaper rings did a good job of trying.

Captain Oxon said the general dilapidation was mostly due to the sea air, the racecourse being barely half a mile from the shore, and no doubt in essence he was right. The sea air had had a free hand for far too long.

Eventually we returned to where my car was parked inside the gate, and looked back to the row of stands: forlorn, deserted, decaying on a chilly early November afternoon, with a salt-laden drizzle just beginning to blur the outlines.

"What's to be done?" said Lord Hagbourne glumly, as we drove through the rows of bungalows on our way home.

"I don't know." I shook my head.

"The place is dead."

I couldn't argue. Seabury had suddenly seemed to me to be past saving. The Friday and Saturday fixtures could be held now, but as things stood the gate money would hardly cover expenses. No company could go on taking a loss indefinitely. Seabury could plug the gap at present by drawing on their reserve funds, but as I'd seen from their balance sheets at Company House, the reserves only amounted to a few thousands. Matters were bound to get worse. Insolvency waited round a close corner. It might be more realistic to admit that Seabury had no future and to sell the land at the highest price offered as soon as possible. People were, after all, crying out for flat land at the seaside. And there was no real reason why the shareholders shouldn't be rewarded for their long loyalty and recent poor dividends and receive eight pounds for each one they had invested. Many would gain if Seabury came under the hammer, and no one would lose. Seabury was past saving: best to think only of the people who would benefit.

My thoughts stopped with a jerk. This, I realized, must be the attitude of the clerk, Mr. Fotherton, and of the manager, Oxon, and of all the executives. This explained why they had made surprisingly little attempt to save the place. They had accepted defeat easily and seen it to be not only harmless but, to many, usefully profitable. As it had been with other courses, big courses like Hurst Park and Birmingham, so it should be with Seabury.

What did it matter that yet another joined the century's ghost ranks of Cardiff, Derby, Bournemouth, Newport? What did it matter if busy people like Inspector Cornish of Dunstable couldn't go racing much because their local course had vanished? What did it matter if Seabury's holidaymakers went to the bingo halls instead?

Chasing owners, I thought, should rise up in a body and demand that Seabury should be preserved, because no racecourse was better for their horses. But of course they wouldn't. You could tell owners how good it was, but unless they were horsemen themselves, it didn't register. They only saw the rotten amenities of the stands, not the splendidly sited well-built fences that positively invited their horses to jump. They didn't know how their horses relished the short springy turf underfoot, or found the arc and cambers of the bends perfect for maintaining an even speed. Corners at many other racecourses threw horses wide and broke up their stride, but not those at Seabury. The original course builder had been brilliant, and regular visits from the inspector of courses had kept his work fairly intact. Fast, true-run, unhazardous racing, that's what Seabury gave.

Or had given, before Kraye.

Kraye and the executive's inertia between them. . . . I stamped on the accelerator in a surge of anger and the car swooped up the side of the South Downs like a bird. I didn't often drive fast any more: I did still miss having two hands on the wheel. At the top, out of consideration for my passenger's nerves, I let the speedometer ribbon slide back to fifty.

He said, "I feel like that about it too."

I glanced at him in surprise.

"The whole situation is infuriating," he said. "Such a good course basically, and nothing to be done."

"It could be saved," I said.

"How?"

"A new attitude of mind. . . ." I trailed off.

"Go on," he said. But I couldn't find the words to tell him politely that he ought to chuck out all the people in power at Seabury; too many of them were probably his ex-school chums or personal friends.

"Suppose," he said after a few minutes, "that you had a free hand, what would you do?"

"One would never get a free hand. That's half the trouble. Someone makes a good suggestion, and someone else squashes it. They end up, often as not, by doing nothing."

"No, Sid, I mean you personally. What would you do?"

"I?" I grinned. "What I'd do would have the National Hunt Committee swooning like Victorian maidens."

"I'd like to know."

"Seriously?"

He nodded. As if he could ever be anything else but serious.

I sighed. "Very well, then. I'd pinch every good crowd-pulling idea that any other course has thought of and put them all into operation on the same day."

125

"What, for instance?"

"I'd take the whole of the reserve fund and offer it as a prize for a big race. I'd make sure the race was framed to attract the really top chasers. Then I'd go round to their trainers personally and explain the situation, and beg for their support. I'd go to some of the people who sponsor Gold Cup races and cajole them into giving five-hundred-pound prizes for all the other races on that day. I'd make the whole thing into a campaign. I'd get Save Seabury discussed on television, and in the sports columns of newspapers. I'd get people interested and involved. I'd make helping Seabury the smart thing to do. I'd get someone like the Beatles to come and present the trophies. I'd advertise free car-parking and free race cards, and on the day I'd have the whole place bright with flags and bunting and tubs of flowers to hide the lack of paint. I'd make sure everyone on the staff understood that a friendly welcome must be given to the customers. And I'd insist that the catering firm use its imagination. I'd fix the meeting for the beginning of April, and pray for a sunny spring day. That," I said, running down, "would do for a start."

"And afterwards?" He was noncommittal.

"A loan, I suppose. Either from a bank or from private individuals. But the executive would have to show first that Seabury could be a success again, like it used to be. No one falls over himself to lend to a dying business. The revival has to come before the money, if you see what I mean."

"I do see," he agreed slowly, "but . . ."

"Yes. But. It always comes to 'but.' But no one at Seabury is going to bother."

We were silent for a long way.

Finally I said, "This meeting on Friday and Saturday—it would be a pity to risk another last-minute disaster. Hunt Radnor Associates could arrange for some sort of guard on the course. Security patrols, that kind of thing."

"Too expensive," he said promptly. "And you've not yet proved that it is really needed. Seabury's troubles still look like plain bad luck to me."

126

"Well, a security patrol might prevent any more of it."

"I don't know. I'll have to see." He changed the subject then, and talked firmly about other races on other courses all the way back to London.

10

Dolly lent me her telephone with resignation on Tuesday morning, and I buzzed the switchboard for an internal call to Missing Persons.

"Sammy?" I said. "Sid Halley, down in Racing. Are you busy?"

"The last teen-ager has just been retrieved from Gretna. Fire away. Who's lost?"

"A man called Smith."

Some mild blasphemy sped three stories down the wire.

I laughed. "I think his name really is Smith. He's a driver by trade. He's been driving a tanker for Intersouth Chemicals for the last year. He left his job and his digs last Wednesday; no forwarding address." I told him about the crash, the suspected concussion and the revelry by night.

"You don't think he was planted on purpose on the job a year ago? His name likely wouldn't be Smith in that case . . . make it harder."

"I don't know. But I think it's more likely he was a bona fide Intersouth driver who was offered a cash payment for exceptional services rendered."

"O.K., I'll try that first. He might give Intersouth as a reference, in which case they'll know if he applies for another job somewhere, or I might trace him through his union. The wife might have worked, too. I'll let you know."

"Thanks."

"Don't forget, when the old man buys you a gold-plated executive desk I want my table back."

"You'll want forever," I said, smiling. It had been Sammy's lunch.

On the table in question lay the slim file on the Andrews case that Jones-boy had unearthed from the basement. I looked round the room.

"Where's Chico?" I asked.

Dolly answered. "Helping a bookmaker to move house."

"He's doing *what?*" I goggled.

"That's right. Long-standing date. The bookmaker is taking his safe with him and wants Chico to sit on it in the furniture van. It had to be Chico, he said. No one else would do. The paying customer is always right, so Chico's gone."

"Damn."

She reached into a drawer. "He left you a tape," she said.

"Undamn, then."

She grinned and handed it to me, and I took it over to the recorder, fed it through onto the spare reel, and listened to it in the routine office way, through the earphones.

"After wearing my plates down to the ankles," said Chico's cheerful voice, "I found out that the worst things your clerk of the course did at Dunstable were to frame a lot of races that did the opposite of attract any decent runners, and be stinking rude to all and sundry. He was quite well liked up to the year before he killed himself. Then everyone says he gradually got more and more crazy. He was so rude to people who worked at the course that half of them wouldn't put up with it and left. And the local tradesmen practically spat when I mentioned his name. I'll fill you in when I see you, but there wasn't anything like Seabury—no accidents or damage or anything like that."

Sighing, I wiped the tape clean and gave it back to Dolly. Then I opened the file on my table and studied its contents.

A Mr. Mervyn Brinton of Reading, Berkshire, had

applied to the agency for personal protection, having had reason to believe that he was in danger of being attacked. He had been unwilling to say why he might be attacked, and refused to have the agency make inquiries. All he wanted was a bodyguard. There was a strong possibility, said the report, that Brinton had tried a little amateurish blackmail, which had backfired. He had at length revealed that he possessed a certain letter, and was afraid of being attacked and having it stolen. After much persuasion by Chico Barnes, who pointed out that Brinton could hardly be guarded for the rest of his life, Brinton had agreed to inform a certain party that the letter in question was lodged in a particular desk drawer in the Racing Section of Hunt Radnor Associates. In fact it was not; and had not at any time been seen by anyone working for the agency. However, Thomas Andrews came, or was sent, to remove the letter, was interrupted by J. S. Halley (whom he wounded by shooting), and subsequently made his escape. Two days later Brinton telephoned to say he no longer required a bodyguard, and as far as the agency was concerned the case was then closed.

The foregoing information had been made available to the police in their investigation into the shooting of Halley.

I shut the file. A drab little story, I thought, of a pathetic little man playing out of his league.

Brinton.

The clerk of the course at Dunstable had also been called Brinton.

I sat gazing at the short file. Brinton wasn't an uncommon name. There was probably no connection at all. Brinton of Dunstable had died a good two years before Brinton of Reading had asked for protection. The only visible connection was that at different ends of the scale both the Dunstable Brinton and Thomas Andrews had earned their living on the racecourse. It wasn't much. Probably nothing. But it nagged.

I went home, collected the car, and drove to Reading.

A nervous, gray-haired elderly man opened the front door on a safety chain, and peered through the gap.

"Yes?"

"Mr. Brinton?"

"What is it?"

"I'm from Hunt Radnor Associates. I'd be mos' grateful for a word with you."

He hesitated, chewing an upper lip adorned with ar untidy pepper-and-salt mustache. Anxious brown eyes looked me up and down and went past me to the white car parked by the curb.

"I sent a check," he said finally.

"It was quite in order," I assured him.

"I don't want any trouble . . . it wasn't my fault that the man was shot." He didn't sound convinced.

"Oh, no one blames you for that," I said. "He's perfectly all right now. Back at work, in fact."

His relief showed, even through the crack. "Very well," he said, and pushed the door shut to take off the chain.

I followed him into the front room of his tall terrace house. The air smelled stale and felt still, as if it had been hanging in the same spot for days. The furniture was of the hard-stuffed and brown shellacked substantial type that in my plywood childhood I had thought the peak of living, unobtainable; and there were cases of tropical butterflies on the walls, and carved ornaments from somewhere like Java or Borneo on several small tables. A life abroad, retirement at home, I thought. From color and heat to suburban respectability in Reading.

"My wife has gone out shopping," he said, still nervously. "She'll be back soon." He looked hopefully out of the lace-curtained window, but Mrs. Brinton didn't oblige him by coming to his support.

I said, "I just wanted to ask you, Mr. Brinton, if you were by any chance related to a William Brinton, one-time clerk of Dunstable racecourse."

He gave me a long agonized stare, and to my consternation sat down on his sofa and began to cry, his shaking hands covering his eyes and the tears splashing down onto his tweed-clad knees.

"Please . . . Mr. Brinton . . . I'm so sorry," I said awkwardly.

He snuffled and coughed, and dragged a handkerchie!

out to wipe his eyes. Gradually the paroxysm passed, and he said indistinctly, "How did you find out? I told you I didn't want anyone asking questions."

"It was quite accidental. Nobody asked any questions, I promise you. Would you like to tell me about it? Then I don't think any questions will need to be asked at all, from anyone else."

"The police . . . ," he said doubtfully, on a sob. "They came before. I refused to say anything, and they went away."

"Whatever you tell me will be in confidence."

"I've been such a fool. I'd like to tell someone, really."

I pictured the strung-up, guilt-ridden weeks he'd endured, and the crying fit became not only understandable but inevitable.

"It was the letter, you see," he said, sniffling softly. "The letter William began to write to me, though he never sent it. I found it in a whole trunk of stuff that was left when he . . . killed himself. I was in Sarawak then, you know, and they sent me a cable. It was a shock . . . one's only brother doing such a . . . a terrible thing. He was younger than me. Seven years. We weren't very close, except when we were children. I wish . . . but it's too late now. Anyway, when I came home I fetched all his stuff round from where it had been stored and put it up in the attic here, all his racing books and things. I didn't know what to do with them, you see. I wasn't interested in them, but it seemed . . . I don't know . . . I couldn't just burn them. It was months before I bothered to sort them out, and then I found the letter. . . ." His voice faltered and he looked at me appealingly, wanting to be forgiven.

"Kitty and I had found my pension didn't go anywhere near as far as we'd expected. Everything is so terribly expensive. The rates . . . we decided we'd have to sell the house again though we'd only just bought it, and Kitty's family are all close. And then . . . I thought . . . . perhaps I could sell the letter instead."

"And you got threats instead of money," I said.

"Yes. It was the letter itself which gave me the idea." He chewed his mustache.

"And now you no longer have it," I said matter-of-factly, as if I knew for certain and wasn't guessing. "When you were first threatened you thought you could still sell the letter if Hunt Radnor kept you safe, and then you got more frightened and gave up the letter, and then canceled the protection because the threats had stopped."

He nodded unhappily. "I gave them the letter because that man was shot. . . . I didn't realize anything like that would happen. I was horrified. It was terrible. I hadn't thought it could be so dangerous, just selling a letter. . . . I wish I'd never found it. I wish William had never written it."

So did I, as it happened.

"What did the letter say?" I asked.

He hesitated, his fear showing. "It might cause more trouble. They might come back."

"They won't know you've told me," I pointed out. "How could they?"

"I suppose not." He looked at me, making up his mind. There's one thing about being small: no one is ever afraid of you. If I'd been big and commanding I don't think he'd have risked it. As it was, his face softened and relaxed and he threw off the last threads of reticence.

"I know it by heart," he said. "I'll write it down for you, if you like. It's easier than saying it."

I sat and waited while he fetched a ball-point pen and a pad of large writing paper and got on with his task. The sight of the letter materializing again in front of his eyes affected him visibly, but whether to fear or remorse or sorrow, I couldn't tell. He covered one side of the page, then tore it off the pad and shakily handed it over.

I read what he had written. I read it twice. Because of these short desperate sentences, I reflected unemotionally, I had come within spitting distance of St. Peter.

"That's fine," I said. "Thank you very much."

"I wish I'd never found it," he said again. "Poor William."

"Did you see this man?" I asked, indicating the letter as I put it away in my wallet.

"No, I wrote to him . . . he wasn't hard to find."

"And how much did you ask for?"

Shamefaced, he muttered, "Five thousand pounds."

Five thousand pounds had been wrong, I thought. If he'd asked fifty thousand, he might have had a chance. But five thousand didn't put him among the big-power boys, it just revealed his mediocrity. No wonder he had been stamped on, fast.

"What happened next?" I asked.

"A big man came for the letter, about four o'clock one afternoon. It was awful. I asked him for the money and he just laughed in my face and pushed me into a chair. No money, he said, but if I didn't hand over the letter at once he'd . . . he'd teach me a thing or two. That's what he said, teach me a thing or two. I explained that I had put the letter in my box at the bank and that the bank was closed and that I couldn't get it until the next morning. He said that he would come to the bank with me the next day, and then he went away."

"And you rang up the agency almost at once? Yes. What made you chose Hunt Radnor?"

He looked surprised. "It was the only one I knew about. Are there any others? I mean, most people have heard of Hunt Radnor, I should think."

"I see. So Hunt Radnor sent you a bodyguard, but the big man wouldn't give up."

"He kept telephoning . . . then your man suggested setting a trap in his office, and in the end I agreed. Oh, I shouldn't have let him, I was such a fool. I knew all the time, you see, who was threatening me, but I couldn't tell your agency because I'd have to admit I'd tried to get money . . . illegally."

"Yes. Well, there's only one more thing. What was he like, the man who came and threatened you?"

Brinton didn't like even the memory of him. "He was very strong. Hard. When he pushed me it was like a wall. I'm not . . . I mean, I've never been good with my fists, or anything like that. If he'd started hitting me I couldn't have stopped him."

"I'm not blaming you for not standing up to him," I pointed out. "I just want to know what he looked like."

"Very big," he said vaguely. "Huge."

"I know it's several weeks ago now, but can't you possibly remember more than that? How about his hair? Anything odd about his face? How old? What class?"

He smiled for the first time, the sad wrinkles folding for a moment into some semblance of faded charm. If he'd never taken his first useless step into crime, I thought, he might still have been a nice gentle innocuous man, fading without rancor toward old age, troubled only by how to make a little pension go a long way. No tearing, destructive guilt.

"It's certainly easier when you ask questions like that. He was beginning to go bald, I remember now. And he had big blotchy freckles on the backs of his hands. It's difficult to know about his age. Not a youth, though; more than thirty, I think. What else did you ask? Oh yes, class. Working class, then."

"English?"

"Oh yes, not foreign. Sort of cockney, I suppose."

I stood up, thanked him, and began to take my leave. He said, begging me still for reassurance, "There won't be any more trouble?"

"Not from me or the agency."

"And the man who was shot?"

"Not from him either."

"I tried to tell myself it wasn't my fault . . . but I haven't been able to sleep. How could I have been such a fool? I shouldn't have let that young man set any trap. . . . I shouldn't have called in your agency . . and it cost another chunk of our savings. . . . I ought never to have tried to get money for that letter."

"That's true, Mr. Brinton, you shouldn't. But what's done is done, and I don't suppose you'll start anything like that again."

"No, no," he said with pain. "I wouldn't. Ever. These last few weeks have been . . ." His voice died. Then he said more strongly, "We'll have to sell the house now,

Kitty likes it here, of course. But what I've always wanted myself is a little bungalow by the sea."

When I reached the office I took out the disastrous letter and read it again, before adding it to the file. Being neither the original nor a photocopy, but only a reproduction from memory, it wasn't of the slightest use as evidence. In the elder Brinton's small tidy script, a weird contrast to the heartbroken contents, it ran:

Dear Mervy, dear big brother,
    I wish you could help me, as you did when I was little. I have spent fifteen years building up Dunstable Racecourse, and a man called Howard Kraye is making me destroy it. I have to frame races which nobody likes. Very few horses come now, and the gate receipts are falling fast. This week I must see that the race-card goes to the printers too late, and the press-room telephones will all be out of order. There will be a terrible muddle. People must think I am mad. I can't escape him. He is paying me as well, but I must do as he says. I can't help my nature, you know that. He has found out about a boy I was living with, and I could be prosecuted. He wants the racecourse to sell for housing. Nothing can stop him getting it. My racecourse, I love it.
    I know I shan't send this letter. Mervy, I wish you were here. I haven't anyone else. Oh dear God, I can't go on much longer, I really can't.

At five to six that afternoon I opened the door of Zanna Martin's office. Her desk was facing me and so was she. She raised her head, recognized me, and looked back at me in a mixture of pride and embarrassment.
"I did it," she said. "If you didn't, I'll kill you."
She had combed her hair even further forward, so that it hung close round her face, but all the same one could see the disfigurement at first glance. I had forgotten, in the days since Friday, just how bad it was.
"I felt the same about you," I said, grinning.

135

"You really did keep your promise?"

"Yes, I did. All day Saturday and Sunday, most of yesterday and most of today, and very nasty it is, too."

She sighed with relief. "I'm glad you've come. I nearly gave it up this morning. I thought you wouldn't do it, and you'd never come back to see if I had, and that I was being a proper idiot."

"Well, I'm here," I said. "Is Mr. Bolt in?"

She shook her head. "He's gone home. I'm just packing up."

"Finished the envelopes?" I said.

"Envelopes? Oh, those I was doing when you were here before? Yes, they're all done."

"And filled and sent?"

"No, the leaflets haven't come back from the printers yet, much to Mr. Bolt's disgust. I expect I'll be doing them tomorrow."

She stood up, tall and thin, put on her coat and tied the scarf over her hair.

"Are you going anywhere this evening?" I asked.

"Home," she said decisively.

"Come out to dinner," I suggested.

"Aunty's legacy won't last long, the way you spend. I think Mr. Bolt has already invested your money. You'd better save every penny until after settlement day."

"Coffee, then, and the flicks?"

"Look," she said hesitantly, "I sometimes buy a hot chicken on my way home. There's a fish-and-chips shop next to the station that sells them. Would you . . . would you like to come and help me eat it? In return, I mean, for Friday night."

"I'd enjoy that," I said, and was rewarded by a pleased, half-incredulous laugh.

"Really?"

"Really."

As before, we went to Finchley by underground, but this time Miss Martin sat boldly where her whole face showed. To try to match her fortitude, I rested my elbow on the seat arm between us. She looked at my hand and then at my face, gratefully, almost as if we were sharing an adventure.

136

As we emerged from the tube station she said, "You know, it makes a great deal of difference if one is accompanied by a man, even—" she stopped abruptly.

"Even," I finished, smiling, "if he is smaller than you and also damaged."

"Oh dear . . . and much younger, as well." Her real eye looked at me with rueful amusement. The glass one stared stonily ahead. I was getting used to it again.

"Let me buy the chicken," I said, as we stopped outside the shop. The smell of hot chips mingled with diesel fumes from a passing lorry. Civilization, I thought. Delightful.

"Certainly not." Miss Martin was firm and bought the chicken herself. She came out with it wrapped in newspaper. "I got a few chips and a packet of peas," she said.

"And I," I said firmly, as we came to an off-license, "am getting some brandy." What chips and peas would do to my digestion I dared not think.

We walked round to the house with the parcels and went through into her room. She moved with a light step.

"In that cupboard over there," she said, pointing, as she peeled off her coat and scarf, "there are some glasses and a bottle of sherry. Will you pour me some? I expect you prefer brandy, but have some sherry if you'd like. I'll just take these things into the kitchen and put them to keep hot."

While I unscrewed the bottles and poured the drinks I heard her lighting her gas stove and unwrapping the parcels. There was dead quiet as I walked across the room with her sherry, and when I reached the door I saw why. She held the chicken in its piece of greaseproof paper absently in one hand; the bag of chips lay open on the table with the box of peas beside it; and she was reading the newspaper they had all been wrapped in.

She looked up at me in bewilderment.

"You," she said. "It's you. This is you."

I looked down where her finger pointed. The fish-and-chips shop had wrapped up her chicken in the Sunday *Hemisphere*.

"Here's your sherry," I said, holding it out to her.

She put down the chicken and took the glass without appearing to notice it.

"Another Halley," she said. "It caught my eye. Of course I read it. And it's your picture, and it even refers to your hand. You are Sid Halley."

"That's right." There was no chance of denying it.

"Good heavens. I've known about you for years. Read about you. I saw you on television, often. My father loved watching the racing, we always had it on when he was alive—" She broke off and then said with increased puzzlement, "Why on earth did you say your name was John and that you worked in a shop? Why did you come to see Mr. Bolt? I don't understand."

"Drink your sherry, put your chicken in the oven before it freezes and I'll tell you." There was nothing else to do: I didn't want to risk her brightly passing on the interesting tidbit of news to her employer.

Without demur she put the dinner to heat, came to sit on the sofa, opposite to where I apprehensively waited in an armchair, and raised her eyebrows in expectation.

"I don't work in a shop," I admitted. "I am employed by a firm called Hunt Radnor Associates."

Like Brinton, she had heard of the agency. She stiffened her whole body and began to frown. As casually as I could, I told her about Kraye and the Seabury shares; but she was no fool and she went straight to the heart of things.

"You suspect Mr. Bolt too. That's why you went to see him."

"Yes, I'm afraid so."

"And me? You took me out simply and solely to find out about him?" Her voice was bitter.

I didn't answer at once. She waited, and somehow her calmness was more piercing than tears or temper could have been. She asked so little of life.

At last I said, "I went to Bolt's office as much to take out his secretary as to see Bolt himself, yes."

The peas boiled over, hissing loudly. She stood up slowly. "At least that's honest."

138

She went into the tiny kitchen and turned out the gas under the saucepan.

I said, "I came to your office this afternoon because I wanted to look at those leaflets Bolt is sending to Seabury shareholders. You told me at once that they hadn't come from the printers. I didn't need to accept your invitation to supper after that. But I'm here."

She stood in the kitchen doorway, holding herself straight with an all too apparent effort.

"I suppose you lied about that too," she said in a quiet rigidly controlled voice, pointing to my arm. "Why? Why did you play such a cruel game with me? Surely you could have got your information without that. Why did you make me change my desk round? I suppose you were laughing yourself sick all day Saturday thinking about it."

I stood up. Her hurt was dreadful.

I said, "I went to Kempton races on Saturday."

She didn't move.

"I kept my promise."

She made a slight gesture of disbelief.

"I'm sorry," I said helplessly.

"Yes. Good night, Mr. Halley. Good night."

I went.

11

Radnor held a Seabury conference the next morning, Wednesday, consisting of himself, Dolly, Chico and me; the result, chiefly, of my having the previous afternoon finally wrung grudging permission from Lord Hagbourne to arrange a twenty-four-hour guard at Seabury for the coming Thursday, Friday and Saturday.

The bulldozing had been accomplished without trouble, and a call to the course that morning had established that the tan was arriving in regular lorry loads and was being spread. Racing, bar any last-minute accidents, was now certain. Even the weather was cooperating. The glass was rising; the forecast was dry, cold and sunny.

Dolly proposed a straight patrol system, and Radnor was inclined to agree. Chico and I had other ideas.

"If anyone intended to sabotage the track," Dolly pointed out, "they would be frightened off by a patrol. Same thing if they were planning something in the stands themselves."

Radnor nodded. "Safest way of making sure racing takes place. I suppose we'll need at least four men to do it properly."

I said, "I agree that we need a patrol tonight, tomorrow night and Friday night, just to play safe. But tomorrow, when the course will be more or less deserted . . . what we need is to pinch them at it, not frighten them off. There's no evidence yet that could be used in a court of law. If we could catch them in mid-sabotage, so to speak, we'd be much better off."

"That's right," said Chico. "Hide and pounce. Much better than scaring them away."

"I seem to remember," said Dolly with a grin, "that the last time you two set a trap the mouse shot the cheese."

"Oh God, Dolly, you slay me," said Chico, laughing warmly and for once accepting her affection.

Even Radnor laughed. "Seriously, though," he said, "I don't see how you can. A racecourse is too big. If you are hiding you can only see a small part of it. And surely if you show yourself your presence would act like any other patrol to stop anything plainly suspicious being done? I don't think it's possible."

"Um," I said. "But there's one thing I can still do better than anyone else in this agency."

"And what's that?" said Chico, ready to argue.

"Ride a horse."

"Oh," said Chico. "I'll give you that, chum."

"A horse," said Radnor thoughtfully. "Well, that's certainly an idea. Nobody's going to look suspiciously at a horse at a racecourse, I suppose. Mobile, too. Where would you get one?"

"From Mark Witney. I could borrow his hack. Seabury's his local course. His stables aren't many miles away."

"But can you still—?" began Dolly, and broke off. "Well, don't glare at me like that, all of you. I can't ride with two hands, let alone one."

"A man called Gregory Philips had his arm amputated very high up," I said, "and went on racing in point-to-points for years."

"Enough said," said Dolly. "How about Chico?"

"He can wear a pair of my jodhpurs. Protective coloring. And lean nonchalantly on the rails."

"Stick insects," said Chico cheerfully.

"That's what you want, Sid?" said Radnor.

I nodded. "Look at it from the worst angle: we haven't anything on Kraye that will stand up. We might not find Smith, the tanker driver, and even if we do, he has everything to lose by talking and nothing to gain. When the racecourse stables burned down a year ago, we couldn't prove it wasn't an accident; an illicit cigarette end. Stable lads do smoke, regardless of bans.

"The so-called drain which collapsed—we don't know if it was dug a day, a week, or six weeks before it did its work. That letter William Brinton of Dunstable wrote to his brother, it's only a copy from memory that we've got, no good at all for evidence. All it proves, to our own satisfaction, is that Kraye is capable of anything. We can't show it to Lord Hagbourne, because I obtained it in confidence, and he still isn't a hundred per cent convinced that Kraye has done more than buy shares. As I see it, we've just got to give the enemy a change to get on with their campaign."

"You think they will, then?"

"It's awfully likely, isn't it? This year there isn't another Seabury meeting until February. A three months' gap. And if I read it right, Kraye is in a hurry now because of the political situation. He won't want to spend fifty thousand buying Seabury and then find building land has been nationalized overnight. If I were him, I'd want to clinch the deal and sell to a developer as quickly as possible. According to the photographs of the share

141

transfers, he already holds twenty-three per cent of the shares. This is almost certainly enough to swing the sale of the company if it comes to a vote. But he's greedy. He'll want more. But he'll only want more if he can get it soon. Waiting for February is too risky. So yes, I do think if we give him a chance that he will organize some more damage this week."

"It's a risk," said Dolly. "Suppose something dreadful happens and we neither prevent it nor catch anyone doing it?"

They kicked it round among the three of them for several more minutes, the pros and cons of the straight patrols versus cat and mouse. Finally Radnor turned back to me and said, "Sid?"

"It's your agency," I said seriously. "It's your risk."

"But it's your case. It's still your case. You must decide."

I couldn't understand him. It was all very well for him to have given me a free hand so far, but this wasn't the sort of decision I would have ever expected him to pass on.

Still . . . "Chico and I, then," I said. "We'll go alone tonight and stay all day tomorrow. I don't think we'll let even Captain Oxon know we're there. Certainly not the foreman, Ted Wilkins, or any of the other men. We'll come in from the other side from the stands, and I'll borrow the horse for mobility. Dolly can arrange official patrol guards with Oxon for tomorrow night—suggest he gives them a warm room, Dolly. He ought to have the central heating on by then."

"Friday and Saturday?" asked Radnor, noncommittally.

"Full guards, I guess. As many as Lord Hagbourne will sub for. The race-going crowds make cat-and-mouse impossible."

"Right," said Radnor, decisively. "That's it, then."

When Dolly, Chico and I had got as far as the door he said, "Sid, you wouldn't mind if I had another look at those photographs? Send Jones-boy down with them if you're not needing them."

"Sure," I agreed. "I've pored over them till I know

142

them by heart. I bet you'll spot something at once that I've missed."

"It often works that way," he said, nodding.

The three of us went back to the Racing Section, and via the switchboard I traced Jones-boy, who happened to be in Missing Persons. While he was on his way down I flipped through the packet of photographs yet again. The share transfers, the summary with the list of bank accounts, the letters from Bolt, the ten-pound notes, and the two sheets of dates, initials and figures from the very bottom of the attaché case. It had been clear all along that these last were lists either of receipts or expenditures, but by now I was certain they were the latter. A certain W.L.B. had received regular sums of fifty pounds a month for twelve months, and the last date for W.L.B. was four days before William Leslie Brinton, clerk of Dunstable Racecourse, had taken the quickest way out. Six hundred pounds and a threat; the price of a man's soul.

Most of the other initials meant nothing to me, except the last one, J.R.S., which looked as if they could be the tanker drivers. The first entry for J.R.S., for one hundred pounds, was dated the day before the tanker overturned at Seabury, the day before Kraye went to Aynsford for the weekend.

In the next line, the last of the whole list, a further sum of one hundred and fifty pounds was entered against J.R.S. The date of this was that of the following Tuesday, three days before I had taken the photographs. Smith had packed up and vanished from his job and his digs on that Tuesday.

Constantly recurring among the other varying initials were two Christian names, Leo and Fred. Each of these was on the regular payroll, it seemed. Either Leo or Fred, I guessed, had been the big man who had visited the frightened Mervyn Brinton. Either Leo or Fred was the "big chap" who had sent Andrews with a gun to Cromwell Road.

I had a score to settle with either Leo or Fred.

Jones-boy came in for the photographs. I tapped them together back into their box and gave them to him.

"Where, you snotty-nosed little coot, is our coffee?"

said Chico rudely. We had been downstairs when Jones-boy did his rounds.

"Coots are bald," observed Dolly coyly, eyeing Jones-boy's luxuriant locks.

Jones-boy unprintably told Chico where he could find his coffee.

Chico advanced a step, saying, "You remind me of the people sitting on the walls of Jerusalem." He had been raised in a church orphanage, after all.

Jones-boy knew the more basic bits of Isaiah. He said callously, "You did it on the doorstep of Barnes cop shop, I believe."

Chico furiously lashed out a fist to Jones-boy's head. Jones-boy jumped back, laughed insultingly, and the box he was holding flew high out of his hand, opening as it went.

"Stop it you two, damn you," shouted Dolly, as the big photographs floated down onto her desk and onto the floor.

"Babes in the wood," remarked Jones-boy, in great good humor from having got the best of the slinging match. He helped Dolly and me pick up the photographs, shuffled them back into the box in no sort of order, and departed grinning.

"Chico," said Dolly severely, "you ought to know better."

"The bossy-mother routine bores me sick," said Chico violently.

Dolly bit her lip and looked away. Chico stared at me defiantly, knowing very well he had started the row and was in the wrong.

"As one bastard to another," I said mildly, "pipe down."

Not being able to think of a sufficiently withering reply fast enough Chico merely scowled and walked out of the room. The show was over. The office returned to normal. Typewriters clattered, someone used the tape recorder, someone else the telephone. Dolly sighed and began to draw up her list for Seabury. I sat and thought about Leo. Or Fred. Unproductively.

After a while I ambled upstairs to Bona Fides, where

144

the usual amount of telephone shouting filled the air. George, deep in a mysterious conversation about moth balls, saw me and shook his head. Jack Copeland, freshly attired in a patchily faded green sleeveless pullover, took time out between calls to say that they were sorry, but they'd made no progress with Kraye. He had, Jack said, very craftily covered his tracks about ten years back. They would keep digging, if I liked. I liked.

Up in Missing Persons Sammy said it was too soon for results on Smith.

When I judged that Mark Witney would be back in his house after exercising his second lot of horses, I rang him up and asked him to lend me his hack, a pensioned-off old steeplechaser of the first water.

"Sure," he said. "What for?"

I explained what for.

"You'd better have my horse box as well," he commented. "Suppose it pours with rain all night? Give you somewhere to keep dry, if you have the box."

"But won't you be needing it? The forecast says clear and dry anyway."

"I won't need it until Friday morning. I haven't any runners until Seabury. And only one there, I may say, in spite of being so close. The owners just won't have it. I have to go all the way to Banbury on Saturday. Damn silly with another much better course on my doorstep."

"What are you running at Seabury?"

He told me, at great and uncomplimentary length, about a half-blind, utterly stupid, one-paced habitual non-jumper with which he proposed to win the novice chase. Knowing him, I guessed he would. We agreed that Chico and I should arrive at his place about eight that evening, and I rang off.

After that I left the office, went across London by underground to Company House in the city, and asked for the files of Seabury Racecourse. In a numbered chair at a long table, surrounded by earnest men and women clerks pouring over similar files and making copious notes, I studied the latest list of investors. Apart from Kraye

145

and his various aliases, which I now recognized on sight from long familiarity with the share-transfer photographs, there were no large blocks in single ownership. No one else held more than 3 per cent of the total: and as 3 per cent meant that roughly £2500 was lying idle and not bringing in a penny in dividends, it was easy to see why no one wanted a larger holding.

Fotherton's name was not on the list. Although this was not conclusive, because a nominee name like "Mayday Investments" could be anyone at all, I was more or less satisfied that Seabury's clerk was not gambling on Seabury's death. All the big share movements during the past year had been to Kraye, and no one else.

A few of the small investors, holding two hundred or so shares each, were people I knew personally. I wrote down their names and addresses, intending to let me see Bolt's circular letter when it arrived. Slower than via Zanna Martin, but surer.

My mind shied away from Miss Martin. I'd had a bad night thinking about her. Her and Jenny, both.

Back in the office I found it was the tail end of the lunch hour, with nearly all the desks still empty. Chico alone was sitting behind his, biting his nails.

"If we're going to be up all night," I suggested, "we'd better take the afternoon off for sleep."

"No need."

"Every need. I'm not as young as you."

"Poor old grandpa." He grinned suddenly, apologizing for the morning. "I can't help it. That Jones-boy gets on my wick."

"Jones-boy can look after himself. It's Dolly—"

"It's not my bloody fault she can't have kids."

"She wants kids like you want a mother."

"But I don't—" he began indignantly.

"Your own," I said flatly. "Like you want your own mother to have kept you and loved you. Like mine did."

"You had every advantage, of course."

"That's right."

146

He laughed. "Funny thing is I.like old Dolly, really. Except for the hen bit."

"Who wouldn't?" I said amicably. "You can sleep on my sofa."

He sighed. "You're going to be less easy than Dolly to work for, I can see that."

"Eh?"

"Don't kid yourself, mate. Sir, I mean." He was lightly ironic.

The other inmates at the office drifted back, including Dolly, with whom I fixed for Chico to have the afternoon free. She was cool to him and unforgiving, which I privately thought would do them both good.

She said, "The first official patrol will start on the racecourse tomorrow at six A.M. Shall I tell them to find you and report?"

"No," I said defiantly. "I don't know where I'll be."

"It had better be the usual then," she said. "They can report to the old man at his home number when they start the job, and again at six A.M. when they go off and the next lot take over."

"And they'll ring him in between if anything happens?" I said.

"Yes. As usual."

"It's as bad as being a doctor," I said smiling.

Dolly nodded, and half to herself she murmured, "You'll find out."

Chico and I walked round to my flat, pulled the curtains, and did our best to sleep. I didn't find it easy at two-thirty in the afternoon: it was the time for racing, not rest. It seemed to me that I had barely drifted off when the telephone rang. I looked at my watch on the way to answer it in the sitting room and found it was only ten to five. I had asked for a call at six.

It was not the telephone exchange, however, it was Dolly.

"A message has come for you by hand, marked 'very urgent.' I thought you might want it before you go to Seabury."

"Who brought it?"

"A taxi driver."

147

"Shunt him round here, then."

"He's gone, I'm afraid."

"Who's the message from?"

"I've no idea. It's in a plain brown envelope, the size we use for interim reports."

"Oh, all right, I'll come back."

Chico had drowsily propped himself up on one elbow on the sofa.

"Go to sleep again," I said. I've got to go and see something at the office. Won't be long."

When I reached the Racing Section again I found that whatever had come for me, something else had gone. The shaky lemon-colored table. I was deskless again.

"Sammy said he was sorry," explained Dolly, "but he has a new assistant and nowhere to park him."

"I had things in the drawer," I complained. Shades of Sammy's lunch, I thought.

"They're here," Dolly said, pointing to a corner of her desk. "There was only the Brinton file, a half bottle of brandy, and some pills. Also I found this on the floor." She held out a flat, crackly cellophane packet.

"The negatives of those photographs are in here," I said, taking it from her. "They were in the box, though."

"Until Jones-boy dropped it."

"Oh, yes." I put the packet of negatives inside the Brinton file and pinched a large rubber band from Dolly to snap round the outside.

"How about that mysterious very urgent message?" I asked.

Dolly silently and considerately slit open the envelope in question, drew out the single sheet of paper it contained and handed it to me. I unfolded it and stared at it in disbelief.

It was a circular, headed Charing, Street and King, Stockbrokers, dated with the following day's date, and it ran:

Dear Sir or Madam,

We have various clients wishing to purchase small parcels of shares in the following lists of minor companies. If you are considering selling your interests in any of

148

these, we would be grateful if you would get in touch with us. We would assure you of a good fair price, based on today's quotation.

There followed a list of about thirty companies, of which I had heard of only one. Tucked in about three-quarters of the way down was Seabury Racecourse.

I turned the page over. Zanna Martin had written on the back in a hurried hand.

This is only going to Seabury shareholders. Not to anyone owning shares in the other companies. The leaflets came from the printers this morning, and are to be posted tomorrow. I hope it is what you want. I'm sorry about last night.

Z.M.

"What is it?" asked Dolly.

"A free pardon," I said lightheartedly, slipping the circular inside the Brinton file along with the negatives. "Also confirmation that Ellis Bolt is not on the side of the angels."

"You're a nut," she said. "And take these things off my desk. I haven't room for them."

I put the pills and brandy in my pocket and picked up the Brinton file.

"Is that better?"

"Thank you, yes."

"So long, then, my love. See you on Friday."

On the walk back to the flat I decided suddenly to go and see Miss Martin. I went straight down to the garage for my car without going up and waking Chico again, and made my way eastward to the city for the second time that day. The rush-hour traffic was so bad that I was afraid I would miss her, but in fact she was ten minutes late in leaving the office and I caught her up just before she reached the underground station.

"Miss Martin," I called. "Would you like a lift home?"

She turned round in surprise.

"Mr. Halley!"

"Hop in."

She hopped. That is to say, she opened the door, picked up the Brinton file which was lying on the passenger seat, sat down, tidily folded her coat over her knees, and pulled the door shut again. The bad side of her face was toward me, and she was very conscious of it. The scarf and the hair were gently pulled forward.

I took a pound of ten-shilling note out of my pocket and gave them to her. She took them smiling.

"The taxi man told our switchboard girl you gave him that for bringing the leaflet. Thank you very much." I swung out through the traffic and headed for Finchley.

She answered obliquely. "That wretched chicken is still in the oven, stone cold. I just turned the gas out yesterday, after you'd gone."

"I wish I could stay this evening instead," I said, "but I've got a job on for the agency."

"Another time," she said tranquilly. "Another time, perhaps. I understand that you couldn't tell me at first who you worked for, because you didn't know whether I was an . . . er, an accomplice of Mr. Bolt's, and afterwards you didn't tell me for fear of what actually happened, that I would be upset. So that's that."

"You are generous."

"Realistic, even if a bit late."

We went a little way in silence. Then I asked, "What would happen to the shares Kraye owns if it were proved he was sabotaging the company? If he were convicted, I mean. Would his shares be confiscated, or would he still own them when he came out of jail?"

"I've never heard of anyone's shares being confiscated," she said, sounding interested. "But surely that's a long way in the future?"

"I wish I knew. It makes a good deal of difference to what I should do now."

"How do you mean?"

"Well . . . an easy way to stop Kraye buying too many more shares would be to tell the racing press and the financial press that a take-over is being attempted. The price would rocket. But Kraye already holds twenty-three per cent, and if the law couldn't take it away from him,

150

he would either stick to that and vote for a sellout, or if he got cold feet he could unload his shares at the higher price and still make a fat profit. Either way, he'd be sitting pretty financially, in jail or out. And either way Seabury would be built on."

"I suppose this sort of thing's happened before?"

"Take-overs, yes, several. But only one other case of sabotage. At Dunstable. Kraye again."

"Haven't any courses survived a take-over bid?"

"Only Sandown, publicly. I don't know of any others, but they may have managed it in secrecy."

"How did Sandown do it?"

"The local council did it for them. Stated loudly that planning permission would not be given for building. Of course the bid collapsed then."

"It looks as though the only hope for Seabury, in that case, is that the council there will act in this same way. I'd try a strong lobby, if I were you."

"You're quite a girl, Miss Martin," I said smiling. "That's a very good idea. I'll go and dip a toe into the climate of opinion at the Town Hall."

She nodded approvingly. "No good lobbying against the grain. Much better to find out which way people are likely to move before you start pushing!"

Finchley came into sight. I said, "You do realize, Miss Martin, that if I am successful at my job, you will lose yours?"

She laughed. "Poor Mr. Bolt. He's not at all bad to work for. But don't worry about my job. It's easy for an experienced stockbroker's secretary to get a good one, I assure you."

I stopped at her gate, looking at my watch. "I'm afraid I can't come in. I'm already going to be a bit late."

She opened the door without ado and climbed out. "Thank you for coming at all." She smiled, shut the door crisply, and waved me away.

I drove back to my flat as fast as I could, fuming slightly at the traffic. It wasn't until I switched off the engine down in the garage and leaned over to pick it up that I discovered the Brinton file wasn't there. And then remembered Miss Martin holding it on her lap during the journey, and me hustling her out of the car. Miss Martin still had Brinton's file. I hadn't time to go back for it, and I couldn't ring her up because I didn't know the name of the owner of the house she lived in. But surely, I reassured myself, surely the file would be safe enough where it was until Friday.

12

Chico and I sat huddled together for warmth in some gorse bushes and watched the sun rise over Seabury Racecourse. It had been a cold clear night with a tingle of naught degrees centigrade about it, and we were both shivering.

Behind us, among the bushes and out of sight, Revelation, one-time winner of the Cheltenham Gold Cup, was breakfasting on meager patches of grass. We could hear the scrunch when he bit down close to the roots, and the faint chink of the bridle as he ate. For some time Chico and I had been resisting the temptation to relieve him of his nice warm rug.

"They might try something now," said Chico hopefully. "First light, before anyone's up."

Nothing had moved in the night, we were certain of that. Every hour I had ridden Revelation at a careful walk round the whole of the track itself, and Chico had made a plimsollshod inspection of the stands at one with the shadows. There had been no one about. Not a sound but the stirring breeze, not a glimmer of light but from the stars and a waning moon.

Our present spot, chosen as the sky lightened and some concealment became necessary, lay at the furthest spot from the stands, at the bottom of the semicircle of track cut off by the road which ran across the course. Scattered bushes and scrub filled the space between the track and boundary fence, enough to shield us from all but closely

152

prying eyes. Behind the boundary fence were the little back gardens of the first row of bungalows. The sun rose bright and yellow away to our left and the birds sang around us. It was half past seven.

"It's going to be a lovely day," said Chico.

At ten past nine there was some activity up by the stands and the tractor rolled onto the course pulling a trailer. I unshipped my race glasses, balanced them on my bent-up knees, and took a look. The trailor was loaded with what I guessed were hurdles, and was accompanied by three men on foot.

I handed the glasses to Chico without comment, and yawned.

"Lawful occasions," he remarked, bored.

We watched the tractor and trailer lumber slowly round the far end of the course, pause to unload, and return for a refill. On its second trip it came close enough for us to confirm that it was in fact the spare hurdles that were being dumped in position, four or five at each flight, ready to be used if any were splintered in the races. We watched for a while in silence. Then I said slowly, "Chico, I've been blind."

"Huh?"

"The tractor," I said. "The tractor. Under our noses all the time."

"So?"

"So the sulfuric acid tanker was pulled over by a tractor. No complicated lifting gear necessary. Just a couple of ropes or chains slung over the top of the tanker and fastened round the axles. Then you unscrew the hatches and stand well clear. Someone drives the tractor at full power up the course, over goes the tanker and out pours the juice. And Bob's your uncle!"

"Every racecourse has a tractor," said Chico thoughtfully.

"That's right."

"So no one would look twice at a tractor on a racecourse. Quite. No one would remark on any tracks it left. No one would mention seeing one on the road. So if you're right, and I'd say you certainly are, it

153

wouldn't necessarily have been that tractor, the racecourse tractor, which was used."

"I'll bet it was, though." I told Chico about the photographed initials and payments. "Tomorrow I'll check the initials of all the workmen here from Ted Wilkins downwards against that list. Any one of them might have been paid just to leave the tractor on the course, lying handy. The tanker went over on the evening before the meeting, like today. The tractor would have been in use then too. Warm and full of fuel. Nothing easier. And afterwards, straight on up the racecourse and out of sight."

"It was dusk," agreed Chico. "As long as no one came along the road in the minutes it took to unhitch the ropes or chains afterwards, they were clear. No traffic diversions, no detours, nothing."

We sat watching the tractor lumbering about, gloomily realizing we couldn't prove a word of it.

"We'll have to move," I said presently. "There's a hurdle just along there, about fifty yards away, where those wings are. They'll be down here over the road soon."

We adjourned with Revelation back to the horse box half a mile away down the road to the west and took the opportunity to eat our own breakfast. When we had finished Chico went back first, strolling along confidently in my jodhpurs, boots and polo-necked jersey, the complete horseman from head to foot. He had never actually sat on a horse in his life.

After a while I followed on Revelation. The men had brought the hurdles down into the semicircular piece of track and had laid them in place. They were now moving further away up the course, unloading the next lot. Unremarked, I rode back to the bushes and dismounted. Of Chico there was no sign for another half hour, and then he came whistling across from the road with his hands in his pockets.

When he reached me he said, "I had another look round the stands. Rotten security, here. No one asked me what I was doing. There are some women cleaning here and there, and some are working in the stable block

154

getting the lads' hostel ready, things like that. I said good morning to them, and they said good morning back." He was disgusted.

"Not much scope for saboteurs," I said morosely. "Cleaners in the stands and workmen on the course."

"Dusk tonight," nodded Chico. "That's the most likely time now."

The morning ticked slowly away. The sun rose to its low November zenith and shone straight into our eyes. I passed the time by taking a photograph of Revelation and another of Chico. He was fascinated by the tiny camera and said he couldn't wait to get one like it. Eventually I put it back into my breeches pocket, and shading my eyes against the sun took my hundredth look up the course.

Nothing. No men, no tractor. I looked at my watch. One o'clock. Lunch hour. More time passed.

Chico picked up the race glasses and swept the course.

"Be careful," I said idly. "Don't look at the sun with those. You'll hurt your eyes."

"Do me a favor."

I yawned, feeling the sleepless night catch up.

"There's a man on the course," he said. "One. Just walking."

He handed me the glasses and I took a look. He was right. One man was walking alone across the racecourse; not round the track but straight across the rough grass in the middle. He was too far away for his features to be distinguishable and in any case he was wearing a fawn duffel coat with the hood up. I shrugged and lowered the glasses. He looked harmless enough.

With nothing better to do we watched him reach the far side, duck under the rails, and move along until he was standing behind one of the fences with only his head and shoulders in our sight.

Chico remarked that he should have attended to nature in the gents' before he left the stands. I yawned again, smiling at the same time. The man went on standing behind the fence.

155

"What on earth is he doing?" said Chico, after about five minutes.

"He isn't doing anything," I said, watching through the glasses. "He's just standing there looking this way."

"Do you think he's spotted us?"

"No, he couldn't. He hasn't any binocs, and we are in the bushes."

Another five minutes passed in inactivity.

"He must be doing *something*," said Chico, exasperated.

"Well, he isn't," I said.

Chico took a turn with the glasses. "You can't see a damn thing against the sun," he complained. "We should have camped up the other end."

"In the car park?" I suggested mildly. "The road to the stables and the main gates runs along the other end. There isn't a scrap of cover."

"He's got a flag," said Chico suddenly. "Two flags. One in each hand. White on the left, orange on the right. He seems to be waving them alternately. He's just some silly nit of a racecourse attendant practicing calling up the ambulance and the vet." He was disappointed.

I watched the flags waving, first white, then orange, then white, then orange, with a gap of a second or two between each wave. It certainly wasn't any form of recognizable signaling: nothing like semaphore. They were, as Chico had said, quite simply the flags used after a fall in a race: white to summon the ambulance for the jockey, orange to get attention for a horse. He didn't keep it up very long. After about eight waves altogether he stopped, and in a moment or two began to walk back across the course to the stands.

"Now what," said Chico, "do you think all that was in aid of?"

He swept the glasses all round the whole racecourse yet again. "There isn't a soul about except him and us."

"He's probably been standing by a fence for months waiting for a chance to wave his flags, and no one has been injured anywhere near him. In the end, the temptation proved too much."

I stood up and stretched, went through the bushes to Revelation, undid the halter with which he was tethered to the bushes, unbuckled the surcingle and pulled off his rug.

"What are you doing?" said Chico.

"The same as the man with the flags. Succumbing to an intolerable temptation. Give me a leg up." He did what I asked, but hung on to the reins.

"You're mad. You said in the night that they might let you do it after this meeting, but they'd never agree to it before. Suppose you smash the fences?"

"Then I'll be in almighty trouble," I agreed. "But here I am on a super jumper looking at a heavenly course on a perfect day, with everyone away at lunch." I grinned "Leave go."

Chico took his hand away, "It's not like you," he said doubtfully.

"Don't take it to heart," I said flippantly, and touched Revelation into a walk.

At this innocuous pace the horse and I went out into the track and proceeded in the direction of the stands. Counter-clockwise, the way the races were run. Still at a walk we reached the road and went across its uncovered Tarmac surface. On the far side of the road lay the enormous dark brown patch of tan, spread thick and firm where the burnt turf had been bulldozed away. Horses would have no difficulty in racing over it.

Once on the other side, on the turf again, Revelation broke into a trot. He knew where he was. Even with no crowds and no noise the fact of being on a familiar racecourse was exciting him. His ears were pricked, his step springy. At fourteen he had been already a year in retirement, but he moved beneath me like a four-year-old. He too, I guessed fancifully, was feeling the satanic tug of a pleasure about to be illicitly snatched.

Chico was right, of course. I had no business at all to be riding on the course so soon before a meeting. It was indefensible. I ought to know better. I did know better. I eased Revelation gently into a canter.

There were three flights of hurdles and three fences more or less side-by-side up the straight, and the water

157

jump beyond that. As I wasn't sure that Revelation would jump the fences in cold blood on his own (many horses won't), I set him at the hurdles.

Once he had seen these and guessed my intention I doubt if I could have stopped him, even if I'd wanted to. He fairly ate up the first flight and stretched out eagerly for the second. After that I gave him a choice, and of the two obstacles lying ahead, he opted for the fence. It didn't seem to bother him that he was on his own. They were excellent fences and he was a Gold Cup winner, born and bred for the job and being given an unexpected, much-missed treat. He flew the fence with all his former dash and skill.

As for me, my feelings were indescribable. I'd sat on a horse a few times since I'd given up racing, but never found an opportunity of doing more than riding out quietly at morning exercise with Mark's string. And here I was, back in my old place, doing again what I'd ached for in the two and a half years. I grinned with irrepressible joy and got Revelation to lengthen his stride for the water jump.

He took it with feet to spare. Perfect. There were no irate shouts from the stands on my right, and we swept away on round the top bend of the course, fast and free. Another fence at the end of the bend—Revelation floated it—and five more stretching away down the far side. It was at the third of these, the open ditch, that the man had been standing and waving the flags.

It's an undoubted fact that emotions pass from rider to horse, and Revelation was behaving with the same reckless exhilaration which gripped me, so after two spectacular leaps over the next two fences we both sped onward with arms open to fate. There ahead was the guard rail, the four-foot-wide open ditch and the four-foot-six fence rising on the far side of it. Revelation, knowing all about it, automatically put himself right to jump.

It came, the blinding flash in the eyes, as we soared into the air. White, dazzling, brain-shattering light, splintering the day into a million fragments and blotting out the world in a blaze as searing as the sun.

I felt Revelation falling beneath me and rolled instinctively, my eyes open and quite unable to see. Then
there was the rough crash on the turf and the return of
vision from light to blackness and up through gray to
normal sight.

I was on my feet before Revelation, and I still had
hold of the reins. He struggled up, bewildered and
staggering, but apparently unhurt. I pulled him forward
into an unwilling trot to make sure of his legs, and was
relieved to find them whole and sound. It only remained
to remount as quickly as possible, and this was in-
furiatingly difficult. With two hands I could have jumped
up easily; as it was I scrambled untidily back into the
saddle at the third attempt, having lost the reins
altogether and bashed my stomach on the pommel of
the saddle into the bargain. Revelation behaved very
well, all things considered. He trotted only fifty yards
or so in the wrong direction before I collected myself
and the reins into a working position and turned him
round. This time we by-passed the fence and all sub-
sequent ones: I cantered him first down the side of the
track, slowed to a trot to cross the road, and steered then
not on round the bottom semicircle but off to the right,
heading for where the boundary fence met the main
London road.

Out of the corner of my eye I saw Chico running in
my direction across the rough grass. I waved him toward
me with a sweep of the arm and reined in and waited
for him where our paths converged.

"I thought you said you could bloody well ride," he
said, scarcely out of breath from the run.

"Yeah," I said. "I thought so once."

He looked at me sharply. "You fell off. I was watching. You fell off like a baby."

"If you were watching . . . the horse fell, if you don't
mind. There's a distinction. Very important to jockeys."
Traffic whizzed along the London road only ten yards

"Nuts," he said. "You fell off."

"Come on," I said, walking Revelation toward the
boundary fence. "There's something to find," I told Chico

159

what. "In one of those bungalows, I should think. At a window or on the roof, or in a garden."

"Sods," said Chico forcefully. "The dirty sods."

I agreed with him.

It wasn't very difficult, because it had to be within a stretch of only a hundred yards or so. We went methodically along the boundary fence toward the London road, stopping to look carefully into every separate little garden, and at every separate little house. A fair number of inquisitive faces looked back.

Chico saw it first, propped into a high leafless branch of a tree growing well back in the second-to-last garden. Traffic whizzed along the London road only ten yeards ahead, and Revelation showed signs of wanting to retreat.

"Look," said Chico, pointing upward.

I looked, fighting a mild battle against the horse. It was five feet high, three feet wide, and polished to a spotless brilliance. A mirror.

"Sods," said Chico again.

I nodded, dismounted, led Revelation back to where the traffic no longer fretted him, and tied the reins to the fence. Then Chico and I walked along to the London road and round into the road of bungalows. Napoleon Close, it said. Napoleon wasn't *that* close, I reflected, amused.

We rang the door of the second bungalow. A man and a woman both came to the door to open it, elderly, gentle, inoffensive and inquiring.

I came straight to the point, courteously. "Do you know you have a mirror in your tree?"

"Don't be silly," said the woman, smiling as at an idiot. She had flat wavy gray hair and was wearing a sloppy black cardigan over a brown wool dress. No color sense, I thought.

"You'd better take a look," I suggested.

"It's not a mirror, you know," said the husband, puzzled. "It's a placard. One of those advertisement things."

"That's right," said his wife contrapuntally. "A placard."

160

"We agreed to lend our tree—"

"For a small sum, really . . . only our pension—"

"A man put up the framework—"

"He said he would be back soon with the poster—"

"A religious one, I believe. A good cause—"

"We wouldn't have done it otherwise—"

Chico interrupted. "I wouldn't have thought it was a good place for a poster. Your tree stands further back than the others. It isn't conspicuous."

"I did think—" began the man doubtfully, shuffling in his checked, woolly bedroom slippers.

"But if he was willing to pay rent for your particular tree, you didn't want to put him off," I finished. "An extra quid or two isn't something you want to pass on next door."

They wouldn't have put it so bluntly, but they didn't demur.

"Come and look," I said.

They followed me round along the narrow path beside their bungalow wall and into their own back garden. The tree stood halfway to the racecourse boundary fence, the sun slanting down through the leafless branches. We could see the wooden back of the mirror, and the ropes which fastened it to the tree trunk. The man and his wife walked round to the front, and their puzzlement increased.

"He said it was for a poster," repeated the man.

"Well," I said as matter-of-factly as I could, "I expect it is for a poster, as he said. But at the moment, you see, it is a mirror. And it's pointing straight out over the racecourse; and you know how mirrors reflect the sunlight? We just thought it might not be too safe, you know, if anyone got dazzled, so we wondered if you would mind us moving it?"

"Why, goodness," agreed the woman, looking with more awareness at our riding clothes, "no one could see the racing with light shining in their eyes."

"Quite. So would you mind if we turned the mirror round a bit?"

"I can't see that it would hurt, Dad," she said doubtfully.

161

He made a nondescript assenting movement with his hand, and Chico asked how the mirror had been put up in the tree in the first place. The man had brought a ladder with him, they said, and no, they hadn't one themselves. Chico shrugged, placed me beside the tree, put one foot on my thigh, one on my shoulder, and was up in the bare branches like a squirrel. The elderly couple's mouths sagged open.

"How long ago?" I asked. "When did the man put up the mirror?"

"This morning," said the woman, getting over the shock. "He came back just now, too, with another rope or something. That's when he said he'd be back with the poster."

So the mirror had been hauled up into the tree while Chico and I had been obliviously sitting in the bushes, and adjusted later when the sun was at the right angle in the sky. At two o'clock. The time, the next day, of the third race, the handicap steeplechase. Some handicap, I thought, a smash of light in the eyes.

White flag: a little bit to the left. Orange flag: a little bit to the right. No flag: dead on target.

Come back tomorrow afternoon and clap a religious poster over the glass as soon as the damage was done, so that even the most thorough search wouldn't reveal a mirror. Just another jinx on Seabury Racecourse. Dead horses, crushed and trampled jockeys. A jinx. Send my horses somewhere else, Mr. Whitney, something always goes wrong at Seabury.

I was way out in one respect. The religious poster was not due to be put in place the following day.

13

"I think," I said gently to the elderly couple, "that it might be better if you went indoors. We will explain to the man who is coming what we are doing to his mirror."

Dad glanced up the path toward the road, put his arm protectively round his wife's woolly shoulders, and said gratefully, "Er . . . yes . . . yes."

They shuffled rapidly through the back door into the bungalow just as a large man carrying an aluminum folding ladder and a large rolled-up paper came barging through their front gate. There had been the squeak of his large, plain, dark blue van stopping, the hollow crunch of the handbrake being forcibly applied, the slam of the door and the scrape of the ladder being unloaded. Chico in the tree crouched quite still, watching.

I was standing with my back to the sun, but it fell full on the big man's face when he came into the garden. It wasn't the sort of face one would naturally associate with religious posters. He was a cross between a heavyweight wrestler and Mount Vesuvius. Craggy, brutally strong and not far off erupting.

He came straight toward me across the grass, dropped the ladder beside him, and said inquiringly, "What goes on?"

"The mirror," I said, "comes down."

His eyes narrowed in sudden awareness and his body stiffened. "There's a poster going over it," he began quite reasonably, lifting the paper roll. Then with a rush the lava burst out, the paper flew wide, and the muscles bunched into action.

It wasn't much of a fight. He started out to hit my face, changed his mind, and ploughed both fists in below the belt. It was quite a long way down for him. Doubling

163

over in pain onto the lawn, I picked up the ladder, and gave him a swinging swipe behind the knees.

The ground shook with the impact. He fell on his side, his coat swinging open. I lunged forward, snatching at the pistol showing in the holster beside his ribs. It came loose, but he brushed me aside with an arm like a telegraph pole. I fell, sprawling. He rolled over into a crouch, picked up the gun from the grass and sneered down into my face. Then he stood up like a released spring and on the way with force and deliberation booted his toecap into my navel. He also clicked back the catch on his gun.

Up in the tree, Chico yelled. The big man turned and took three steps toward him, seeing him for the first time. With a choice of targets, he favored the one still in a state to resist. The hand with the pistol pointed at Chico.

"Leo," I shouted. Nothing happened. I tried again.

"Fred!"

The big man turned his head a fraction back to me and Chico jumped down onto him from ten feet up.

The gun went off with a double crash and again the day flew apart in shining splintering fragments. I sat on the ground with my knees bent up, groaning quietly, cursing fluently, and getting on with my business.

Drawn by the noise, the inhabitants of the bungalows down the line came out into their back gardens and looked in astonishment over the fences. The elderly couple stood palely at their window, their mouths again open. The big man had too big an audience now for murder.

Chico was overmatched for size and nearly equaled in skill. He and the big man threw each other round a bit while I crept doubled up along the path into the front garden as far as the gate, but the battle was a foregone conclusion, bar the retreat.

He came alone, crashing up the path, saw me hanging on to the gate and half raised the gun. But there were people in the road now, and more people peering out of opposite windows. In scorching fury he whipped at my head with the barrel, and I avoided it by letting go of the gate and collapsing on the ground again. Behind the gate, with the bars nice and comfortingly between me and his boot.

He crunched across the pavement, slammed into the van, cut his cogs to ribbons and disappeared out onto the London road in a cloud of dust.

Chico came down the garden path staggering, with blood sloshing out of a cut eyebrow. He looked anxious and shaken.

"I thought you said you could bloody well fight," I mocked him.

He came to a halt beside me on his knees. "Blast you." He put his fingers to his forehead and winced at the result.

I grinned at him.

"You were running away," he said.

"Naturally."

"What have you got here?" He took the little camera out of my hand. "Don't tell me," he said, his face splitting into an unholy smile. "Don't tell me."

"It's what we came for, after all."

"How many?"

"Four of him. Two of the van."

"Sid, you slay me, you really do."

"Well," I said, "I feel sick." I rolled over and retched what was left of my breakfast onto the roots of the privet hedge. There wasn't any blood. I felt a lot better.

"I'll go and get the horse box," said Chico, "and pick you up."

"You'll do nothing of the sort," I said, wiping my mouth on a handkerchief. "We're going back into the garden. I want that bullet."

"It's halfway to Seabury," he protested, borrowing my handkerchief to mop the blood off his eyebrow.

"What will you bet?" I said. I used the gate again to get up, and after a moment or two was fairly straight. We presented a couple of reassuring grins to the audience, and retraced our way down the path into the back garden.

The mirror lay in sparkling pointed fragments all over the lawn.

"Pop up the tree and see if the bullet is there, in the

wood. It smashed the mirror. It might be stuck up there. If not, we'll have to comb the grass."

Chico went up the aluminum ladder that time.

"Of all the luck," he called. "It's here." I watched him take a penknife out of his pocket and carefully cut away at a section just off-center of the backboard of the ex-mirror. He came down and held the little misshapen lump out to me on the palm of his hand. I put it carefully away in the small waist pockets of my breeches.

The elderly couple had emerged like tortoises from their bungalow. They were scared and puzzled, understandably. Chico offered to cut down the remains of the mirror, and did, but we left them to clear up the resulting firewood.

As an afterthought, however, Chico went across the garden and retrieved the poster from a soggy winter rosebed. He unrolled it and showed it to us, laughing.

BLESSED ARE THE MEEK, FOR THEY SHALL INHERIT THE EARTH.

"One of them," said Chico, "has a sense of humor."

Much against his wishes, we returned to our observation post in the scrubby gorse.

"Haven't you had enough?" he said crossly.

"The patrols don't get here till six," I reminded him. "And you yourself said that dusk would be the likely time for them to try something."

"But they've already done it."

"There's nothing to stop them from rigging up more than one booby trap," I pointed out. "Especially as that mirror thing wouldn't have been one hundred per cent reliable, even if we hadn't spotted it. It depended on the sun. Good weather forecast, I know, but weather forecasts are as reliable as a perished hot-water bottle. A passing cloud would have wrecked it. I would think they have something else in mind."

"Cheerful," he said resignedly. He led Revelation away along the road to stow him in the horse box, and was gone a long time.

When he came back he sat down beside me and said, "I went all round the stables. No one stopped me or

166

asked what I was doing. Don't they have *any* security here? The cleaners have all gone home, but there's a woman cooking in the canteen. She said I was too early, to come back at half past six. There wasn't anyone about in the stands block except an old geezer with snuffles mucking about with the boiler."

The sun was lower in the sky and the November afternoon grew colder. We shivered a little and huddled inside our jerseys.

Chico said, "You guessed about the mirror before you set off round the course."

"It was a possibility, that's all."

"You could have ridden along the boundary fence, looking into the gardens like we did afterwards, instead of haring off over all those jumps."

I grinned faintly. "Yes. As I told you, I was giving in to temptation."

"Screwy. You must have known you'd fall."

"Of course I didn't. The mirror mightn't have worked very effectively. Anyway, it's better to test a theory in a practical way. And I just wanted to ride round there. I had a good excuse if I were hauled up for it. So I went. And it was grand. So shut up."

He laughed. "All right." Restlessly he stood up again and said he would make another tour. While he was gone I watched the racecourse with and without the binoculars, but not a thing moved on it.

He came back quietly and dropped down beside me.

"As before," he said.

"Nothing here, either."

He looked at me sideways. "Do you feel as bad as you look?"

"I shouldn't be surprised," I said. "Do you?"

He tenderly touched the area round his cut eyebrow. "Worse. Much worse. Soggy bad luck, his slugging away at your belly like that."

"He did it on purpose," I said idly, "and it was very informative."

"Huh?"

"It showed he knew who I was. He wouldn't have needed to have attacked us like that if we'd just been people come over from the racecourse to see if we could shift the mirror. But when he spoke to me he recognized me, and he knew I wouldn't be put off by any poster eyewash. And his sort don't mildly back down and retreat without paying you off for getting in their way. He just hit where he knew it would have most effect. I actually saw him think it."

"But how did he know?"

"It was he who sent Andrews to the office," I said. "He was the man Mervyn Brinton described: big, going a bit bald, freckles on the back of his hands, cockney accent. He was strong-arming Brinton, and he sent Andrews to get the letter that was supposed to be in the office. Well, Andrews knew me, and I knew him. He must have gone back and told our big friend Fred that he had shot me in the stomach. My death wasn't reported in the papers, so Fred knew I was still alive and would put the finger on Andrews at once. Andrews wasn't exactly a good risk to Fred, just a silly spiv with no sense, so Fred, I guess, marched him straight off to Epping Forest and left him for the birds. Who did a fair job, I'll give them that."

"Do you think," said Chico slowly, "that the gun Fred had today . . . is that why you wanted the bullet?"

I nodded. "That's right. I tried for the gun too, but no dice. If I'm going on with this sort of work, pal, you'll have to teach me a spot of judo."

He looked down doubtfully. "With that hand?"

"Invent a new sport," I said. "One-armed combat."

"I'll take you to the club," he said, smiling. "There's an old Jap there who'll find a way if anyone can."

"Good."

Up at the far end of the racecourse a horse box turned in off the main road and trundled along toward the stables. The first of the next day's runners had apparently arrived.

Chico went to have a look.

I sat on in fading daylight, watching nothing happen, hugging myself against the cold and the reawakened grinding ache in my gut, and thinking evil thoughts about Fred. Not Leo. Fred.

There were four of them, I thought. Kraye, Bolt, Fred and Leo.

I had met Kraye: he knew me only as Sid, a despised hanger-on in the home of a retired admiral he had met at his club and had spent a weekend with.

I had met Bolt: he knew me as John Halley, a shop assistant wanting to invest a gift from an aunt.

I had met Fred: he knew my whole name, and that I worked for the agency, and that I had turned up at Seabury.

I did not know if I had met Leo. But Leo might know me. If he had anything to do with racing, he definitely did.

It would be all right, I thought, as long as they did not connect all the Halleys and Sids too soon. But there was my wretched hand, which Kraye had pulled out of my pocket, which Fred could have seen in the garden, and which Leo, whoever he was, might have noticed almost anywhere in the last six days, thanks to my promise to Miss Martin. Miss Martin, who worked for Bolt. A proper merry-go-round, I thought wryly.

Chico materialized out of the dusk. "It was Ping Pong, running in the first tomorrow. All aboveboard," he said. "And nothing doing anywhere, stand or course. We might as well go."

It was well after five. I agreed, and got up stiffly.

"That Fred," said Chico, casually giving me a hand, "I've been thinking. I've seen him before, I'm certain. At race meetings. He's not a regular. Doesn't work for a bookie, or anything like that. But he's about. Cheap rings, mostly."

"Let's hope he doesn't burrow," I said.

"I don't see why he should," he said seriously. "He can't possibly think you'd connect him with Andrews, or with Kraye. All you caught him doing was fixing a poster in a tree. If I were him, I'd be sleeping easy."

"I called him Fred," I said.

"Oh," said Chico glumly. "So you did."

We reached the road and started along it toward the horse box.

"Fred must be the one who does all the jobs," said

Chico. "Digs the false drains, sets fire to stables, and drives tractors to pull over tankers. He's big enough for anything.

"He didn't wave the flag. He was up the tree at the time."

"Um. Yes. Who did?"

"Not Bolt," I said. "It wasn't fat enough for Bolt, even in a duffel coat. Possibly Kraye. More likely Leo, whoever he is."

"One of the workmen, or the foreman. Yes. Well, that makes two of them for overturning tankers and so on."

"It would be easier for two," I agreed.

Chico drove the horse box back to Mark's, and then, to his obvious delight, my Merc back to London.

14

Chief Inspector Cornish was pleased but trying to hide it.

"I suppose you can chalk it up to your agency," he said as if it were debatable.

"He walked slap into us, to be fair."

"And slap out again," he said dryly.

I grimaced. "You haven't met him."

"You want to leave that sort to us," he said automatically.

"Where were you, then?"

"That's a point," he admitted, smiling.

He picked up the matchbox again and looked at the bullet. "Little beauty. Good clear markings. Pity he had a revolver, though, and not an automatic. It would have been nice to have had cartridge cases as well."

"You're greedy," I said.

He looked at the aluminum ladder standing against his wall, and at the poster on his desk, and at the rush-job photographs. Two clear prints of the van showing its number plates and four of Fred in action against Chico. Not exactly posed portraits, those, but four different, characteristic and recognizable angles taken in full sunlight.

"With all this lot to go on, we'll trace him before he draws breath."

"Fine," I said. And the sooner Fred was immobilized the better, I thought. Before he did any more damage to Seabury. "You'll need a tiger net to catch him. He's a very tough baby, and he knows judo. And unless he has the sense to throw it away, he'll still have that gun."

"I'll remember," he said. "And thanks." We shook hands amicably as I left.

It was results day at Radnor's, too. As soon as I got back Dolly said Jack Copeland wanted me up in Bona Fides. I made the journey.

Jack gleamed at me over the half-moons, pleased with his department. "George's got him. Kraye. He'll tell you."

I went over to George's desk. George was fairly smirking but after he'd talked for two minutes, I allowed he'd earned it.

"On the off-chance," he said, "I borrowed a bit of smooth quartz Kraye recently handled in the Geology Museum and got Sammy to do the prints on it. Two or three different sets of fingers came out, so we photographed the lot. None of them were on the British files, but I've given them the run-around with the odd pal in Interpol and so on, just in case. And brother, have we hit pay dirt or have we."

"We have?" I prompted, grinning.

"And how. Your friend Kraye is in the ex-con library of the state of New York."

"What for?"

"Assault."

"Of a girl?" I asked.

George raised his eyebrows. "A girl's father. Kraye had beaten the girl, apparently with her permission. She didn't complain. But her father saw the bruises and raised

171

the roof. He said he'd get Kraye on a rape charge, though it seems the girl had been perfectly willing on that count. too. But it looked bad for Kraye, so he picked up a chair and smashed it over the father's head and scampered. They caught him boarding a plane for South America and hauled him back. The father's brain was damaged. There are long medical details, but what it all boils down to is that he couldn't coordinate properly afterwards. Kraye got off on the rape charge, but served four years for attacking the father.

"Three years after that he turned up in England with some money and a new name, and soon acquired a wife. The one who divorced him for cruelty. Nice Chap."

"Yes indeed," I said. "What was his real name?"

"Wilbur Potter," said George sardonically. "And you'll never guess. He was a geologist by profession. He worked for a construction firm, surveying. Always moving about. Character assessments: slick, a pusher, a good talker. Cut a few corners, always had more money than his salary, threw his weight about, but nothing indictable. The assault on the father was his first brush with the law. He was thirty-four at the time."

"Messy, I said. "The whole thing."

"Very," George agreed.

"But sex violence and fraudulent take-overs aren't much related," I complained.

"You might as well say it is impossible to have boils and cancer at the same time. Something drastically wrong with the constitution, and two separate symptoms."

"I'll take your word for it," I said.

Sammy up in Missing Persons had done more than photograph Kraye's fingerprints, he had almost found Smith.

"Intersouth rang us this morning," he purred. "Smith gave them as a reference. He's applied for a driving job in Birmingham."

"Good," I said.

"We should have his address by this afternoon."

Downstairs in Racing I reached for Dolly's telephone and got through to Charing, Street and King.

"Mr. Bolt's secretary speaking," said the quiet voice.

"Is Mr. Bolt in?" I asked.

"I'm afraid not . . . er, who is that speaking, please?"

"Did you find you had a file of mine?"

"Oh. . . ." She laughed. "Yes, I picked it up in your car. I'm so sorry."

"Do you have it with you?"

"No," she said, "I didn't bring it here. I thought it might be better not to risk Mr. Bolt seeing it, as it's got Hunt Radnor Associates printed on the outside along with a red sticker saying 'Ex Records, care of Sid Halley.' "

"Yes, it would have been a disaster," I agreed with feeling.

"I left it at home. Do you want it in a hurry?"

"No, not really. As long as it's safe, that's the main thing. How would it be if I came over to fetch it the day after tomorrow—Sunday morning? We could go for a drive, perhaps, and have some lunch."

There was a tiny pause. Then she said strongly, "Yes, please. Yes."

"Have the leaflets gone out?" I asked.

"They went yesterday."

"See you on Sunday, Miss Martin."

I put down Dolly's telephone to find her looking at me quizzically. I was again squatting on the corner of her desk, the girl from the typing pool having in my absence reclaimed her chair.

"The mouse got away again, I understand," she said. "Some mouse."

Chico came into the office. The cut on his eyebrow looked red and sore, and all the side of his face showed grayish bruising.

"Two of you," said Dolly disgustedly, "and he knocked you about like kids."

Chico took this a lot better than if she had fussed maternally over his injury.

"It took more than two Lilliputians to peg down

173

Gulliver," he said with good humor. (They had a large library in the children's orphanage.)

"But only one David to slay Goliath."

Chico made a face at her, and I laughed.

"And how are our collywobbles today?" he asked me ironically.

"Better than your looks."

"You know why Sid's best friends won't tell him?" said Chico.

"Why?" said Dolly, seriously.

"He suffers from halley-tosis."

"Oh God," said Dolly. "Take him away, someone. Take him away. I can't stand it."

On the ground floor I sat in a padded maroon armchair in Radnor's drawing-room office and listened to him saying there were no out-of-the-ordinary reports from the patrols at Seabury.

"Fison has just been on the telephone. Everything is normal for a race day, he says. The public will start arriving very shortly. He and Thom walked all round the course just now with Captain Oxon for a thorough check. There's nothing wrong with it, that they can see."

There might be something wrong with it that they couldn't see. I was uneasy.

"I might stay down there tonight, if I can find a room," I said.

"If you do, give me a ring at home, during the evening."

"Sure." I had disturbed his dinner, the day before, to tell him about Fred and the mirror.

"Could I have those photographs back, if you've finished with them?" I asked. "I want to check that list of initials against the racecourse workmen at Seabury."

"I'm sorry, Sid, I haven't got them."

"Are they back upstairs?"

"No, no, they aren't here at all. Lord Hagbourne has them."

"But why?" I sat up straight, disturbed.

"He came here yesterday afternoon. I'd say on bal-ince he is almost down on our side of the fence. I didn't get the usual caution about expenses, which is a good sign. Anyway, what he wanted was to see the proofs you told him we held which show it was Kraye who is buying the shares. Photographs of share transfer certificates. He knew about them. He said you'd told him."

"Yes, I did."

"He wanted to see them. That was reasonable, and I didn't want to risk tipping him back into indecision, so I showed them to him. He asked me very courteously if he could take them to show them to the Seabury executive. They held a meeting this morning, I believe. He thought they might be roused to some effective action if they could see for themselves how big Kraye's holding is."

"What about the other photographs? The others that were in the box."

"He took them all. They were all jumbled up, and he was in a hurry. He said he'd sort them out himself later."

"He took them to Seabury?" I said uneasily.

"That's right. For the executive meeting this morning." He looked at his watch. "The meeting must be on at this moment, I should think. If you want them you can ask him for them as soon as you get there. He should have finished with them by then."

"I wish you hadn't let him take them," I said.

"It can't do any harm. Even if he lost them we'd still have the negatives. You could get another print done tomorrow, of your list."

The negatives, did he but know it, were inaccessibly tucked into a mislaid file in Finchley. I didn't confess. Instead I said, unconvinced, "All right. I suppose it won't matter. I'll get on down there, then."

I packed an overnight bag in the flat. The sun was pouring in through the windows, making the blues and greens and blond wood furniture look warm and friendly. After two years the place was at last beginning to feel like home. A home without Jenny. Happiness without

175

Jenny. Both were possible, it seemed. I certainly felt more myself than at any time since she left.

The sun was still shining, too, at Seabury. But not on a very large crowd. The poor quality of the racing was so obvious as to be pathetic: and it was in order that such a rotten gaggle of weedy quadrupeds could stumble and scratch their way round to the winning post, I reflected philosophically, that I had tried to pit my inadequate wits against Lord Hagbourne, Captain Oxon, the Seabury executive, Kraye, Bolt, Fred, Leo, old Uncle Tom Cobley and all.

There were no mishaps all day. The horses raced nonchalantly over the tan patch at their speedy crawl, and no light flashed in their eyes as they knocked hell out of the fences on the far side. Round one to Chico and me.

As the fine weather put everyone in a good mood, a shred of Seabury's former vitality temporarily returned to the place: enough, anyway, for people to notice the dinginess of the stands and remark that it was time something was done about it. If they felt like that, I thought, a revival shouldn't be impossible.

The Senior Steward listened attentively while I passed on Miss Martin's suggestion that Seabury council should be canvassed, and surprisingly said that he would see it was promptly done.

In spite of these small headways, however, my spine wouldn't stop tingling. Lord Hagbourne didn't have the photographs.

"They are only mislaid, Sid," he said soothingly. "Don't make such a fuss. They'll turn up."

He had put them down on the table round which the meeting had been held, he said. After the official business was over, he had chatted, standing up. When he turned back to pick up the box, it was no longer there. The whole table had been cleared. The ashtrays were being emptied. The table was required for lunch. A white cloth was being spread over it.

What, I asked, had been the verdict of the meeting, anyway? Er, um, it appeared the whole subject had been shelved for a week or two: no urgency was felt. Shares changed hands slowly, very slowly. But they had agreed that Hunt Radnor could carry on for a bit.

I hesitated to go barging into the executive's private room just to look for a packet of photographs, so I asked the caterers instead. They hadn't seen it, they said, rushing round me. I tracked down the man and woman who had cleared the table after the meeting and laid it for lunch.

Any amount of doodling on bits of paper, said the waitress, but no box of photographs, and excuse me love, they're waiting for these sandwiches. She agreed to look for it, looked, and came back shaking her head. It wasn't there, as far as she could see. It was quite big, I said despairingly.

I asked Mr. Fotherton, clerk of the course; I asked Captain Oxon; I asked the secretary and anyone else I could think of who had been at the meeting. None of them knew where the photographs were. All of them, busy with their racing jobs, said much the same as Lord Hagbourne.

"Don't worry, Sid, they're bound to turn up."

But they didn't.

I stayed on the racecourse until after the security patrols changed over at six o'clock. The in-comers were the same men who had been on watch the night before, four experienced and sensible ex-policemen, all middle-aged. They entenched themselves comfortably in the press room, which had windows facing back and front, effective central heating, and four telephones; better headquarters than usual on their night jobs, they said.

Between the last race (three thirty) and six o'clock, apart from hunting without success for the photographs and driving Lord Hagbourne round to Napoleon Close for a horrified firsthand look at the smashed-up mirror, I persuaded Captain Oxon to accompany me on a thorough nook-and-cranny checkup of all the racecourse buildings.

He came willingly enough, his stiffness of earlier in the week having been thawed, I supposed, by the comparative success of the day; but we found nothing and no one that shouldn't have been there.

I drove into Seabury and booked into the Seafront Hotel, where I had often stayed in the past. It was only half full. Formerly, on racing nights, it had been crammed. Over a brandy in the bar the manager lamented with me the state of trade.

"Race meetings used to give us a boost every three weeks nearly all the winter. Now hardly anyone comes, and I hear they didn't even ask for the January fixtures this year. I tell you, I'd like to see that place blooming again, we need it."

"Ah," I said. "Then write to the Town Council and say so."

"That wouldn't help," he said gloomily.

"You never know. It might. Do write."

"All right, Sid. Just to please you then. For old time's sake. Let's have another brandy on the house."

I had an early dinner with him and his wife and afterward went for a walk along the seashore. The night was dry and cold and the onshore breeze smelled of seaweed. The banked pebbles scrunched into trickling hollows under my shoes and the winter sand was as hard-packed as rock. Thinking about Kraye and his machinations, I had strolled quite a long way eastward, away from the racecourse, before I remembered I had said I would ring Radnor at his home during the evening.

There was nothing much to tell him. I didn't hurry, and it was nearly ten o'clock when I got back to Seabury. The modernizations didn't yet run to telephones in all the bedrooms at the hotel, so I used the kiosk outside on the promenade, because I came to it first.

It wasn't Radnor who answered, but Chico, and I knew at once from his voice that things had gone terribly wrong.

"Sid . . . ," he said. "Sid . . . look, pal, I don't know how to tell you. You'll have to have it straight. We've been trying to reach you all the evening."

"What . . . ?" I swallowed.

"Someone bombed your flat."

"Bombed," I said stupidly.

"A plastic bomb. It blew the street wall right out. All the flats round yours were badly damaged, but yours . . . well, there's nothing there. Just a big hole with disgusting black sort of cobwebs. That's how they knew it was a plastic bomb. The sort the French terrorists used. . . . Sid, are you there?"

"Yes."

"I'm sorry, pal. I'm sorry. But that's not all. They've done it to the office, too." His voice was anguished. "It went off in the Racing Section. But the whole place is cracked open. It's . . . it's bloody ghastly."

"Chico."

"I know. I know. The old man's round there now, just staring at it. He made me stay here because you said you'd ring, and in case the racecourse patrols want anything. No one was badly hurt, that's the only good thing. Half a dozen people were bruised and cut, at your flats. And the office was empty, of course."

"What time . . . ?"

"The bomb in the office went off about an hour and a half ago, and the one in your flat was just after seven. The old man and I were round there with the police when they got the radio message about the office. The police seem to think that whoever did it was looking for something. The people who live underneath you heard someone moving about upstairs for about two hours shortly before the bomb went off, but they just thought it was you making more noise than usual. And it seems everything in your flat was moved into one pile in the sitting room and the bomb put in the middle. The police said it meant that they hadn't found what they were looking for and were destroying everything in case they had missed it."

"Everything . . . ," I said.

"Not a thing was left. God, Sid, I wish I didn't have to . . . but there it is. Nothing that was there exists any more."

The letters from Jenny when she loved me. The only photograph of my mother and father. The trophies I won racing. The lot. I leaned numbly against the wall.

"Sid, are you still there?"

179

"Yes."

"It was the same thing at the office. People across the road saw lights on and someone moving about inside, and just thought we were working late. The old man said we must assume they still haven't found what they were looking for. He wants to know what it is."

"I don't know," I said.

"You must."

"No. I don't."

"You can think on the way back."

"I'm not coming back, not tonight. It can't do any good. I think I'll go out to the racecourse again, just to make sure nothing happens there too."

"All right. I'll tell him when he calls. He said he'd be over in Cromwell Road all night, very likely."

We rang off and I went out of the kiosk into the cold night air. I thought that Radnor was right. It was important to know what it was that the bomb merchants had been looking for. I leaned against the outside of the box, thinking about it. Deliberately not thinking about the flat, the place that had begun to be home, and all that was lost. That had happened before in one way or another. The night my mother died, for instance. And I'd ridden my first winner the next day.

To look for something, you had to know it existed. If you used bombs, destroying it was more important than finding it. What did I have, which I hadn't had long (or they would have searched before) which Kraye wanted obliterated.

There was the bullet which Fred had accidentally fired into the mirror. They wouldn't find that, because it was somewhere in a police ballistics laboratory. And if they had thought I had it, they would have looked for it the night before.

There was the leaflet Bolt had sent out, but there were hundreds of those, and he wouldn't want the one I had, even if he knew I had it.

There was the letter Mervyn Brinton had rewritten for me, but if it were that it meant . . .

I went back into the telephone box, obtained Mervyn

Brinton's number from the directory inquiries, and rang him up.

To my relief, he answered.

"You are all right, Mr. Brinton?"

"Yes, yes. What's the matter?"

"You haven't had a call from the big man? You haven't told anyone about my visit to you, or that you know your brother's letter by heart?"

He sounded scared. "No. Nothing's happened. I wouldn't tell anyone. I never would."

"Fine," I reassured him. "That's just fine. I was only checking."

So it was not Brinton's letter.

The photographs, I thought. They had been in the office all the time until Radnor gave them to Lord Hagbourne yesterday afternoon. No one outside the agency, except Lord Hagbourne and Charles, had known they existed. Not until this morning, when Lord Hagbourne took them to the Seabury executive meeting, and lost them.

Suppose they weren't lost, but stolen. By someone who knew Kraye, and thought he ought to have them. From the dates on all those documents Kraye would know exactly when the photographs had been taken. And where.

My scalp contracted. I must assume, I thought, that they had now connected all the Halleys and Sids.

Suddenly fearful, I rang up Aynsford. Charles himself answered, calm and sensible.

"Charles, please will you do as I ask, at once, and no questions? Grab Mrs. Cross, go out and get in the car and drive well away from the house, and ring me back at Seabury 79411. Got that? Seabury 79411."

"Yes," he said, and put down the telephone. Thank God, I thought, for a naval training. There might not be much time. The office bomb had exploded an hour and a half ago; London to Aynsford took the same.

Ten minutes later the phone began to ring. I picked up the receiver.

"They say you're in a call box," Charles said.

"That's right. Are you?"

"No, the pub down in the village. Now, what's it all about?"

I told him about the bombs, which horrified him, and about the missing photographs.

"I can't think what else it can be that they are looking for."

"But you said that they've got them.

"The negatives," I said.

"Oh. Yes. And they weren't in your flat or the office?"

"No. Quite by chance, they weren't."

"And you think if they're still looking, that they'll come to Aynsford?"

"If they are desperate enough, they might. They might think you would know where I keep things. . . . And even have a go at making you tell them. I asked you to come out quick because I didn't want to risk it. If they are going to Aynsford, they could be there at any minute now. It's horribly likely they'll think of you. They'll know I took the photos in your house."

"From the dates. Yes. Right. I'll get to the local police and ask for a guard on the house at once."

"Charles, one of them . . . well, if he's the one with the bombs, you'll need a squad." I described Fred and his van, together with its number.

"Right." He was still calm. "Why would the photographs be so important to them? Enough to use bombs, I mean?"

"I wish I knew."

"Take care."

"Yes," I said.

I did take care. Instead of going back into the hotel, I rang it up.

The manager said, "Sid, where on earth are you, people have been trying to reach you all the evening—the police too."

"Yes, Joe, I know. It's all right. I've talked to the police in London. Now, has anyone actually called at the hotel, wanting me?"

"There's someone up in your room, yes. Your father-in-law, Admiral Roland."

"Oh really? Does he look like an admiral?"

"I suppose so." He sounded puzzled.

"A gentleman?"

"Yes, of course." Not Fred, then.

"Well, he isn't my father-in-law. I've just been talking to him in his house in Oxfordshire. You collect a couple of helpers and chuck my visitor out."

I put down the receiver sighing. A man up in my room meant everything I'd brought to Seabury would very likely be ripped to bits. That left me with just the clothes I stood in, and the car—

I fairly sprinted round to where I'd left the car. It was locked, silent and safe. No damage. I patted it thankfully, climbed in, and drove out to the racecourse.

15

All was quiet as I drove through the gates and switched off the engine. There were lights on—one shining through the windows of the press room, one outside the weighing-room door, one high up somewhere on the stands. The shadows in between were densely black. It was a clear night with no moon.

I walked across to the press room, to see if the security patrols had anything to report.

They hadn't.

All four of them were fast asleep.

Furious, I shook the nearest. His head lolled like a pendulum, but he didn't wake up. He was sitting slumped into his chair. One of them had his arms on the table and his head on his arms. One of them sat on the floor, his head on the seat of the chair and his arms hanging down. The fourth lay flat, face downward, near the opposite wall.

The stupid fools, I thought. Ex-policemen letting themselves be put to sleep like infants. It shouldn't have been possible. One of their first rules in guard work was to take their own food and drink with them and not accept sweets from strangers.

I stepped round their heavily breathing hulks and picked up one of the press telephones to ring Chico for reinforcements. The line was dead. I tried the three other instruments. No contact with the exchange on any of them.

I would have to go back and ring up from Seabury, I thought. I went out of the press room but in the light pouring out before I shut the door I saw a dim figure walking toward me from the direction of the gate.

"Who's that?" he called imperiously, and I recognized his voice. Captain Oxon.

"It's only me, Sid Halley," I shouted back. "Come and look at this."

He came on into the light, and I stood aside for him to go into the press room.

"Good heavens. What on earth's the matter with them?"

"Sleeping pills. And the telephones don't work. You haven't seen anyone about who ought not to be?"

"No. I haven't heard anything except your car. I came down to see who had come."

"How many lads are there staying overnight in the hostel? Could we use some of those to patrol the place while I ring the agency to get some more men?"

"I should think they'd love it," he said. "There are about five of them. They shouldn't be in bed yet. We'll go over and ask them, and you can use the telephone from my flat to ring your agency."

"Thanks," I said. "That's fine."

I looked round the room at the sleeping men. "I think perhaps I ought to see if any of them tried to write a message. I won't be a minute."

He waited patiently while I looked under the head and folded arms of the man at the table and under the man on the floor, and all round the one with his head on the chair seat, but none of them had even reached for a pencil. Shrugging, I looked at the remains of their supper, lying on the table. Half-eaten sandwiches on greaseproof paper, dregs of coffee in cups and thermos flasks, a couple of apple cores, some cheese sections and empty wrappings, and an unpeeled banana.

"Found anything?" asked Oxon.

I shook my head in disgust. "Not a thing. They'll have terrible headaches when they wake up, and serve them right."

"I can understand you being annoyed. . . ." he began. But I was no longer really listening. Over the back of the chair occupied by the first man I had shaken was hanging a brown leather binoculars case, and on its lid were stamped three black initials: L.E.O. Leo. *Leo.*

"Something the matter?" asked Oxon.

"No." I smiled at him and touched the strap of the binoculars. "Are these yours?"

"Yes. The men asked if I could lend them some. For the dawn, they said."

"It was very kind of you."

"Oh. Nothing." He shrugged, moving out into the night. "You'd better make that phone call first. We'll tackle the boys afterwards."

I had absolutely no intention of walking into his flat.

"Right," I said.

We went out of the door, and I closed it behind us.

A familiar voice, loaded with satisfaction, spoke from barely a yard away. "So you've got him, Oxon. Good."

"He was coming—" began Oxon in anxious anger, knowing that "got him" was an exaggeration.

"No," I said, and turned and ran for the car.

When I was barely ten yards from it someone turned the lights on. The headlights of my own car. I stopped dead.

Behind me one of the men shouted and I heard their feet running. I wasn't directly in the beam, but silhouetted against it. I swerved off to the right, toward the gate. Three steps in that direction, and the headlights of a car turning in through it caught me straight in the eyes.

There were more shouts, much closer, from Oxon and Kraye. I turned, half-dazzled, and saw them closing in. Behind me now the incoming car rolled forward. And the engine of my Mercedes purred separately into life.

I ran for the dark. The two cars, moving, caught me

again in their beams. Kraye and Oxon ran where they pointed.

I was driven across and back toward the stands like a coursed hare, the two cars behind inexorably finding me with their lights and the two men running with reaching, clutching hands. Like a nightmare game of "He," I thought wildly, with more than a child's forfeit if I were caught.

Across the parade ring, across the flat Tarmac stretch beyond it, under the rails of the unsaddling enclosure and along the inside of the door into the trainers' luncheon room and through there without stopping into the kitchen. And weaving on from there out into the members' lunch room, round acres of tables with upturned chairs, through the far door into the wide passage which cut like a tunnel along the length of the huge building, across it, and up a steep stone staircase emerging halfway up the open steps of the stands, and sideways along them as far as I could go. The pursuit was left behind.

I sank down, sitting with one leg bent to run, in the black shadow where the low wooden wall dividing the members from Tattersalls cut straight down the steps separating the stands into two halves. On top of the wall wire netting stretched up too high to climb: high enough to keep out the poorer customers from gate crashing the expensive ring.

At the bottom of the steps lay a large expanse of members' lawn stretching to another metal mesh fence, chest high, and beyond that lay the whole open expanse of racecourse. Half a mile across it to the London road to Seabury, with yet another barrier, the boundary fence, to negotiate.

It was too far. I knew I couldn't do it. Perhaps once, with two hands for vaulting, with a stomach which didn't already feel as if it were tearing into more holes inside. But not now. Although I always mended fast, it was only two weeks since I had found the short walk to Andrews' body very nearly too much; and Fred's well-aimed attentions on the previous day had not been therapeutic.

Looking at it straight: if I ran, it had to be successful. My kingdom for a horse, I thought. Any reasonable cowboy would have had Revelation hitched to the rails, ready for a flying leap into the saddle and a thundering exit. I had a hundred-and-fifty-mile-an-hour little white Mercedes, and someone else was sitting in it.

To run and be caught running would achieve nothing and be utterly pointless.

Which left just one alternative.

The security patrol hadn't been drugged for nothing. Kraye wasn't at Seabury for his health. Some more damage had been planned for this night. Might already have been done. There was just a chance, if I stayed to look, that I could find out what it was. Before they found *me*. Naturally.

If I ever have any children, they won't get me playing hide-and-seek.

Half an hour later the grim game was still in progress. My own car was now parked on the racecourse side of the stands, on the Tarmac in Tattersalls where the bookies had called that afternoon. It was facing the stands with the headlights full on. Every inch of the steps was lit by them, and since the car had arrived there I had not been able to use that side of the building at all.

The other car was similarly parked inside the racecourse gates, its headlights shining on the fronts of the weighing room, bars, dining rooms, cloakrooms and offices.

Presuming that each car still had a watching occupant, that left only Kraye and Oxon, as far as I could guess, to run me to ground; but I became gradually sure that there were three, not two, after me in the stands. Perhaps one of the cars was empty. But which? And it would be unlikely to have its ignition key in place.

Bit by bit I covered the whole enormous block. I didn't know what I was looking for, that was the trouble. It could have been anything from a plastic bomb downward, but if past form was anything to go by, it was something which could appear accidental. Bad luck. A jinx. Open, recognizable sabotage would be ruinous to the scheme.

Without a surveyor, I couldn't be certain that part of the steps would not collapse the following day under the weight of the crowd, but I could find no trace of any structural damage at all, and there hadn't been much time: only five or six hours since the day's meeting ended.

There were no large quantities of food in the kitchen; the caterers appeared to have removed what had been left over ready to bring fresh the next day. A large double-doored refrigerator was securely locked. discounted the possibility that Kraye could have thought of large-scale food poisoning.

All the fire extinguishers seemed to be in their places, and there were no smoldering cigarette ends near tins of paraffin. Nothing capable of spontaneous combustion I suppose another fire, so soon after the stables, might have been too suspicious.

I went cautiously, carefully, every nerve-racking step of the way, peering round corners, easing through doors, fearing that at any moment one of them would pounce on me from behind.

They knew I was still there, because everywhere they went they turned on lights, and everywhere I went turned them off. Opening a door from a lighted room onto a dark passage made one far too easy to spot; turned off the lights before I opened any door. There had been three lights in the passage itself, but I had broken them early on with a broom from the kitchen.

Once when I was in the passage, creeping from the men's lavatories to the Tattersalls bar, Kraye himself appeared at the far end, the members' end, and began walking my way. He came in through the faint glow from the car's headlights, and he hadn't seen me. One stride took me across the passage, one jump and a wriggle into the only cover available, the heap of equipment the book makers had left there out of the weather, overnight.

These were only their metal stands, their folded umbrellas, the boxes and stools they stood on: a thin, spiky, precarious heap. I crouched down beside them, praying I wouldn't dislodge anything.

Kraye's footsteps scraped hollowly as he trod toward my ineffective hiding place. He stopped twice, opening doors and looking into the storerooms which were in places built back under the steps of the stands. They were mostly empty or nearly so, and offered nothing to me. They were too small, and all dead ends: if I were found in one of them, I couldn't get out.

The door of the bar I had been making for suddenly opened, spilling bright light into the passage between me and Kraye.

Oxon's voice said anxiously, "He can't have got away."

"Of course not, you fool," said Kraye furiously. "But if you'd had the sense to bring your keys over with you we'd have had him long ago." Their voices echoed up and down the passage.

"It was your idea to leave so much unlocked. I could go back and fetch them."

"He'd have too much chance of giving us the slip. But we're not getting anywhere with all this dodging about. We'll start methodically from this end and move down."

"We did that to start with," complained Oxon. "And we missed him. Let me go back for the keys. Then as you said before, we can lock all the doors behind us and stop him doubling back."

"No," said Kraye decisively. "There aren't enough of us. You stay here. We'll go back to the weighing room and start all together."

They began to walk away. The bar door was still open, lighting up the passage, which I didn't like. If anyone came in from the other end, he would see me for sure.

I shifted my position to crawl away along the wall for better concealment, and one of the bookmakers' metal tripods slid down and clattered off the side of the pile with an echoing noise like a dozen demented machine guns.

There were shouts from the two men down the passage.

"There he is."

"Get him."

I stood up and ran.

The nearest opening in the wall was a staircase up to a suite of rooms above the changing room and members' dining room. I hesitated a fraction of a second and then passed it. Up those steps were the executive's rooms and offices. I didn't know my way round up there, but Oxon did. He had a big enough advantage already in his knowledge of the building without my giving him a bonus.

I ran on, past the gents' cloaks, and finally in through the last possible door, that of a long, bare, dirty room smelling of beer. It was a sort of extra, subsidiary bar, and all it now contained was a bare counter backed by empty shelves. I nearly fell over a bucket full of crinkled metal bottle tops which someone had carelessly left in my way, and then wasted precious seconds to dart back to put the bucket just inside the door I'd come in by.

Kraye and Oxon were running. I snapped off the lights, and with no time to get clear through the far door out into the paddock, where anyway I would be lit by car headlights, I scrambled down behind the bar counter.

The door jerked open. There was a clatter of the bucket and a yell, and the sound of someone falling. Then the light snapped on again, showing me just how tiny my hiding place really was, and two bottle tops rolled across the floor into my sight.

"For God's sake," yelled Kraye in anger. "You clumsy, stupid fool. Get up. Get up." He charged down the room to the far door, the board floor bouncing slightly under his weight. From the clanking, cursing, and clattering of bottle tops I imagined that Oxon was extricating himself from the bucket and following. If it hadn't been so dangerous it would have been funny.

Kraye yanked the outside door open, stepped outside and yelled across to the stationary car to ask where I had gone. I felt rather than saw Oxon run down the room to join him. I crawled round the end of the counter, sprinted for the door I had come in by, flipped off the light again, slammed the door, and ran back up the passage. There was a roar from Kraye as he fumbled back into the darkened room; and long before they had emerged into the passage again, kicking bottle tops in all directions, I was safe in the opening of a little offshoot lobby to the kitchen.

The kitchens were safest for me because there were so many good hiding places and so many exits, but it wasn't much good staying there because I had searched them already.

I was fast running out of places to look. The boiler room had given me an anxious two minutes as its only secondary exit was into a dead-end storeroom containing, as far as I could see, nothing but vast oil tanks with pipes and gauges. They were hard against the walls: nowhere to hide. The boiler itself roared, keeping the central heating going all through the night.

The weighing room was even worse, because it was big and entirely without cover. It contained nothing it shouldn't have, just tables, chairs, notices pinned on the walls, and the weighing machine itself. Beyond, in the changing room, there were rows of pegs with saddles on, the warm, banked-up coke stove in the corner, and a big wicker basket full of helmets, boots, weight cloths and other equipment left by the valets overnight. A dirty cup and saucer. A copy of *Playboy*. Several raincoats. Racing colors on pegs. A row of washed breeches hanging up to dry. It was the most occupied-looking part of the stands, the place I felt most at home in and where I wanted to go to ground, like an ostrich in familiar sand. But on the far side of the changing room lay only the washroom, another dead end.

Opening out of the weighing room on the opposite side to the changing room was the Steward's room, where in the past like all jockeys I'd been involved in cases of objections-to-the-winner. It was a bare room: large table, chairs round it, sporting pictures, small threadbare carpet. A few of the Stewards' personal possessions lay scattered about, but there was no concealment.

A few doors here and there were locked, in spite of Oxon's having left the keys in his flat. As usual I had the bunch of lock pickers in my pocket; and with shortened breath I spent several sticky minutes letting myself into one well-secured room off the members' bar. It proved to be the liquor store: crates of spirits, champagne, wine and beer. Beer from floor to ceiling, and a porter's trolley to transport it. It was a temptation to lock myself in there, and wait for the caterers to rescue me in the morning. This was one door that Oxon would not expect to find me on the far side of.

In the liquor store I might be safe. On the other hand, if I were safe the racecourse might not be. Reluctantly I left again; but I didn't waste time locking up. With the pursuit out of sight, I risked a look upstairs. It was warm and quiet, and all the lights were on. I left them on, figuring that if the watchers in the cars saw them go out they would know too accurately where I was.

Nothing seemed to be wrong. On one side of a central lobby there was the big room where the executive held their meetings and ate their lunch. On the other side there was a sort of drawing room furnished with light armchairs, with two cloakrooms leading off it at the back. At the front, through double glass doors, it led out into a box high up on the stands. The private box for directors and distinguished guests, with a superb view over the whole course.

I didn't go there. Sabotage in the royal box wouldn't stop a race meeting to which royalty weren't going anyway. And besides, whoever was in my car would see me opening the door.

Retreating, I went back, right through the dining-board room and out into the service room on the far side. There I found a storeroom with plates, glass and cutlery, and in the storeroom also a second exit. A small service lift down to the kitchens. It worked with ropes like the one in the office on Cromwell Road . . . like the office lift *had* worked, before the bomb.

Kraye and Oxon were down in the kitchen. Their angry voices floated up the shaft, mingled with a softer murmuring voice which seemed to be arguing with them. Since for once I knew where they all were, I returned with some boldness to the ground again. But I was worried. There seemed to be nothing at all going wrong in the main building. If they were organizing yet more damage somewhere out on the course itself, I didn't see how I could stop it.

While I was still dithering rather aimlessly along the passage the kitchen door opened, the light flooded on, and I could hear Kraye still talking. I dived yet again for the nearest door and put it between myself and them.

I was, I discovered, in the ladies' room, where I hadn't been before, and there was no second way out. Only a double row of cubicles, all with the doors open, a range of washbasins, mirrors on the walls with a wide shelf beneath them, a few chairs, and a counter like that in the bar. Behind the counter there was a rail with coat hangers.

There were heavy steps in the passage outside. I slid instantly behind and under the counter and pressed myself into a corner. The door opened.

"He won't be in here," said Kraye. "The light's still on."

"I looked in here not five minutes ago, anyway," agreed Oxon.

The door closed behind them and their footsteps went away. I began to breathe again and my thudding heart slowed down. But for a couple of seconds only. Across the room, someone coughed.

I froze. I couldn't believe it. The room had been empty when I came in, I was certain. And neither Kraye nor Oxon had stayed. . . . I stretched my ears, tense, horrified.

Another cough. A soft, single cough.

Try as I could I could hear nothing else. No breathing. No rustle of clothing, no movement. It didn't make sense. If someone in the room knew I was behind the counter, why didn't they do something about it? If they didn't know, why were they so unnaturally quiet?

In the end, taking a conscious grip on my nerves, I slowly stood up.

The room was empty.

Almost immediately there was another cough. Now that my ears were no longer obstructed by the counter, I got a clearer idea of its direction. I swung toward it. There was no one there.

I walked across the room and stared down at the washbasin. Water was trickling from one of the taps. Even while I looked at it the tap coughed. Almost laughing with relief I stretched out my hand and turned it off.

The metal was very hot. Surprised, I turned the water on again. It came spluttering out of the tap, full of air bubbles and very hot indeed. Steaming. How stupid, I thought, turning it off again, to have the water so hot at this time of night. . . .

Christ, I thought. The boiler.

16

Kraye and Oxon's so-called methodical end-to-end search, which had just failed to find me in the ladies', was proceeding from the members' end of the stand toward Tattersalls. The boiler, like myself, was in the part they had already put behind them. I switched out the ladies'-room lights, carefully eased into the passage and via the kitchen, the members' dining room, the gentlemen's cloaks and another short strip of passage returned to the boiler room.

Although there was no door through, I knew that in the far side of the inside wall lay to the left of the weighing room and to the right the changing room, with the dividing wall between. From both those rooms, when it was quiet, as it was that night, one could quite clearly hear the boiler's muffled roar.

The light that I had switched off was on again in the boiler room. I looked round. It all looked as normal as it had before, except . . . except that away to the right there was a very small pool of water on the floor.

Boilers. We had had a lesson on them at school. Sixteen or seventeen years ago, I thought hopelessly. But I remembered very well the way the master had begun the lesson.

"The first thing to learn about boilers," he said, "is that they explode."

He was an excellent teacher: the whole class of forty boys listened from then on with avid interest. But since then the only acquaintance I'd had with boilers was down in the basement of the flats, where I sometimes drank a cup of orange tea with the caretaker. A tough ex-naval stoker, he was, and a confirmed student of racing form. Mostly we'd talked about horses, but sometimes about his job. There were strict regulations for boilers, he'd said, and regular official inspections every three months, and he was glad of it, working alongside them every day.

The first thing to learn about boilers is that they explode.

It's no good saying I wasn't frightened, because I was. If the boiler burst it wasn't simply going to make large new entrances into the weighing room and changing room, it was going to fill every cranny near it with scalding tornadoes of steam. Not a death I looked on with much favor.

I stood with my back against the door and tried desperately to remember that long-ago lesson, and to work out what was going wrong.

It was a big steam boiler. An enormous cylinder nine feet high and five feet in diameter. Thick steel, with dark red antirust paint peeling off. Fired at the bottom not by coke, which it had been built for, but by the more modern roaring jet of burning oil. If I opened the fire door I would feel the blast of its tremendous heat.

The body of the cylinder would be filled almost to the top with water. The flame boiled the water. The resulting steam went out of the top under its own fierce pressure in a pipe which—I followed it with my eye—led into a large yellow-painted round-ended cylinder slung horizontally near the ceiling. This tank looked rather like a zeppelin. It was, if I remembered right, a calorifier. Inside it, the steampipe ran in a spiral, like an immobile spring. The tank itself was supplied from the mains with the water which was to be heated, the water going to the central heating radiators, and to the hot taps in the kitchen, the cloakrooms and the jockeys' washrooms. The scorching heat from the spiral steampipe instantly passed into the water touching it, so that the cold water entering the calorifier was made very hot in the short time before it left at the other end.

The steam, however, losing its heat in the process, gradually condensed back into water. A pipe led down the wall from the calorifier into a much smaller tank, an ordinary square one, standing on the floor. From the bottom of this, yet another pipe tracked right back across the room and up near the boiler itself to a bulbous metal contraption just higher than my head. An electric pump. It finished the circuit by pumping the condensed water up from the tank on the floor and returning it to the boiler, to be boiled, steamed and condensed all over again. Round and round, continuously.

So far, so good. But if you interfered with the circuit so that the water didn't get back into the boiler, and at the same time kept the heat full on at the bottom, all the water inside the cylinder gradually turned to steam. Steam, which was strong enough to drive a liner, or pull a twelve-coach train, but could in this case only get out at all through a narrow, closely spiraled pipe.

This type of boiler, built not for driving an engine but only for heating water, wasn't constructed to withstand enormous pressures. It was a tossup, I thought, whether when all the water had gone the fast-expanding air and steam found a weak spot to break out of before the flames burned through the bottom. In either case, the boiler would blow up.

On the outside of the boiler there was a water guage, a foot-long vertical glass tube held in brackets. The level of water in the tube indicated the level of water in the boiler. Near the top of the gauge a black line showed what the water level ought to be. Two thirds of the way down a broad red line obviously acted as a warning. The water in the gauge was higher than the red line by half an inch.

To put it mildly, I was relieved. The boiler wasn't bulging. The explosion lay in the future, which gave me more time to work out how to prevent it. As long as it would take Oxon and Kraye to decide on a repeat search, perhaps.

I could simply have turned out the flame, but Kraye and Oxon would notice that the noise had stopped, and merely light it again. Nothing would have been gained. On the other hand, I was sure that the flame was higher than it should have been at night, because the water in the ladies' tap was nearly boiling.

Gingerly I turned the adjusting wheel on the oil line. Half a turn. A full turn. The roaring seemed just as loud. Another turn, and that time there was a definite change. Half a turn more. It was perceptibly quieter. Slowly I inched the wheel around more, until quite suddenly the roar turned to a murmur. Too far. Hastily I reversed. At that point where the murmur was again a roar, I left it.

I looked consideringly at the square tank of condensed water on the floor. It was this, overflowing, which was making the pool of water; and it was overflowing because the contents were not being pumped back into the boiler. If they've broken the pump, I thought despairingly, I'm done. I didn't know the first thing about electric pumps.

Another sentence from that faraway school lesson floated usefully through my mind. *For safety's sake, every boiler must have two sources of water.*

I chewed my lower lip, watching the water trickle down the side of the tank onto the floor. Even in the few minutes I had been there the pool had spread. One source of water was obviously knocked out. Where and what was the other?

There were dozens of pipes in the boiler room; not only oil pipes and water pipes, but all the electric cables were installed inside tubes as well. There were about six separate pipes with stopcocks on them. It seemed to me that all the water for the entire building came in through the boiler room.

Two pipes, apparently rising mains, led from the floor up the wall and into the calorifier. Both had stopcocks, which I tested. Both were safely open. There was no rising main leading directly into the boiler.

By sheer luck I was halfway round the huge cylinder looking for an inlet pipe when I saw the lever-type door handle move down. I leaped for the only vestige of cover, the space between the boiler and the wall. It was scorching hot there: pretty well unbearable.

Kraye had to raise his voice to make himself heard over the roaring flame.

"You're sure it's still safe?"

"Yes, I told you, it won't blow up for three hours yet. At least three hours."

"The water's running out already," Kraye objected.

"There's a lot in there." Oxon's voice came nearer. I could feel my heart thumping and hear the pulse in my ears. "The level's not down to the caution mark on the guage yet," he said. "It won't blow for a long time after it goes below that."

"We've got to find Halley," Kraye said. "Got to." If Oxon moved another step he would see me. "I'll work from this end; you start again from the other. Look in every cupboard. The little rat has gone to ground somewhere."

Oxen didn't answer audibly. I had a sudden glimpse of his sleeve as he turned, and I shrank back into my hiding place.

Because of the noise of the boiler I couldn't hear them go away through the door, but eventually I had to risk that they had. The heat where I stood was too appalling. Moving out into the ordinarily hot air in the middle of the room was like diving into a cold bath. And Oxon and Kraye had gone.

I slipped off my jacket and wiped the sweat off my face with my shirt sleeves. Back to the problem: water supply.

The pump *looked* all right. There were no loose wires, and it had an undisturbed, slightly greasy, slightly dirty appearance. With luck, I thought, they hadn't damaged the pump, they'd blocked the pipe where it left the tank. I took off my tie and shirt as well, and put them with my jacket on the grimy floor.

The lid of the tank came off easily enough, and the water, when I tested it, proved to be no more than uncomfortably hot. I drank some in my cupped palm. The running and the heat had made me very thirsty, and

198

although I would have preferred it iced, no water could have been purer, or more tasteless, though I was not inclined to be fussy on that point.

I stretched my arm down into the water, kneeling beside the tank. As it was only about two feet deep, I could touch the bottom quite easily, and almost at once my searching fingers found and gripped a loose object. I pulled it out.

It was a fine mesh filter, which should no doubt have been in place over the opening of the outlet pipe.

Convinced now that the pipe was blocked from this end, I reached down again into the water. I found the edge of the outlet, and felt carefully into it. I could reach no obstruction. Bending over further, so that my shoulder was half in the water, I put two fingers as far as they would go into the outlet. I could feel nothing solid, but there did seem to be a piece of string. It was difficult to get it between two fingers firmly enough to pull as hard as was necessary, but gradually with a series of little jerks I managed to move the plug backward into the tank.

It came away finally so suddenly that I nearly overbalanced. There was a burp from the outer pipe of the tank and on the other side of the room a sharp click from the pump.

I lifted my hand out of the water to see what had blocked the pipe, and stared in amazement. It was a large mouse. I had been pulling its tail.

Accidental sabotage, I thought. The same old pattern. However unlikely it was that a mouse should dive into a tank, find the filter conveniently out of place, and get stuck just inside the outlet pipe, one would have a hard job proving that it was impossible.

I carefully put the sodden little body out of sight in the small gap between the tank and the wall. With relief I noticed that the water level was already going down slightly, which meant that the pump was working properly and the boiler would soon be more or less back to normal.

I splashed some more water out of the tank to make a larger pool should Kraye or Oxon glance in again, and replaced the lid. Putting on my shirt and jacket I followed with my eyes the various pipes in and out of the boiler. The lagged steam exit pipe to the calorifier. The vast chimney flue for the hot gases from the burning oil. The inlet pipe from the pump. The water gauge. The oil pipe. There had to be another water inlet somewhere, partly for safety, partly to keep the steam circuit topped up.

I found it in the end running alongside and behind the inlet pipe from the pump. It was a gravity feed from a stepped series of three small unobtrusive tanks fixed high on the wall. Filters, I reckoned, so that the main's water didn't carry its mineral salts into the boiler and fur it up. The filter tanks were fed by a pipe which branched off one of the rising mains and had its own stopcock.

Reaching up, I tried to turn it clockwise. It didn't move. The main's water was cut off. With satisfaction I turned it on again.

Finally, with the boiler once more working exactly as it should, I took a look at the water gauge. The level had already risen to nearly halfway between the red and black marks. Hoping fervently Oxon wouldn't come back for another check on it, I went over to the door and switched off the light.

There was no one in the passage. I slipped through the door, and in the last three inches before shutting it behind me stretched my hand back and put the light on again. I didn't want Kraye knowing I'd been in there.

Keeping close to the wall, I walked softly down the passage toward the Tattersalls end. If I could get clear of the stands there were other buildings out that way to give cover. The barn, cloakrooms and tote building in the silver ring. Beyond these lay the finishing straight, the way down to the tan patch and the bisecting road. Along that, bungalows, people and telephones.

That was when my luck ran out.

17

was barely two steps past the door of the Tattersalls
ar when it opened and the lights blazed out onto my
ptoeing figure. In the two seconds it took Oxon to real-
e what he was seeing I was six running paces down
ward the way out.

His shouts echoed in the passage mingled with others
urther back, and I still thought that if Kraye too were
ehind me I might have a chance. But when I was within
n steps of the end another figure appeared there,
urrying, called by the noise.

I skidded nearly to a stop, sliding on one of the scat-
ered bottle tops, and crashed through the only possible
oor, into the same empty bar as before. I raced across
ne board floor, kicking bottle tops in all directions, but
never got to the far door. It opened before I reached
, and that was the end.

Doria Kraye stood there, maliciously triumphant. She
as dressed theatrically in white slender trousers and
shiny short white jacket. Her dark hair fell smoothly,
r face was as flawlessly beautiful as ever, and she held
ock-steady in one elegantly long-figured hand the little
22 automatic I had last seen in a chocolate box at the
ottom of her dressing case.

"The end of the line, buddy boy," she said. "You
tay just where you are."

I hesitated on the brink of trying to rush her.

"Don't risk it," she said. "I'm a splendid shot. I
ouldn't miss. Do you want a kneecap smashed?"

There was little I wanted less. I turned round slowly.
here were three men coming forward into the long room.
raye, Oxon and Ellis Bolt. All three of them looked
s if they had long ago got tired of the chase and were
oing to take it out on the quarry.

"Will you walk," said Doria behind me, "or [
dragged?'

I shrugged. "Walk."

All the same, Kraye couldn't keep his hands off n
When, following Doria's instructions, I walked past hi
to go back out through the passage he caught hold
my jacket at the back of the neck and kicked my leg
I kicked back, which wasn't too sensible, as I present
ended up on the floor. There was nothing like little me
bottle tops for giving you a feeling of falling on lit
metal bottle tops, I thought, with apologies to Micha
Flanders and Donald Swan.

"Get up," said Kraye. Doria stood beside him, poir
ing at me with the gun.

I did as he said.

"Right," said Doria. "Now, walk down the passa
and go into the weighing room. And Howard, for God
sake wait till we get there, or we'll lose him again. Wal
buddy boy. Walk straight down the middle of tl
passage. If you try anything, I'll shoot you in the leg."

I saw no reason not to believe her. I walked dow
the center of the passage with her too close behind f
escape, and with the two men bringing up the rear.

"Stop a minute," said Kraye, outside the boil
room.

I stopped. I didn't look round.

Kraye opened the door and looked inside. The lig
spilled out, adding to that already coming from the oth
open doors along the way.

"Well?" said Oxon.

"There's more water on the floor." He sounde
pleased, and shut the door without going in for a furth
look. Not all of my luck had departed, it seemed.

"Move," he said. I obeyed.

The weighing room was as big and bare as ever.
stopped in the middle of it and turned round. The fo
of them stood in a row, looking at me, and I didn't .
all like what I read in their faces.

"Go and sit there," said Doria, pointing.

I went on across the floor and sat where she said, c
the chair of the weighing machine. The pointer in

202

nediately swung round the clock face to show my weight. Nine stone seven. It was, I was remotely interested to see, exactly ten pounds less than when I had last raced. Bullets would solve any jockey's weight problem, I thought.

The four of them came closer. It was some relief to find that Fred wasn't among them, but only some. Kraye was emitting the same livid fury as he had twelve days go at Aynsford. And then, I had merely mildly insulted his wife.

"Hold his arms," he said to Oxon. Oxon was one of those thin wiry men of seemingly limitless strength. He came round behind me, clamped his fingers round my elbows and pulled them back. With concentration Kraye hit me several times in the face.

"Now," he said. "Where are they?"

"What?" I said indistinctly.

"The negatives."

"What negatives?"

He hit me again and hurt his own hand. Shaking it out and rubbing his knuckles, he said, "You know what negatives. The films you took of my papers."

"Oh, those."

"Those." He hit me again, but less hard.

"In the office," I mumbled.

He tried a slap to save his knuckles. "Office," I said.

He tried with his left hand, but it was clumsy. After that he sucked his knuckles and kept his hands to himself.

Bolt spoke for the first time, in his consciously beautiful voice. "Fred wouldn't have missed them, especially as there was no reason for them to be concealed. He's too thorough."

If Fred wouldn't have missed them, the bombs had been pure spite. I licked the inside of a split lip and thought about what I would like to do to Fred.

"Where in the office?" said Kraye.

"Desk."

"Hit him," said Kraye. "My hand hurts."

Bolt had to go, but it wasn't his sort of thing.

"Try with this," said Doria, offering Bolt the gun,

203

but it was luckily so small he couldn't hold it effectively.

Oxon let go of my elbows, came round to the front and looked at my face.

"If he's decided not to tell you, you won't get it out of him like that," he said.

"I told you," I said.

"Why not?" said Bolt.

"You're hurting yourselves more than him. And you want my opinion, you won't get anything out him at all."

"Don't be silly," said Doria scornfully. "He's small."

Oxon laughed without mirth.

"If Fred said so, the negatives weren't at his office asserted Bolt again. "Nor in his flat. And he didn't brin them with him. Or at least, they weren't in his luggag at the hotel."

I looked at him sideways, out of an eye which wa beginning to swell. And if I hadn't been so quick to hav him flung out of my hotel room, I thought sourly, I wouldn't have driven in through the racecourse gate exactly the wrong moment. But I couldn't have foresee it, and it was too late to help.

"They weren't in his car either," said Doria. "B this was." She put her hand into her shining white pock and brought out my baby camera. Kraye took it fro her, opened the case, and saw what was inside. The vei in his neck and temples became congested with bloo In a paroxysm of fury he threw the little black toy acro the room so that it hit the wall with a disintegratin crash.

"Sixteen millimeter," he said savagely. "Fred mu have missed them."

Bolt said obstinately, "Fred would find a needle a haystack. And those films wouldn't have been hi den."

"He might have them in his pocket," suggeste Doria.

"Take your coat off," Kraye said. "Stand up."

I stood up, and the base plate of the weighing machin

204

wobbled under my feet. Oxon pulled my coat down over the back of my shoulders, gave a tug to get the sleeves off, and passed the jacket to Kraye. His own hand he thrust into my trouser pocket. In the right one, under my tie, he found the bunch of lock pickers.

"Sit down," he said. I did so, exploring with the back of my hand some of the damage to my face. It could have been worse, I thought resignedly, much worse. I would be lucky if that were all.

"What are those?" said Doria curiously, taking the jingling collection from Oxon.

Kraye snatched them from her and slung them after the camera. "Skeleton keys," he said furiously. "What he used to unlock my cases."

"I don't see how he could," said Doria, "with that . . that . . . claw." She looked down where it lay on my lap.

A nice line in taunts, I thought, but a week too late. Thanks to Miss Martin, I was at last learning to live with the claw. I left it where it was.

"Doria," said Bolt calmly, "would you be kind enough to go over to the flat and wait for Fred to ring? He may already have found what we want at Aynsford."

I turned my head and found him looking straight at me, assessingly. There was a detachment in the eyes, an unmoved quality in the rounded features; and I began to wonder whether his stolid coolness might not in the end prove even more difficult to deal with than Kraye's rage.

"Aynsford," I repeated thickly. I looked at my watch. If Fred had really taken his bombs to Aynsford, he should by now be safely in the bag. One down, four to go. Five of them altogether, not four. I hadn't thought of Doria being an active equal colleague of the others. My mistake.

"I don't want to," said Doria, staying put.

Bolt shrugged. "It doesn't matter. I see that the negatives aren't at Aynsford, because the thought of Fred looking for them there doesn't worry Halley one little bit."

The thought of what Fred might be doing at Aynsford

205

or to Charles himself didn't worry any of them eithe
But more than that I didn't like the way Bolt wa
reasoning. In the circumstances, a clear-thinking opponer
was something I could well have done without.

"We must have them," said Kraye intensely. "W
must. Or be certain beyond doubt that they wer
destroyed." To Oxon he said, "Hold his arms again."

"No," I said, shrinking back.

"Ah, that's better. Well?"

"They were in the office." My mouth felt stiff.

"Where?"

"In Mr. Radnor's desk, I think."

He stared at me, eyes narrowed, anger half unde
control, weighing up whether I were telling the truth of
not. He certainly couldn't go to the office and mak
sure.

"Were," said Bolt suddenly.

"What?" asked Kraye, impatiently.

"Were," said Bolt. "Halley said were. The negative
were in the office. Now that's very interesting indeed
don't you think?"

Ooxn said, "I don't see why."

Bolt came close to me and peered into my face.
didn't meet his eyes, and anything he could read from
my bruised features he was welcome to.

"I think he knows about the bombs," he said finally.

"How?" said Doria.

"I should think he was told at the hotel. People i
London must have been trying to contact him. Yes,
think we can take it for granted he knows about th
bombs."

"What difference does that make?" said Oxon.

Kraye knew. "It means he thinks he is safe saying th
negatives were in the office, because we can't prove the
weren't."

"They were," I insisted, showing anxiety.

Bolt pursed his full moist lips. "Just how clever i
Halley?" he said.

"He was a jockey," said Oxon flatly, as if tha
automatically meant an I.Q. of 70.

Bolt said, "But they took him on at Hunt Radnor's."

206

"I told you before," said Oxon patiently, "I asked various people about that. Radnor took him on as an advisor, but never gave him anything special to do, and if that doesn't show that he wasn't capable of much, I don't know what does. Everyone knows that his job is only a face-saver. It sounds all right, but it means nothing really. Jobs are quite often given in that way to top jockeys when they retire. No one expects them to *do* much, it's just their name that's useful for a while. When their news value has gone, they get the sack."

This all-too-true summing up of affairs depressed me almost as deeply as my immediate propects.

"Howard?" said Bolt.

"I don't know," said Kraye slowly. "He doesn't strike me as being in the least clever. Very much the opposite. I agree he did take those photographs, but I think you are quite right in believing he doesn't know why we want them destroyed."

That, too, was shatteringly correct. As far as I had been able to see, the photographs proved nothing conclusively except that Kraye had been buying Seabury shares under various names with Bolt's help. Kraye and Bolt could not be prosecuted for that. Moreover the whole of Seabury executive had seen the photographs at the meeting that morning, so their contents were no secret.

"Doria?" Bolt said.

"He's a slimy, spying little creep, but if he was clever he wouldn't be sitting where he is."

You couldn't argue with that, either. It had been farily certain all along that Kraye was getting help from somebody working at Seabury, but even after knowing about clerk of the course Brinton's unwilling collaboration at Dunstable, I had gone on assuming that the helper at Seabury was one of the laborers. I hadn't given more than a second's flicker of thought to Oxon, because it didn't seem reasonable that it should be him. In destroying the racecourse he was working himself out of a job, and good jobs for forty-year-old ex-army captains weren't plentiful enough to be lost lightly. As he certainly wasn't mentally affected like Brinton, he wasn't being blackmailed into doing it against his will. I had thought him silly and self-important, but not a rogue. As Doria said, had I been clever enough to suspect him, I wouldn't be sitting where I was.

Bolt went on discussing me as if I weren't there, and as if the decision they would come to would have ordinary everyday consequences.

He said, "You may all be right, but I don't think so, because since Halley has been on the scene everything's gone wrong. It was he who persuaded Hagbourne to get the course put right, and he who found the mirror as soon as it was up. I took him without question for what he said he was when he came to see me—a shop assistant. You two took him for a wretched little hanger-on of no account. All that, together with the fact that he opened your locked cases and took good clear photographs on a miniature camera, adds up to just one thing to me. Professionalism. Even the way he sits there saying nothing is professional. Amateurs call you names and try to impress you with how much they know. All he has said is that the negatives were in the office. I consider we ought to forget every previous impression we have of him and think of him only as coming from Hunt Radnor."

They thought about this for five seconds. Then Kraye said, "We'll have to make sure about the negatives."

Bolt nodded. If reason hadn't told me what Kraye meant, his wife's smile would have. My skin crawled.

"How?" she said interestedly.

Kraye inspected his grazed knuckles. "You won't beat it out of him," said Oxon. "Not like that. You haven't a hope."

"Why not?" said Bolt.

Instead of replying, Oxon turned to me. "How many races did you ride with broken bones?"

I didn't answer. I couldn't remember anyway.

"That's ridiculous," said Doria scornfully. "How could he?"

"A lot of them do," said Oxon. "And I'm sure he was no exception."

"Nonsense," said Kraye.

Oxon shook his head. "Collarbones, ribs, forearms

208

they'll ride with cracks in any of those if they can keep the owners and trainers from finding out."

Why couldn't he shut up, I thought savagely. He was making things much much worse; as if they weren't appalling enough already.

"You mean," said Doria with sickening pleasure, "that he can stand a great deal?"

"No," I said. "No." It sounded like the plea it was. "You can only ride with cracked bones if they don't hurt."

"They must hurt," said Bolt reasonably.

"No," I said. "Not always." It was true, but they didn't believe it.

"The negatives were in the office," I said despairingly. "In the office."

"He's scared," said Doria delightedly. And that too was true.

It struck a chord with Kraye. He remembered Aynsford. "We know where he's most easily hurt," he said. "That hand."

"No," I said in real horror.

They all smiled.

My whole body flushed with uncontrollable fear. Racing injuries were one thing: they were quick, one didn't expect them, and they were part of the job.

To sit and wait and know that a part of one's self which had already proved a burden was about to be hurt as much as ever was quite something else. Instinctively I put my arm up across my face to hide from them that I was afraid, but it must have been obvious.

Kraye laughed insultingly. "So there's your brave clever Mr. Halley for you. It won't take much to get the truth."

"What a pity," said Doria.

They left her standing in front of me holding the little pistol in an unswerving pink-nailed hand while they went out and rummaged for what they needed. I judged the distance to the door, which was all of thirty feet, and wondered whether the chance of a bullet on the way

209

wasn't preferable to what was going to happen if I stayed where I was.

Doria watched my indecision with amusement.

"Just try it, buddy boy. Just try it."

I had read that to shoot accurately with an automatic pistol took a great deal of skill and practice. It was possible that all Doria had wanted was the power feeling of owning a gun and that she couldn't aim it. On the other hand she was holding it high and with a nearly straight arm, close to where she could see along the sights. On balance, I thought her claim to be a splendid shot had too much probability to be risked.

It was a pity Doria had such a vicious soul inside her beautiful body. She looked gay and dashing in her white Courrèges clothes, smiling a smile which seemed warm and friendly and was as safe as the yawn of a python. She was the perfect mate for Kraye, I thought. Fourth, fifth, sixth time lucky, he'd found a complete complement to himself. If Kraye could do it, perhaps one day I would too . . . but I didn't know if I would even see tomorrow.

I put the back of my hand up over my eyes. My whole face hurt, swollen and stiff, and I was developing a headache. I decided that if I ever got out of this I wouldn't try any more detecting. I had made a proper mess of it.

The men came back, Oxon from the Stewards' room lugging a wooden spoke-backed chair with arms, Kraye and Bolt from the changing room with the yard-long poker from the stove and the rope the wet breeches had been hung on to dry. There were still a couple of pegs clinging to it.

Oxon put the chair down a yard or two away and Doria waved the gun a fraction to indicate I should sit in it. I didn't move.

"God," she said disappointedly, "you really are a little worm, just like at Aynsford. Scared to a stand-still."

"He isn't a shop assistant," said Bolt sharply. "And don't forget it."

I didn't look at him. But for him and his rejection

of Charles's usefully feeble Halley image, I might not have been faced with quite the present situation.

Oxon punched me on the shoulder. "Move," he said.

I stood up wearily and stepped off the weighing machine. They stood close round me. Kraye thrust out a hand, twisted it into my shirt, and pushed me into the chair. He, Bolt and Oxon had a fine old time tying my arms and legs to the equivalent wooden ones with the washing line. Doria watched, fascinated.

I remembered her rather unusual pleasures.

"Like to change places?" I said tiredly.

It didn't make her angry. She smiled slowly, put her gun in a pocket, and leaned down and kissed me long and hard on the mouth. I loathed it. When at length she straightened up she had a smear of my blood on her lip. She wiped it off onto her hand, and thoughtfully licked it. She looked misty-eyed and languorous, as if she had had a profound sexual experience. It made me want to vomit.

"Now," said Kraye. "Where are they?" He didn't seem to mind his wife kissing me. He understood her, of course.

I looked at the way they had tied the rope tightly round and round my left forearm, leaving the wrist bare, palm downward. A hand, I thought. What good, anyway, was a hand that didn't work.

I looked at their faces, one by one. Doria, rapt. Oxon, faintly surprised. Kraye confident, flexing his muscles. And Bolt, calculating and suspicious. None of them within a mile of relenting.

"Where are they?" Kraye repeated, lifting his arm.

"In the office," I said helplessly.

He hit my wrist with the poker. I'd hoped he might at least try to be subtle, but instead he used all his strength and with that one first blow smashed the whole shooting match to smithereens. The poker broke through the skin. The bones cracked audibly like sticks.

I didn't scream only because I couldn't get enough breath to do it. Before that moment I would have said I knew everything there was to know about pain, but it seems one can always learn. Behind my shut eyes the

211

world turned yellow and gray, like sun shining through mist, and every inch of my skin began to sweat. There had never been anything like it. It was too much, too much. And I couldn't manage any more.

"Where are they?" said Kraye again.

"Don't," I said. "Don't do it." I could hardly speak.

Doria sighed deeply.

I opened my eyes a slit, my head lolling weakly back, too heavy to hold up. Kraye was smiling, pleased with his efforts. Oxon looked sick.

"Well?" said Kraye.

I swallowed, hesitating still.

He put the tip of the poker on my shattered bleeding wrist and gave a violent jerk. Among other things it felt like a fizzing electric shock, up my arm into my head and down to my toes. Sweat started sticking my shirt to my chest and my trousers to my legs.

"Don't," I said. "Don't." It was a croak, a capitulation, a prayer.

"Come on, then," said Kraye, and jolted the poker again.

I told them. I told them where to go.

18

They decided it should be Bolt who went to fetch the negatives.

"What is this place?" he said. He hadn't recognized the address.

"The home of . . . a . . . girl friend."

He dispassionately watched the sweat run in trickles down my face. My mouth was dry. I was very thirsty.

"Say . . . I sent you," I said, between jagged breaths. "I . . . asked her . . . to keep them safe. . . . They . . . are with . . . several other things. . . . The package . . .

you want . . . has a name on it . . . a make of film
. . . Jigoro . . . Kano."

"Jigoro Kano. Right," Bolt said briskly.

"Give me . . . ," I said, "some morphine."

Bolt laughed. "After all the trouble you've caused
us? Even if I had any, I wouldn't. You can sit there and
sweat it out."

I moaned. Bolt smiled in satisfaction and turned
away.

"I'll ring you as soon as I have the negatives," he said
to Kraye. "Then we can decide what to do with Halley.
I'll give it some thought on the way up." From his tone
he might have been discussing the disposal of a block
of worthless stocks.

"Good," said Kraye. "We'll wait for your call over
in the flat."

They began to walk toward the door. Oxon and Doria
hung back, Doria because she couldn't tear her fascinated,
dilated eyes away from watching me, and Oxon for more
practical reasons.

"Are you just going to leave him here?" he asked in
surprise.

"Yes. Why not?" said Kraye. "Come on, Doria
darling. The best is over."

Unwillingly she followed him, and Oxon also.

"Some water," I said. "Please."

"No," said Kraye.

They filed past him out of the door. Just before he
shut it he gave me a last look compounded of triumph,
contempt and satisfied cruelty. Then he switched off all
the lights and went away.

I heard the sound of a car starting up and driving off.
Bolt was on his way. Outside the windows the night was
black. Darkness folded round me like a fourth dimension.
As the silence deepened I listened to the low hum of the
boiler roaring safely on the far side of the wall. At least,
I thought, I don't have to worry about that as well. Small,
small consolation.

The back of the chair came only as high as my
shoulders and gave no support to my head. I felt deathly
tired. I couldn't bear to move: every muscle in my body

213

seemed to have a private line direct to my left wrist, and merely flexing my right foot had me panting. I wanted to lie down flat. I wanted a long cold drink. I wanted to faint. I went on sitting in the chair, wide awake, with a head that ached and weighed a ton, and an arm which wasn't worth the trouble.

I thought about Bolt going to Zanna Martin's front door, and finding that his own secretary had been helping me. I wondered for the hundredth time what he would do about that: whether he would harm her. Poor Miss Martin, whom life had already hurt too much.

Not only her, I thought. In the same file was the letter Mervyn Brinton had written out for me. If Bolt should see that, Mervyn Brinton would be needing a bodyguard for life.

I thought about the people who had bourne the beatings and brutalities of the Nazis and of the Japanese and had often died without betraying their secrets. I thought about the atrocities still going on throughout the world, and the ease with which man could break man. In Algeria, they said, unbelievable things had been done. Behind the Iron Curtain, brainwashing wasn't all. In African jails, who knew?

Too young for World War Two, safe in a tolerant society, I had had no thought that I should ever come to such a test. To suffer or to talk. The dilemma that stretched back to antiquity. Thanks to Kraye, I now knew what it was like at first hand. Thanks to Kraye, I didn't understand how anyone could keep silent unto death.

I thought: I wanted to ride round Seabury Racecourse again, and to go back into the weighing room, and to sit on the scales; and I've done all those things.

I thought: a fortnight ago I couldn't let go of the past. I was clinging to too many ruins, the ruins of my marriage and my racing career and my useless hand. They were gone for good now, all of them. There was nothing left to cling to. And every tangible memory of my life had blown away with a plastic bomb. I was rootless and homeless: and liberated.

What I refused to think about was what Kraye might still do during the next few hours.

214

Bolt had been gone for a good long time when at last Kraye came back. It had seemed half eternity to me, but even so I was in no hurry for it to end.

Kraye put the light on. He and Doria stood just inside the doorway, staring across at me.

"You're sure there's time?" said Doria.

Kraye nodded, looking at his watch. "If we're quick."

"Don't you think we ought to wait until Ellis rings?" she said. "He might have thought of something better."

"He's late already," said Kraye impatiently. They had clearly been arguing for some time. "He should have rung by now. If we're going to do this, we can't wait any longer."

"All right," she shrugged. "I'll go and take a look."

"Be careful. Don't go in."

"No," she said. "Don't fuss."

They both came over to where I sat. Doria looked at me with interest, and liked what she saw.

"He looks ghastly, doesn't he? Serves him right."

"Are you human?" I said.

A flicker of awareness crossed her lovely face, as if deep down she did indeed know that everything she had enjoyed that night was sinful and obscene, but she was too thoroughly addicted to turn back. "Shall I help you?" she said to Kraye, not answering me.

"No. I can manage. He's not very heavy."

She watched with a smile while her husband gripped the back of the chair I was sitting in and began to tug across the floor toward the wall. The jerks were almost past bearing. I grew dizzy with the effort of not yelling my head off. There was no one close enough to hear me if I did. Not the few overnight stable lads fast asleep three hundred yards away. Only the Krayes, who would find it sweet.

Doria licked her lips, as if at a feast.

"Go on," said Kraye. "Hurry."

"Oh, all right," she agreed crossly, and went out through the door into the passage.

Kraye finished pulling me across the room, turned the chair round so that I was facing the wall with my

215

knees nearly touching it and stood back, breathing deepl
from the exertion.

On the other side of the wall the boiler gently roare
One could hear it more clearly at such close quarter:
I knew I had no crashing explosion, no flying brick:
no killing steam to worry about. But the sands wer
running out fast, all the same.

Doria came back and said in a puzzled voice, "
thought you said there would be water all down th
passage."

"That's right."

"Well, there isn't. Not a drop. I looked into the boile
room and it's as dry as a bone."

"It can't be. It's nearly three hours since it starte
over-flowing. Oxon warned us it must be nearly read
to blow. You must be wrong."

"I'm not," she insisted. "The whole thing look
perfectly normal to me."

"It can't be." Kraye's voice was sharp. He went o
in a hurry to see for himself, and came back eve
faster.

"You're right. I'll go and get Oxon. I don't know ho
the confounded thing works." He went straight on o
of the main door, and I heard his footsteps running. The
was no urgency except his own anger. I shivered.

Doria wasn't certain enough of the boiler's safety
spend any time near me, which was about the first rea
good thing which had happened the whole night. N
did she find the back of my head worth speaking t
she liked to see her worms squirm. Perhaps she had ev
lost her appetite, now things had gone wrong. She wait
uneasily near the door for Kraye to come back, fiddlin
with the catch.

Oxon came with him, and they were both runnin
They charged across the weighing room and out in
the passage.

I hadn't much left anyway, I thought. A few tatte
of pride, perhaps. Time to nail them to the mast.

The two men walked softly into the room and do
to where I sat. Kraye grasped the chair and swung
violently round. The weighing room was quiet, u

disturbed. There was only blackness through the window. So that was that.

I looked at Kraye's face, and wished on the whole that I hadn't. It was white and rigid with fury. His eyes were two black pits.

Oxon held the mouse in his hand. "It must have been Halley," he said, as if he'd said it before. "There's no one else."

Kraye put his right hand down on my left, and systematically began to take his revenge. After three long minutes I passed out.

I clung to the dark, trying to hug it round me like a blanket, and it obstinately got thinner and thinner, lighter and lighter, noisier and noisier, more and more painful, until I could no longer deny that I was back in the world.

My eyes unstuck themselves against my will.

The weighing room was full of people. People in dark uniforms. Policemen. Policemen coming through every door. Bright yellow lights at long last shining outside the window. Policemen carefully cutting the rope away from my leaden limbs.

Kraye and Doria and Oxon looked smaller, surrounded by the dark blue men. Doria in her brave white suit instinctively and unsuccessfully tried to flirt with her captors. Oxon, disconcerted to his roots, faced the facts of life for the first time.

Kraye's fury wasn't spent. His eyes stared in hatred across the room.

He shouted, struggling in strong restraining arms, "Where did you send him? Bolt. Where did you send him?"

"Ah, Mr. Potter," I said into a sudden oasis of silence. "Mr. Wilbur Potter. Find out. But not from me."

19

Of course I ended up where I had begun, flat on my back in a hospital. But not for so long, that time. I had a pleasant sunny room with a distant view of the sea, some exceedingly pretty nurses and a whole stream of visitors. Chico came first, as soon as they would let him, on the Sunday afternoon.

He grinned down at me.

"You look bloody awful."

"Thanks very much."

"Two black eyes, a scabby lip, a purple and yellow complexion and a three-day beard. Glamorous."

"It sounds it."

"Do you want to look?" he asked, picking up a hand mirror from a chest of drawers.

I took the mirror and looked. He hadn't exaggerated. I would have faded into the background in a horror movie.

Sighing, I said, "X certificate, definitely."

He laughed, and put the mirror back. His own face still bore the marks of battle. The eyebrow was healing, but the bruise showed dark right down his cheek.

"This is a better room than you had in London," he remarked, strolling over to the window. "And it smells O.K. For a hospital, that is."

"Pack in the small talk and tell me what happened," I said.

"They told me not to tire you."

"Don't be an ass."

"Well, all right. You're a bloody rollicking nit in many ways, aren't you?"

"It depends how you look at it," I agreed peaceably.

"Oh sure, sure."

"Chico, give," I pleaded. "Come on."

218

"Well, there I was harmlessly snoozing away in Radnor's armchair with the telephone on one side and some rather good chicken sandwiches on the other, dreaming about a willing blonde and having a ball, when the front doorbell rang." He grinned. "I got up, stretched and went to answer it. I thought it might be you, come back after all and with nowhere to sleep. I knew it wouldn't be Radnor, unless he'd forgotten his key. And who else would be knocking on his door at two o'clock in the morning? But there was this fat geezer standing on the doorstep in his city pin-stripes, saying you'd sent him. 'Come in, then,' I said, yawning my head off. He came in, and I showed him into Radnor's sort of study place, where I'd been sitting.

" 'Sid sent you?' I asked him. 'What for?' He said he understood your girl friend lived here. God, mate, don't ever try snapping your mouth shut at the top of a yawn. I nearly dislocated my jaw. Could he see her, he said. Sorry it was so late, but it was extremely important.

" 'She isn't here,' I said. 'She's gone away for a few days. Can I help you?'

" 'Who are you?' he said, looking me up and down.

"I said I was her brother. He took a sharpish look at the sandwiches and the book I'd been reading, which had fallen on the floor, and he could see I'd been asleep, so he seemed to think everything was O.K., and he said, 'Sid asked me to fetch something she is keeping for him. Do you think you could help me find it?'

" 'Sure,' I said. 'What is it?'

"He hesitated a bit but he could see that it would look too weird if he refused to tell me, so he said, 'It's a packet of negatives. Sid said your sister had several things of his, but the packet I want has a name on it, a make of films. Jigoro Kano.'

" 'Oh?' I said innocently. 'Sid sent you for a packet marked Jigoro Kano?'

" 'That's right,' he said, looking round the room. 'Would it be in here?'

" 'It certainly would,' I said."

Chico stopped, came over beside the bed, and sat on the edge of it, by my right toe.

219

"How come you know about Jigoro Kano?" he said seriously.

"He invented judo," I said. "I read it somewhere."

Chico shook his head. "He didn't really invent it. In 1882 he took all the best bits of hundreds of versions of jujitsu and put them into a formal sort of order, and called it judo."

"I was sure you would know," I said, grinning at him.

"You took a very sticky risk."

"You had to know. After all, you're an expert. And there were all those years at your club. No risk. I knew you'd know. As long as I'd got the name right, that is. Anyway, what happened next?"

Chico smiled faintly.

"I tied him into a couple of knots. Armlocks and so on. He was absolutely flabbergasted. It was really rather funny. Then I put a bit of pressure on. You know. The odd thumb screwing down onto a nerve. God, you should have heard him yell. I suppose he thought he'd wake the neighbors, but you know what London is. No one took a blind bit of notice. So then I asked him where you were, when you sent him. He didn't show very willing, I must say, so I gave him a bit more. Poetic justice, wasn't it, considering what they'd just been doing to you? I told him I could keep it up all night, I'd hardly begun. There was a whole bookful I hadn't touched on. It shook him, it shook him bad."

Chico stood up restlessly and walked about the room.

"You know?" he said wryly. "He must have had a lot to lose. He was a pretty tough cookie, I'll give him that. If I hadn't been sure that you'd sent him to me as a sort of S.O.S., I don't think I'd have had the nerve to hurt him enough to bust him."

"I'm sorry," I said.

He looked at me thoughtfully. "We both learned about it, didn't we? You on the receiving end, and me . . . I didn't like it. Doing it, I mean. I mean, the odd swipe or two and a few threats, that's usually enough, and it doesn't worry you a bit, you don't give it a second

220

thought. But I've never hurt anyone like that before. Not seriously, on purpose, beyond bearing. He was crying, you see. . . ."

Chico turned his back to me, looking out of the window.

There was a long pause. The moral problems of being on the receiving end were not so great, I thought. It was easier on the conscience altogether.

At last Chico said, "He told me, of course. In the end."

"Yes."

"I didn't leave a mark on him, you know. Not a scratch. . . . He said you were at Seabury Racecourse. Well, I knew that was probably right, and that he wasn't trying the same sort of misdirection you had, because you'd told me yourself that you were going there. He said that you were in the weighing room and that the boiler ~~would soon~~ soon blow up. He said that he hoped it would kill you. He seemed half out of his mind with rage about you. How he should have known better than to believe you, he should have realized that you were as slippery as a snake, he'd been fooled once before. . . . He said he'd taken it for granted you were telling the truth when you broke down and changed your story about the negatives being in the office, because you . . . because you were begging for mercy and morphine and God knows what."

"Yes," I said. "I know all about that."

Chico turned away from the window, his face lightening into a near grin. "You don't say," he said.

"He wouldn't have believed it if I'd given in sooner, or less thoroughly. Kraye would have, but not him. It was very annoying."

"Annoying," said Chico. "I like that word." He paused, considering. "At what moment exactly did you think of sending Bolt to me?"

"About half an hour before they caught me," I admitted. "Go on. What happened next?"

"There was a ball of string on Radnor's writing desk, so I tied old Fatso up with that in an uncomfortable position. Then there was the dicey problem of who to

221

ring up to get the rescue squads on the way. I mean, the Seabury police might think I was some sort of a nut, ringing up at that hour and telling such an odd sort of story. At the best, they might send a bobby or two out to have a look, and the Krayes would easily get away. And I reckoned you'd want them rounded up red-handed, so to speak. I couldn't get hold of Radnor on account of the office phones being plasticated. So, well, I rang Lord Hagbourne."

"You didn't!"

"Well, yes. He was O.K., he really was. He listened to what I told him about you and the boiler and the Krayes and so on, and then he said, 'Right,' he'd see that half the Sussex police force turned up at Seabury Racecourse as soon as possible."

"Which they did."

"Which they did," agreed Chico. "To find that my old pal Sid had dealt with the boiler himself, but was otherwise in a fairly ropey state."

"Thanks." I said. "For everything."

"Be my guest."

"Will you do me another favor?"

"Yes, what?"

"I was supposed to take someone out to lunch today. She'll be wondering why I didn't turn up. I'd have got one of the nurses to ring her, but I still don't know her telephone number."

"Are you talking about Miss Zanna Martin? The poor old duck with the disaster area on a face?"

"Yes," I said, surprised.

"Then don't worry. She wasn't expecting you. She knows you're here."

"How?"

"She turned up at Bolt's office yesterday morning, to deal with the mail apparently, and found a policeman waiting on the doorstep with a search warrant. When he had gone she put two and two together smartly and trailed over to Cromwell Road to find out what was going on. Radnor had gone down to Seabury with Lord Hagbourne, but I was there poking about in the ruins, and we sort of swapped info. She was a bit upset about

222

you, mate, in a quiet sort of way. Anyhow, she won't be expecting you to take her out to lunch."

"Did she say anything about having one of our files?"

"Yes. I told her to hang on to it for a day or two. There frankly isn't anywhere in the office to put it."

"All the same, you go over to where she lives as soon as you get back, and collect it. It's the Brinton file. And take great care of it. The negatives Kraye wanted are inside it."

Chico stared. "You're not serious."

"Why not?"

"But everyone—Radnor, Lord Hagbourne, even Kraye and Bolt, and the police—everyone has taken it for granted that what you said first was right, that they were in the office and were blown up."

"It's lucky they weren't," I said. "Get some more prints made. We've still got to find out why they were so hellishly important. And don't tell Miss Martin they were what Kraye wanted."

The door opened and one of the pretty nurses came in.

"I'm afraid you'll have to go now," she said to Chico. She came close beside the bed and took my pulse. "Haven't you any sense?" she exclaimed, looking at him angrily. "A few quiet minutes was what we said. Don't talk too much, and don't let Mr. Halley talk at all."

"You try giving *him* orders," said Chico cheerfully, "and see where it gets you."

"Miss Martin's address," I began.

"No," said the nurse severely. "No more talking."

I told Chico the address.

"See what I mean?" he said to the nurse. She looked down at me and laughed. A nice girl behind the starch.

Chico went across the room and opened the door.

"So long, then, Sid. Oh, by the way, I brought this for you to read. I thought you might be interested."

He pulled a glossy booklet folded lengthwise out of an inner pocket and threw it over onto the bed. It fell just out of my reach, and the nurse picked it up to give t me. Then suddenly she held on to it tight.

223

"Oh no," she said. "You can't give him that!"

"Why not?" said Chico. "What do you think he is, a baby?"

He went out and shut the door. The nurse clung to the booklet, looking very troubled. I held out my hand for it.

"Come on."

"I think I ought to ask the doctors. . . ."

"In that case," I said, "I can guess what it is. Knowing Chico. So be a dear and hand it over. It's quite all right."

She gave it to me hesitantly, waiting to see my reaction when I caught sight of the bold words on the cover: *Artificial Limbs. The Modern Development.*

I laughed. "He's a realist," I said. "You wouldn't expect him to bring fairy stories."

20

When Radnor came the next day he looked tired, dispirited and ten years older. The military jauntiness had gone from his bearing, there were deep lines around his eyes and mouth, and his voice was lifeless.

For some moments he stared in obvious distress at the white-wrapped arm which stopped abruptly four inches below the elbow.

"I'm sorry about the office," I said.

"For God's sake—"

"Can it be rebuilt? How bad is it?"

"Sid—"

"Are the outside walls still solid, or is the whole place a write-off?"

"I'm too old," he said, giving in, "to start again."

"It's only bricks and mortar that are damaged. You haven't got to start again. The agency is you, not the

uilding. Everyone can work for you just as easily
omewhere else."

He sat down in an armchair, rested his head back,
nd closed his eyes.

"I'm tired," he said.

"I don't suppose you've had much sleep since it hap-
ened."

"I am seventy-one," he said flatly.

I was utterly astounded. Until that day I would have
ut him in the late fifties.

"You can't be."

"Time passes," he said. "Seventy-one."

"If I hadn't suggested going after Kraye it wouldn't
ave happened," I said with remorse. "I'm so sorry . . .
o sorry. . . ."

He opened his eyes. "It wasn't your fault. If it was
nyone's it was my own. You wouldn't have let
agbourne take those photographs to Seabury, if it had
en left to you. I know you didn't like it, that I'd given
em to him. Letting the photographs go to Seabury was
e direct cause of the bombs, and it was my mistake,
ot yours."

"You couldn't possibly tell," I protested.

"I should have known better, after all these years. I
ink . . . perhaps I may not see so clearly . . . con-
quences, things like that." His voice died to a low,
iserable murmur. "Because I gave the photographs to
agbourne, you lost your hand."

"No," I said decisively. "It's ridiculous to start
aming yourself for that. For heaven's sake snap out
it. No one in the agency can afford to have you in this
ame of mind. What are Dolly and Jack Copeland and
mmy and Chico and all the others to do if you don't
ck up the pieces?"

He didn't answer.

"My hand was useless, anyway," I said. "And if I'd
en willing to give in to Kraye I needn't have lost it. It
had nothing whatever to do with you."

He stood up.

"You told Kraye a lot of lies," he said.

"That's right."

225

"But you wouldn't lie to me."

"Naturally not."

"I don't believe you."

"Concentrate on it. It'll come in time."

"You don't show much respect for your elders."

"Not when they behave like bloody fools," I agre
dryly.

He blew down his nostrils, smoldering inwardly. E
all he said was, "And you? Will you still work
me?"

"It depends on you. I might kill us all next time."

"I'll take the risk."

"All right then. Yes. But we haven't finished this tin
yet. Did Chico get the negatives?"

"Yes. He had two sets of prints done this mornin
One for him, and he gave me one to bring to you. .
said you'd want them, but I didn't think—"

"But you did bring them?" I urged.

"Yes, they're outside in my car. Are you sure—?"

"For heaven's sake," I said in exasperation. "I c
hardly wait."

By the following day I had acquired several m
pillows, a bedside telephone and a reputation for be
a difficult patient.

The agency restarted work that morning, squeez
into Radnor's own small house. Dolly rang to say it v
absolute hell, there was only one telephone instead
thirty, the blitz spirit was fortunately in operation,
to worry about a thing, there was a new word going rou
the office, it was Halley-lujah, and good-bye, some
else's turn now.

Chico rang a little later from a call box.

"Sammy found that driver, Smith," he said. "He w
to see him in Birmingham yesterday. Now that Kray
in jug Smith is willing to turn Queen's evidence.
agreed that he did take two hundred and fifty quid, j
for getting out of his cab, unclipping the chains wh
the tanker had gone over, and sitting on the side of
road moaning and putting on an act. Nice e
money."

"Good," I said.

"But that's not all. The peach of it is he still has the money, most of it, in a tin box, saving it for a deposit on a house. That's what tempted him, apparently, needing money for a house. Anyway, Kraye paid him the second installment in tenners, from one of the blocks you photographed in his case. Smith still has one of the actual tenners in the pictures. He agreed to part with that for evidence, but I can't see anyone making him give the rest back, can you?"

"Not exactly!"

"So we've got Kraye nicely tied up on malicious damage."

"That's terrific," I said. "What are they holding him on now?"

"Gross bodily harm. And the others for aiding and abetting."

"Consecutive sentences, I trust."

"You'll be lucky."

I sighed. "All the same, he still owns twenty-three per cent of Seabury's shares."

"So he does," agreed Chico gloomily.

"How bad exactly is the office?" I asked.

"They're surveying it still. The outside walls look all right, it's just a case of making sure. The inside was pretty well gutted."

"We could have a better layout," I said. "And a lift."

"So we could," he said happily. "And I'll tell you something else which might interest you."

"What?"

"The house next door is up for sale."

I was asleep when Charles came in the afternoon, and he watched me wake up, which was a pity. The first few seconds of consciousness were always the worst: I had the usual hellish time, and when I opened my eyes, there he was.

"Good God, Sid," he said in alarm. "Don't they give you anything?"

I nodded, getting a firmer grip on things.

227

"But with modern drugs, surely . . . I'm going complain."

"No."

"But Sid—"

"They do what they can, I promise you. Don't loo so upset. It'll get better in a few days. Just now it's bore, that's all. Tell me about Fred."

Fred had already been at the house when the poli guard arrived at Aynsford. Four policemen had go there, and it took all four to hold him, with Charles goir back and helping as well.

"Did he do much damage?" I asked. "Before t police got there?"

"He was very methodical, and very quick. He h been right through my desk, and all the wardroom. Eve envelope, folder and notebook had been ripped apa and the debris was all in a heap, ready to be destroye He'd started on the dining room when the police arrive He was very violent. And they found a box of plast explosive lying on the hall table, and some more out the van." He paused. "What made you think he wou come?"

"They knew I took the photographs at Aynsford, b how would they know I got them developed in Londo I was afraid they might think I'd had them done locall and that they'd think you'd know where the negativ were, as it was you who inveigled Kraye down there the first place."

He smiled mischievously. "Will you come to Aynsfo for a few days when you get out of here?"

"I've heard that somewhere before," I said. "N thanks."

"No more Krayes," he promised. "Just a rest."

"I'd like to, but there won't be time. The agency in a dicky state. And I've just been doing to my bo what you did to me at Aynsford."

"What's that?"

"Kicking him out of depression into action."

His smile twisted in amusement.

"Do you know how old he is?" I said.

"About seventy, why?"

I was surprised. "I'd no idea he was that age, until e told me yesterday."

Charles squinted at the tip of his cigar. He said, "You ways thought I asked him to give you a job, didn't u? And guaranteed your wages."

I made a face at him, embarrassed.

"You may care to know it wasn't like that at all. I dn't know him personally, only by name. He sought e out one day in the club and asked me if I thought u'd be any good at working with him. I said yes, I ought you would. Given time."

"I don't believe it."

He smiled. "I told him you played a fair game of ess. Also that you had become a jockey simply through rcumstances, because you were small and your mother ed, and that you could probably succeed at something se just as easily. He said that from what he'd seen of u racing you were the sort of chap he needed. He told e then how old he was. That's all. Nothing else. Just w old he was. But we both understood what he was ying."

"I nearly threw it away," I said. "If it hadn't been r you—"

"Oh yes," he said wryly. "You have a lot to thank e for. A lot."

Before he went I asked him to look at the photographs, t he studied them one by one and handed them back aking his head.

Chief Inspector Cornish rang up to tell me Fred was t only in the bag but sewn up.

"The bullets match all right. He drew the same gun the men who arrested him, but one of them fortunately rew a vase at him and knocked it out of his hand before could shoot."

"He was a fool to keep that gun after he had shot ndrews."

"Stupid. Crooks often are, or we'd never catch them. d he didn't mention his little murder to Kraye and e others, so they can't be pinched as accessories to that. ty. But it's quite clear he kept it quiet. The Sussex force

said that Kraye went berserk when he found (
Apparently he mostly regretted not having known ab
your stomach while he had you in his clutches."

"Thank God he didn't!" I exclaimed with feeling.

Cornish's chuckle came down the wire. "Fred
supposed to look for Brinton's letter at your age
himself, but he wanted to go to a football match up ne
or something, and sent Andrews instead. He said
didn't think there's be a trap, or anything subtle
that. Just an errand, about on Andrews' level. He
he only lent him the gun for a lark, he didn't m
Andrews to use it, didn't think he'd be so silly. But t
Andrews went back to him scared stiff and said he'd s
you, so Fred says he suggested a country ramble in
ping Forest and the gun went off by accident. I ask y
try that on a jury! Fred says he didn't tell Kraye beca
he was afraid of him."

"What! Fred afraid?"

"Kraye seems to have made an adverse impress
on him."

"Yes, he's apt to do that," I said.

I read Chico's booklet from cover to cover. One
to thank the thalidomide children, it appeared, for
speed-up of modern techniques. As soon as my arm
properly healed I could have a versatile gas-powe
tool-hand with a swiveling wrist, activated by sm
pistons and controlled by valves, and operated by
shoulder muscles. The main snag to that, as far as I c
gather, was that one always had to carry the small
cylinders about, strapped on, like a permanent
diver.

Much more promising, almost fantastic, was the la
invention of British and Russian scientists, the m
electric arm. This worked entirely by harnessing the
electric currents generated in one's own remain
muscles, and the booklet cheerfully said it was eas
to fit on someone whose amputation was recent.
less one had lost of a limb, the better were one's char
of success. That put me straight in the guinea seats.

Finally, said the booklet with a justifiable flourish

trumpets, at St. Thomas' Hospital they invented a miraculous new myo-electric hand which could do practically everything a real one could except grow nails.

I missed my real hand, there was no denying it. Even in its deformed state it had had its uses, and I suppose that any loss of so integral a part of oneself must prove a radical disturbance. My unconscious mind did its best to reject the facts: I dreamed each night that I was whole, riding races, tying knots, clapping—anything which required two hands. I awoke to the frustrating stump.

The doctors agreed to inquire from St. Thomas' how soon I could go there.

On Wednesday morning I rang up my accountant and asked when he had a free day. Owing to an unexpected cancellation of plans, he said, he would be free on Friday. I explained where I was and roughly what had happened. He said that he would come to see me, he didn't mind the journey, a breath of sea air would do him good.

As I put the telephone down my door opened and Lord Hagbourne and Mr. Fotherton came tentatively through it. I was sitting on the edge of the bed in a dark blue dressing gown, my feet in slippers, my arm in a cradle inside a sling, chin freshly shaved, hair brushed, and the marks of Kraye's fists fading from my face. My visitors were clearly relieved at these encouraging signs of revival, and relaxed comfortably into the armchairs.

"You're getting on well, then, Sid?" said Lord Hagbourne.

"Yes, thank you."

"Good, good."

"How did the meeting go?" I asked. "On Saturday?"

Both of them seemed faintly surprised at the question.

"Well, you did hold it, didn't you?" I said anxiously.

"Why, yes," said Fotherton. "We did. There was a moderately good gate, thanks to the fine weather." He was a thin, dry man with a long face molded into drooping lines of melancholy, and on that morning he kept smoothing three fingers down his cheek as if he were nervous.

Lord Hagbourne said, "It wasn't only your security

231

men who were drugged. The stable lads all woke up feeling muzzy, and the old man who was supposed to look after the boiler was asleep on the floor in the canteen. Oxon had given them all a glass of beer. Naturally, your men trusted him."

I sighed. One couldn't blame them too much. I might have drunk with him myself.

"We had the inspector in yesterday to go over the boiler thoroughly," said Lord Hagbourne. "It was nearly due for its regular check anyway. They said it was too old to stand much interference with its normal working, and that it was just as well it hadn't been put to the test. Also that they thought that it wouldn't have taken as long as three hours to blow up. Oxon was only guessing."

"Charming," I said.

"I sounded out Seabury council," said Lord Hagbourne. "They're putting the racecourse down on their agenda for next month. Apparently a friend of yours, the manager of the Seafront Hotel, has started a petition in the town urging the council to take an interest in the racecourse on the grounds that it gives a seaside town prestige and free advertising and is good for trade."

"That's wonderful," I said, very pleased.

Fotherton cleared his throat, looked hesitantly at Lord Hagbourne, and then at me.

"It has been discussed . . . ," he began. "It has been decided to ask you if you . . . er . . . would be interested in taking on . . . in becoming clerk of the course at Seabury?"

"Me?" I exclaimed, my mouth falling open in astonishment.

"It's getting too much for me, being clerk of two courses," he said, admitting it a year too late.

"You saved the place on the brink of the grave," said Lord Hagbourne with rare decisiveness. "We all know it's an unusual step to offer a clerkship to a professional jockey so soon after he's retired, but Seabury executive are unanimous. They want you to finish the job."

They were doing me an exceptional honor. I thanked them, and hesitated, and asked if I could think it over.

232

"Of course, think it over," said Lord Hagbourne. "But say yes."

I asked them then to have a look at the box of photographs, which they did. They both scrutinized each print carefully, one by one, but they could suggest nothing at the end.

Miss Martin came to see me the next afternoon, carrying some enormous, sweet-smelling bronze chrysanthemums. A transformed Miss Martin, in a smart dark-green tweed suit and shoes chosen for looks more than sturdy walking. Her hair had been restyled so that it was shorter and curved in a bouncy curl onto her cheek. She had even tried a little lipstick and powder, and had tidied her eyebrows into a shapely line. The scars were just as visible, the facial muscles as wasted as ever, but Miss Martin had come to terms with them at last.

"How super you look," I said truthfully.

She was embarrassed, but very pleased. "I've got a new job. I had an interview yesterday, and they didn't even seem to notice my face. Or at least they didn't say anything. In a bigger office, this time. A good bit more than I've earned before, too."

"How splendid," I congratulated her sincerely.

"I feel new," she said.

"I too."

"I'm glad we met." She smiled, saying it lightly. "Did you get that file back all right? Your young Mr. Barnes came to fetch it."

"Yes, thank you."

"Was it important?"

"Why?"

"He seemed very odd when I gave it to him. I thought he was going to tell me something about it. He kept starting to, and then he didn't."

I would have words with Chico, I thought.

"It was only an ordinary file," I said. "Nothing to tell."

On the off-chance, I got her to look at the photographs. Apart from commenting on the many examples of her own typing, and expressing surprise that anybody should

233

have bothered to photograph such ordinary papers, she had nothing to say.

She rose to go, pulling on her gloves. She still automatically leaned forward slightly, so that the curl swung down over her cheek.

"Good-bye, Mr. Halley. And thank you for changing everything for me. I'll never forget how much I owe you."

"We didn't have that lunch," I said.

"No." She smiled, not needing me any more. "Never mind. Some other time." She shook hands. "Good-bye."

She went serenely out of the door.

"Good-bye, Miss Martin," I said to the empty room. "Good-bye, good-bye, good-bye." I sighed sardonically at myself, and went to sleep.

Noel Wayne came loaded on Friday morning with a bulging briefcase of papers. He had been my accountant ever since I began earning big money at eighteen, and he probably knew more about me than anyone else on earth. Nearly sixty, bald except for a gray fringe over the ears, he was a small, round man with alert black eyes and a slow-moving mills-of-God mind. It was his advice more than my knowledge which had turned my earnings into a modest fortune via the stock markets, and I seldom did anything of any importance financially without consulting him first.

"What's up?" he said, coming straight to the point as soon as he had taken off his overcoat and scarf.

I walked over to the window and looked out. The weather had broken. It was drizzling, and a fine mist lay over the distant sea.

"I've been offered a job," I said. "Clerk of the course at Seabury."

"No!" he said, as astonished as I had been. "Are you going to accept?"

"It's tempting," I said. "And safe."

He chuckled behind me. "Good. So you'll take it."

"A week ago I definitely decided not to do any more detecting."

"Ah."

"So I want to know what you think about me buying a partnership in Radnor's agency."

He checked.

"I didn't think you even liked the place."

"That was a month ago. I've changed since then. And I won't be changing back. The agency is what I want."

"But has Radnor *offered* a partnership?"

"No. I think he might have eventually, but not since someone let a bomb off in the office. He's hardly likely to ask me to buy a half share of the ruins. And he blames himself for this." I pointed to the sling.

"With reason?"

"No," I said rather gloomily. "I took a risk which didn't come off."

"Which was?"

"Well, if you need it spelled out, that Kraye would only hit hard enough to hurt, not to damage beyond repair."

"I see." He said it calmly, but he looked horrified. "And do you intend to take similar risks in future?"

"Only if necessary."

"You always said the agency didn't do much crime work," he protested.

"It will from now on, if I have anything to do with it. Crooks make too much misery in the world." I thought of the poor Dunstable Brinton. "And listen, the house next door is for sale. We could knock the two into one. Radnor's is bursting at the seams. The agency has expanded a lot even in the two years I've been there. There seems more and more demand for his sort of service. Then the head of Bona Fides, that's one of the departments, is a natural to expand as an employment consultant on the management level. He has a gift for it. And insurance—Radnor's always neglected that. We don't have an insurance investigation department. I'd like to start one. Suspect insurance claims, you know. There's a lot of work in that."

"You're sure Radnor will agree, if you suggest a partnership?"

"He may kick me out. I'd risk it though. What do you think?"

"I think you've gone back to how you used to be," he said thoughtfully. "Which is good. Nothing but good. But . . . well, tell me what you really think about that." He nodded at my chopped-off arm. "None of your flippant lies, either. The truth."

I looked at him and didn't answer.

"It's only a week since it happened," he said, "and as you still look the color of a grubby sheet I suppose it's hardly fair to ask. But I want to know."

I swallowed. There were some truths which really couldn't be told. I said instead, "It's gone. Gone, like a lot of other things I used to have. I'll live without it."

"Live, or exist?"

"Oh live, definitely. Live." I reached for the booklet Chico had brought, and flicked it at him. "Look."

He glanced at the cover and I saw the faint shock in his face. He didn't have Chico's astringent brutality. He looked up and saw me smiling.

"All right," he said soberly. "Yes. Invest your money in yourself."

"In the agency," I said.

"That's what I mean," he said. "In the agency. In yourself."

He said he'd need to see the agency's books before a definite figure could be reached, but we spent an hour discussing the maximum he thought I should prudently offer Radnor, what return I could hope for in salary and dividends, and what I should best sell to raise the sum once it was agreed.

When we had finished I trotted out once more the infuriating photographs.

"Look them over, will you?" I said. "I've shown them to everyone else without result. These photographs were the direct cause of the bombs in my flat and the office and of me losing my hand, and I can't see why. It's driving me ruddy well mad."

"The police . . . ," he suggested.

"The police are only interested in the one photograph of a ten-pound note. They looked at the others, said they could see nothing significant, and gave them back to Chico. But Kraye couldn't have been worried about that bank note, it was ten thousand to one we'd come across it again. No, it's something else. Something not obviously criminal, something Kraye was prepared to go to any lengths to obliterate immediately. Look at the time factor. Oxon only pinched the photographs just before lunch, down at Seabury. Kraye lived in London. Say Oxon rang him and told him to come and look: Oxon couldn't leave Seabury, it was a race day. Kraye had to go to Seabury himself. Well, he went down and looked at the photographs and saw . . . what? What? My flat was being searched by five o'clock."

Noel nodded in agreement. "Kraye was desperate. Therefore there was something to be desperate about." He took the photographs and studied them one by one.

Half an hour later he looked up and stared blankly out the window at the wet, gray skies. For several minutes he stayed completely still, as if in a state of suspended animation: it was his way of concentrated thinking. Finally he stirred and sighed. He moved his short neck as if it were stiff, and lifted the top photograph off the pile.

"This must be the one," he said.

I nearly snatched it out of his hand.

"But it's only the summary of the share transfers," I said in disappointment. It was the sheet headed S.R., Seabury Racecourse, which listed in summary form all Kraye's purchases of Seabury shares. The only noticeable factor in what had seemed to me merely a useful at-a-glance view of his total holding, was that it had been typed on a different typewriter, and not by Miss Martin. This hardly seemed enough reason for Kraye's hysteria.

"Look at it carefully," said Noel. "The three left-hand columns you can disregard, because I agree they are simply a tabulation of the share transfers, and I can't see any discrepancies."

"There aren't," I said. "I checked that."

"How about the last column, the small one on the right?"

"The banks?"

237

"The banks."

"What about them?" I said.

"How many different ones are there?"

I looked down the long list, counting. "Five. Barclays, Piccadilly. Westminster, Birmingham. British Linen Bank, Glasgow. Lloyds, Doncaster. National Provincial, Liverpool."

"Five bank accounts, in five different towns. Perfectly respectable. A very sensible arrangement in many ways. He can move round the country and always have easy access to his money. I myself have accounts in three different banks: it avoids muddling my clients' affairs with my own."

"I know all that. I didn't see any significance in his having several accounts. I still don't."

"Hm," said Noel. "I think it's very likely that he has been evading income tax."

"Is that all?" I said disgustedly.

Noel looked at me in amusement, pursing his lips. "You don't understand in the least, I see."

"Well, for heaven's sake, you wouldn't expect a man like Kraye to pay up every penny he was liable for like a good little citizen."

"You wouldn't," agreed Noel, grinning broadly.

"I'll agree he might be worried. After all, they sent Al Capone to jug in the end for tax evasion. But over here, what's the maximum sentence?"

"He'd only get a year, at the most," he said, "but—"

"And he would have been sure to get off with a fine. Which he won't do now, after attacking me. Even so for that he'll only get three or four years, I should think and less for the malicious damage. He'll be out and operating again far too soon. Bolt, I suppose, will be struck off, or whatever it is with stockbrokers."

"Stop talking," he said, "and listen. While it's quite normal to have more than one bank account, an inspector of taxes, having agreed to your tax liability, may ask you to sign a document stating that you have disclosed to him *all* your bank accounts. If you fail to mention one or two, it constitutes a fraud, and if you are discovered you can then be prosecuted. So, suppose Kray

238

has signed such a document, omitting one or two or even three of the five accounts? And then he finds a photograph in existence of his most private papers, listing all five accounts as undeniably his?"

"But no one would have noticed," I protested.

"Quite. Probably not. But to him it must have seemed glaringly dangerous. Guilty people constantly fear their guilt will be visible to others. They're vibratingly sensitive to anything which can give them away. I see quite a lot of it in my job."

"Even so, bombs are pretty drastic."

"It would entirely depend on the sum involved," he said primly.

"Huh?"

"The maximum fine for income tax evasion is twice the tax you didn't pay. If, for example, you amassed ten thousand pounds but declared only two, you could be fined a sum equal to twice the tax on eight thousand pounds. With surtax and so on, you might be left with almost nothing. A nasty setback."

"To put it mildly," I said in awe.

"I wonder," Noel said thoughtfully, putting the tips of his fingers together, "just how much undeclared loot Kraye had got stacked away in his five bank accounts?"

"It must be a lot," I said, "for bombs."

"Quite so."

There was a long silence. Finally I said, "One isn't required either legally or morally to report people to the Inland Revenue."

He shook his head.

"But we could make a note of those five banks, just in case?"

"If you like," he agreed.

"Then I think I might let Kraye have the negatives and the new sets of prints," I said. "Without telling him I know why he wants them."

Noel looked at me inquiringly, but didn't speak.

I grinned faintly. "On condition that he makes a free, complete and outright gift to Seabury Racecourse Company of his twenty-three per cent holding."